# THE PROFESSOR'S DAUGHTER

# The PROFESSOR'S DAUGHTER

· A NOVEL ·

# EMILY RABOTEAU

HENRY HOLT AND COMPANY · NEW YORK

This is a work of fiction. All characters and events portrayed in this novel either are products of the author's imagination or are used fictitiously.

Henry Holt and Company, LLC
*Publishers since 1866*
115 West 18th Street
New York, New York 10011

Henry Holt® is a registered trademark of
Henry Holt and Company, LLC.

Distributed in Canada by H. B. Fenn and Company Ltd.
Library of Congress Cataloging-in-Publication Data

Raboteau, Emily.
    The professor's daughter / Emily Raboteau.—1st ed.
        p. cm.
    ISBN-13: 978-0-8050-7506-9
    ISBN-10: 0-8050-7506-2
    1. Women college students—Fiction. 2. College teachers—Family relationships—
Fiction. 3. African American college teachers—Fiction. 4. Racially mixed people—
Fiction. 5. Fathers and daughters—Fiction. 6. Interracial marriage—Fiction.
7. Coma—Patients—Fiction. 8. Princeton (N.J.)—Fiction. I. Title.

PS3618.A326P76 2005
813'.6—dc22                                                                    2004054004

Henry Holt books are available for special promotions
and premiums. For details contact: Director, Special Markets.

First Edition 2005

Some of the chapters in this novel have appeared
elsewhere in slightly different form: "Bernie and Me" in the
*Chicago Tribune, Callaloo,* and *African Voices;* "Bernard Jr.'s Uncle Luscious"
and "Rash" in *The Missouri Review;* "The Origins of Little Willa" in
*The Hartford Courant;* "Respiration" in *Callaloo;* "The Death of Deb Levine"
in *Story Quarterly,* "The Man with the One-String Guitar" in
*Transition,* and "Beulah's Quilt in the House of Sticks" in *Tin House.*

Designed by Victoria Hartman

Printed in the United States of America
1   3   5   7   9   10   8   6   4   2

For my father,
Albert J. Raboteau II,
who paved the way

As she fell asleep, she placed one soft hand
over her land. It was a gesture of belonging.

—Bessie Head, *A Question of Power*

# BERNIE AND ME

Bernie-ism 18.1:
It is a privilege to be able to invent oneself. It is also a burden.

My big brother Bernard took great pains to learn how to talk Black. Street Black. Prophet Black. Angry Black. Which wasn't something you heard a lot of where we grew up. It started when his voice suddenly changed. One day, he spoke in the smooth tenor treble of a choir-boy angel, and the next he possessed the devilish bass of Barry White. Once he was blessed with that depth, Bernie culled some of the diction from our father's brilliant friend, Professor Lester Wright, and pulled the rest from Public Enemy. The result was stunning.

It pissed off our mom. "Talk like yourself, Bernie. Please," she'd say. If he was in a good mood, he'd touch the fingertips of one hand against the fingertips of the other and answer, "Mother Lynn, I am nobody but myself. Do I make you uneasy? Let's examine your fear." Pure Professor Lester. Perfector of charm. If he was in a bad mood, he'd just snarl, *"Step off, bitch,"* and Mom would lean over the kitchen sink and cry into a dishrag. He shaved his head like Michael Jordan. He was a teenager. He had transformed.

When we were little, people remarked on two things about us.

The first thing was how we got along so well. Bernie and I never fought because I adored him too much. He told me once he thought we were the same person in two different bodies and that's why he'd never hurt me. It wasn't that he adored me back. It was that he considered me an extension of himself. *I wasn't finished yet when I came. I came too fast and I left some of me behind. That was you. So you came afterwards to finish me up.*

The second thing was that we didn't look black, although Bernie came closer: fuller lips, darker skin, flatter nose. Still, most people would guess Bengali or Brazilian when meeting him for the first time. Until his voice changed and they heard him speak. Then he would make more sense to them.

I remain a question mark. When people ask me what I am, which is not an everyday question, but one I get asked every day, I want to tell them about Bernie. I don't, of course. I just tell them what color my parents are, which is to say, my father is black and my mother is white.

People don't usually believe me. *You look _____ (fill in the blank) Puerto Rican, Algerian, Israeli, Italian, Suntanned, or maybe Like you Got Some Indian Blood, but you don't look like you got any Black in you. No way! Your father must be real light-skinned.*

In fact, he isn't, but somehow in the pooling pudding of genes, our mom's side won out in the category of hair. And this is really what makes you black in the eyes of others. It's not the bubble of your mouth, the blood in your veins, the blackness of your skin or the Bantu of your butt. It ain't your black-eyed peas and greens. It's not your rhythm or your blues or your rage or your pride. It's your hair. The kink and curl of it, loose or tight, just so long as it resembles an afro. And ours didn't. That is why when Bernie shaved his head, he started to pass for the whole of one half of what he was. Even more than talking the talk, that was the act that did it for him.

My big brother Bernie is a vegetable now. Mom keeps him on a cot in the living room. Him and his wires and tubes and bags of fluid and breathing machines and the shit-and-piss pot. She gives him sponge baths three times a week. When I go down to visit, I wipe the dribble from his chin and I think about him dribbling basketballs. Before. Now he has burnt basketball skin. No hair at all (afro or otherwise). Half a face.

Bernie was tragic long before that, though, because he was too beautiful and because he was Bernard III. He was a legacy.

His looks were more of a curse than a blessing, really. People just couldn't stop staring at him. Our mother put our father through grad school at Berkeley by pawning Bernie off as a child model. He had that third world poster-child appeal. That red-brown skin and those soupspoon mud-water eyes.

We still have Bernie, framed in a diaper ad that hangs in the upstairs bathroom. There's baby Bernie before I came along, a little brown buddha staring out at you over your morning crap, one fat fist raised next to his adorable face in a gesture of benediction or defiance, depending on how you look at it. I asked our mom to take it down after the accident because I thought it was tasteless. What with him having to wear diapers at night now as a grown man and all. That just made her sniffle and twist the plastic pearl buttons on her nightgown so I let it go.

But he was beautiful. The way a leopard is. Or twilight.

My father is black and my mother is white and my brother is a vegetable. When we were small the vegetable told me stories. The stories began when we moved from the West Coast to the East Coast. I remember elaborate stories under the blankets or in the back seat of the car on a long night trip, the highway winding before us, unfathomably long.

❧

The highway is winding behind us. I am six and my brother is seven. We are driving cross-country from Oakland where kids like us are a dime a dozen, double dutching on asphalt and break dancing on cardboard dance floors under helicopter skies. Bernie and me in the back seat with the U-haul bumping behind, playing hock-a-loogie flip-the-bird to the cars in the lanes on our sides. Bernie and me and our ashy knees. Dad is zigzagging up and down America for our education instead of going in a straight line because that is what our dad is like. Only PBS and no Barbie dolls.

We stop in Salt Lake City and Bernie steals some salt peanuts for us to share.

"Here, Em," he says, and we're crunching them and tossing the shells on the ground. My dad says, "Where did you get those?" and Bernie says, "Huh?" My dad says take them back and Bernie says why, we already ate half. Mom says do it anyway because they're not yours and stealing is wrong, and Dad slaps Bernie full in the face and says:

*"NO. The reason you don't steal is because that is exactly what they expect you to do."*

Everyone in Salt Lake City is looking at us. They're flying kites over the windy lake. One is a dragon. One is a diamond. Bernie takes the peanuts back with five fingers on his face and my mother turns to my dad and she says to him:

"I guess they expect to see you hitting your children too." She goes after Bernie and pets him like a puppy dog. She loves him best. I suck on a peanut shell until it turns soft on my tongue.

We stop at Mount Rushmore and Dad tells us about the big heads and Mom says, "Isn't that something?" Bernie says, "No. It would be something if you painted some clown faces on 'em and put a roller coaster in front."

And we all laugh because Bernie always makes us laugh.

We go to the Badlands and there is no one and nothing all around, like we are the last people on the earth. The clouds are like long white hair falling sideways. Dad tells us about Sitting Bull and the Sioux and the Ghost Dances and Bernie tells me he can see their ghosts dancing real slow over by the hill and I ask him do they have bows and arrows. He says, "No. They're crying."

We pass through Wisconsin to see Grammy Livy and Pops snoring through his nose in his armchair with the cigar ashing down his sweater and all Aunt Patty's kids on the walls in their first communion clothes, but not me and Bernie. Pops has a nose like a strawberry. His feet are battleships and his big toes poke through his socks. He wakes up and says, "Who are you, then?" Bernie says we're your grandkids, Pops, and Pops says there's only one way to prove it. "Can you hold your liquor?"

"That's not funny," says our mom.

There is a mah-jongg box on the mantelpiece and we want to see inside but it's not for kids to touch. Grammy Livy has a pinchy mouth. She gives us all turkey and Wonderbread with margarine on it and Jell-O for dessert except it's called ambrosia salad because of the coconut snow on top and the baby oranges floating inside. She stares and stares at Bernie. Bernie asks her does he have a booger on his face. Nobody says much. Mom slams the door on the way out so hard the windows rattle.

"Did your dad smoke cigars?" Bernie asks our dad.

"No," says our dad. Our dad's mom and dad are dead.

"Did your Nan make Jell-O?" I ask.

"You'd catch her with her pants down sooner than you'd catch her making Jell-O. She knew how to cook food with flavor."

Mom wacks Dad with her pocketbook. "Shut up, Bernard."

"All right, Lynn," he says, "but just because you know I'm right." He pats her on the behind and we all get back in the car.

We drive by a metal rainbow in St. Louis. Bernie tells me look at the pot of gold at the bottom. I can't see it. All I see is a paper cup rolling in the wind. I pretend I can see it because I believe Bernie can.

We stop at a Bob's Big Boy in Arkansas and we sit at a table for twenty-five minutes and the waitress still isn't coming. We're hungry. Our mom says we should go but our dad says no, we stay. So we're staying.

Everyone in Bob's Big Boy is staring at us and when I stare back, they look at their hamburgers. Nobody is saying anything. It's like a library, only evil. My dad has a stone face like a Mount Rushmore man. His fists are stones on the table and his knuckles are tight white like ice cubes. My mom isn't saying anything. Bernie is scribble-scrabbling on his paper place mat with Bob's Big Boy crayons. He draws a hangman hanging and gives it to Dad. He wants him to guess who it is. Dad looks at it.

"Guess who it is."

"That's not a very nice picture," Dad says. He crumples it up and pushes it away.

"I'm hungry," Bernie says.

Mom waves to the waitress. The waitress is pretending not to look. She has black hair near her scalp and then it turns yellow like strings of corn.

"Hey, lady! I'm hungry," says Bernie. "My little sister's hungry too!" The waitress pretends she can't hear. She goes into the kitchen.

Everyone is looking at us from the corner of their eyes. I don't know why they don't like us. My lip starts to shake. Nobody is moving. I want to go. I feel like crying but my brother is smiling. Everyone is staring at Bernie. Bernie slides off his chair and turns into Michael Jackson. He starts to do the moonwalk on Bob's Big Boy's black-and-white floor. Dad says *sit down* but Bernie doesn't do it.

Dad's face breaks open. "Quit acting the fool, boy!" he says, and he gets up and storms out and the bells on the door jinglejangle. Everyone starts eating their hamburgers. Bernie rolls his eyes. Mom's staring at the chair where Dad isn't. She's biting her fingernails.

"I'm fucking hungry, Mom," says Bernie.

"I know, honey," she says. "Let's go somewhere else." She puts a dollar on the table even though we didn't eat anything and she forgets to tell Bernie to mind his potty mouth.

We leave and Bernie has his hand full with Bob's Big Boy crayons but nobody makes him take them back. My father is mad and my mother is sad and my brother is bad. I think we will be driving forever.

"There's this kid, Johnny, and his sister, Raisa," Bernie wakes me up to tell me at a Motel 6 while our parents are fast asleep in the next bed.

"This kid Johnny has a hole in his pocket. I don't mean a hole in his pocket like what a quarter falls through, but like a black hole from outer space that's rolled up in a ball and sitting in his pocket sort of like it's a marble only it's a black hole. Understand?"

"Yes," I say even though I don't.

"So when they need to get away, Johnny takes the ball out of his pocket and throws it on the ground and it turns into the hole. Then him and Raisa can jump in and get away. Only one time they jumped in and they ended up on the other side of the world but it's not China. It's this country where it's only giants that live there."

"Good giants or bad giants?"

"Dumb giants."

"Oh."

"And Johnny made a serious mistake. He forgot to put the hole back in his pocket for them to get back. He lost it. So they're stuck there."

"Forever?"

"Yes." Bernie rolls over so his back is to me. "Go back to sleep."

I dream about the giants and I tell Bernie about it when I wake up. He says what were their names and I say Rushmore Fishmore and Bob's Big Boy. Bernie smiles at me and says we had the same dream.

Our dad's mom and dad are dead but he has his grand-aunt, Nan Zanobia, at the bottom of Mississippi and a hundred second cousins and we never met any of them before. When we get there Nan Zan is watering the flowers, and when she sees us she drops the hose and puts her hand over her mouth. Nan Zan is old old.

"Good Lord, Bernard Jr., is that you?" she says and she comes running at us with her arms reaching out and she tells my dad he's a sight for sore eyes it's been too long and are these your pretty babies, lemme get a good look at them.

"You must be Bernard Number Three!" she says, and she makes Bernie turn around in a circle and she laughs and she claps once and says, "Woooo, look out for this one! Girls gonna flock to him like flies to honey! Look at them daddy-longlegs lashes!"

"What happened to Bernard Number One?" asks Bernie, but Nan Zan doesn't say anything. She looks at me instead. Her eyes are scary blue. I think maybe she can't hear so good 'cause she's so old. I hope she'll say my eyelashes are like daddy-longlegs even though I know they aren't.

"You must be little Emma. Girl, you came out with some good hair. Let's see your kitchen." I don't know what she's talking about and then she sneaks her fingers in the back of my hair and she says there's no naps in my kitchen. Dad tells her there's no such thing as good hair or bad hair and Nan Zan says, "Hush, Bernard Jr. You ain't a woman so you don't know."

Nan Zan lives in a shotgun shack and there's so many cousins I can't remember all their names and she cooks us fried shrimps and okra and rice and black-eyed peas and lemonade to drink and watermelon and pralines with pecans picked right off the pecan tree by the boy cousins.

Bernie goes with the boy cousins and their BB gun and I go with the girl cousins. They can't keep their fingers out of my hair and the one called Sweetie Pop gets out her coconut hair grease and she's slathering it on and they're all pulling and twisting, yank, yank, yank. It hurts and I say stop, please stop, and they call me stuck-up white prissy and won't let me play jacks. The boy cousins come back whooping and hollering with a dead owl in a brown paper bag. It's got a BB in its neck.

We drive and drive. We drive up to the Blue Mountains in Tennessee and the sun is setting low but it's not night yet and the humpty-bumpty mountains really do look blue and the air looks blue and soft and my brother Bernie looks blue in the seat next to me. I think he is asleep but then he opens his eyes halfway and he says Dad, and my dad says yes son. Bernie says did God make the mountains or are we all just guessing. My dad doesn't say anything so Mom says it was God, Bernie, of course it was God made them.

We drive and we drive and we are finally there which is Princeton where our dad is going to be a professor and my mom says wake up! We're here. Every lawn is big and has a garden and in every garden there are tiny sparks of light and my dad says those are fireflies and

Bernie squashes one and wipes the glow on my forehead and I scream and my mom and dad laugh.

❧

Our house. It wasn't the biggest house on the block, but it was the biggest house we'd ever seen. In the front were a shaggy craggy blue spruce and a row of smooth slate flagstones leading to the big red door. In the back were a splintering porch, a blossoming dogwood tree, and a garage with a magic door that opened at the push of a button. Downstairs were a bay window with a bench, a busted dumbwaiter and a chandelier. Upstairs were a bathtub with claws and four bedrooms with buckling wallpaper. The walls in my room were freckled with fading forget-me-nots. In California, I used to share a room with my brother. We used to sleep in a bunk bed with me on the bottom and Bernie on top. Now the bunk bed was divided. I poked my fingers in the posts where the screws used to go. "Can't I sleep with you?" I asked him over and over again. He told me don't be a baby. I was supposed to be happy to have my own room.

Our mom filled the house with upscale, slightly damaged yard sale finds. She was a sucker for a bargain. "Can you believe they were selling this rocking chair for only twenty dollars?" she'd marvel. "I talked them down to fifteen. She threw in this exercise bike for free and the only thing wrong with it is the handlebars are a little crooked." Or, "This is an original Tiffany's lamp, with only a hairline crack. She wasn't thinking straight when she sold it to me. They're going through a divorce." She bought our dining room table at a garage sale. It was a gorgeous mahogany oval with leaves that refused to fold down.

She wanted to convert the basement den into a game room. She stocked it with jigsaw puzzles and board games: Clue, Yahtzee,

Battleship, Monopoly, Scrabble, Parcheesi, and Life, but these were not popular with our dad (because he always won), nor with Bernie (because he always lost). She taught me the rules to canasta, crazy eights, and cribbage with kitchen matchsticks. I played with her from time to time, at a lopsided vintage card table, but it wasn't long before the den turned into the TV room. Later, it was the room where Bernie lifted weights.

The house was a perpetual mess. The stairs were cluttered, the counters were sticky, the attic was overrun with squirrels. Our mother wasn't a disciplined housekeeper. She tried inventing systems to involve Bernie and me in cleaning: color-coded pie charts and graphs designating which kid needed to do what chore on which day, but she wasn't consistent with these methods and usually wound up doing everything herself. Our dad did not help her.

This was our house. A place of fine, broken things. A place where games were aborted. A place of uncontrolled mess. It was an old house, with plenty of hiding places. The walls talked at night. My brother was no longer the ceiling to my sleep. Without him above me, I had nightmares of the house blowing down.

⚜

Our dad won a Guggenheim and a Fulbright. When I was in the third grade he went to Ghana and the Ivory Coast to research West African marriage ceremonies. He was gone for a long time. He returned with a goatskin drum for Bernie and a tiny giraffe carved out of wood for me, and for Mom a bolt of kente cloth that she spread over the dining room table. I got scared when he walked in the door. He'd shaved his beard while he was away and I didn't recognize his face. He looked like a stranger.

His book, *When I Left My Father's House: Slave Weddings of the African Diaspora,* won the National Historical Society Book Award.

He spent more and more time in libraries or holed up in his office at home, listening to scratchy slave narrative recordings, over and over again. Sometimes he didn't come home at night. Once when he needed to do some research in the photo archives at the Schomburg he had to bring us with him because our mom had the flu.

I think that was our first time in New York. It was definitely our first time in Harlem. It was cold, January or February maybe, but there were lots of men outside on their brownstone stoops drinking out of paper bags without gloves or scarves, just their collars turned up against the wind.

They get quiet when we walk by and look at us with their rheumy eyes. My dad nods at them but they don't nod back. I'm worried they will take my gold Christmas charm bracelet so I make sure it's hidden underneath my coat sleeve. "How's the hot chocolate?" Bernie asks one of them. The man grins and lifts his paper bag like he is toasting my brother.

Inside the Schomburg there is a poem on the marble floor. I read it to myself while our dad checks our coats and I don't know why but it makes me feel like crying. Bernie asks me to read it to him. *I've known rivers: / I've known rivers ancient as the world and older than the flow / of human blood in human veins.* Bernie walks along the words as I speak them slowly. *My soul has grown deep like the rivers.* When I get to the part about the Mississippi's muddy bosom going all golden in the sunset I have to stop because I am crying. Our dad comes and asks me what's wrong. Bernie knows I don't want to say anything.

"Sometimes we just feel sad," he says.

When we leave the Schomburg later that afternoon there is a dead dog taking up a parking space by the curb and a lady honking at him because she wants to park there. One of the dog's eyeballs has popped out of its socket and is strung a few inches from the face by a thin pink string of ligament. The eye is as big as a Ping-Pong ball. It is gazing at the sky. Down the street is a dreadlocked bum wrapped in a wet sleeping bag. He is rocking himself and chanting *Diiiiime-nickel-penny. Please help! Diiiiime-nickel-penny! Please help!* Bernie tries to give the man his winter hat so he can keep warm but the man doesn't take it.

*Diiiiime-nickel penny. Please help!*

On the train home I think about the poem and the dog and the man and I start crying again. Bernie tells our dad that if he really wants to know, I am crying because I am wondering about our grandfather. That isn't true. I don't really know why I am crying. It's Bernie who's always asking about Bernard Number One. Mom says it's not a story to pass on to children. Our dad looks out the train window. He doesn't say anything. He doesn't even give me his handkerchief.

> Bernie-ism 11.8 (eleven years, eight months):
> I'm so dyslexic, I'm dyxlecis. Dog is God and Em is Me.

My brother couldn't read until he was eleven. I was ten and Bernie was eleven and he was reading comic books and I was reading *Wuthering Heights*. But he had friends and I didn't have any except for Hadas who lived around the corner and had a wandering eye. Our first Halloween in Princeton we went trick-or-treating with some kids from the neighborhood. I was Sojourner Truth and nobody knew who that was so I hated my costume and wanted to go home whereas Bernie was making himself adored by breaking raw eggs into every mailbox up and down the block. It was no better the next year when I dressed up like Miss Havisham from *Great Expectations*. "What are you supposed to be?" they asked.

The question had begun.

"What does it feel like to have a black father?" one of the Williams twins asked me on the school bus during a class trip to Thomas Edison's laboratory in West Orange.

I didn't understand. It hadn't occurred to me that I should feel different than she did. "It feels fine," I answered, but inside the Black Mariah, I began to wonder.

"This is the first motion picture studio," the tour guide explained, then showed us a reel from *The Great Train Robbery.* We learned that when people first saw that movie, eighty years before, they believed the train was real and hid beneath their seats. The other kids laughed but I was worried. When the train came toward us, I held my hand up at arm's length, as if to stop it. My hand was caught in the dusty projection light, magnified in monstrous black distortion on the screen.

For my eighth birthday, my mother invited all of the girls in my class to the Kendall Park roller rink. "Why'd you invite *her*?" Lindsey Mallard asked me, pointing at Brigitte on her wobbly skates. "Don't you know she's *black*?"

"I know," I said, turning red beneath the disco lights.

"Is she your friend?" she sneered.

"No," I protested. I was telling the truth. None of them were my friends.

That winter was the season of the Stork Baby. My mother, being somewhat frantic and behind in her Christmas shopping, brought me with her to the Toys "Я" Us to pick out a Stork Baby doll, but the shelves were bare. We stood on the customer service line for over an hour. "It's a two-week wait for a Stork Baby," the clerk reported.

My mom was astonished. "Two weeks?"

"That's right, lady. Unless you want a black doll. We got them in storage. You can get a black doll today."

"Do you want a black doll, Emma?" my mom asked.

"I'm not sure," I said. It didn't seem like they were as good.

"We'll take one of each," my mother decided. She signed our name to the white-baby waitlist. We walked out with the black baby that day.

I had two dolls, but I hated them both. They were pug-faced and ugly. I cut off their yarn hair, and spoiled their faces with purple marker. I was disturbed. For nearly a month I pretended to swallow my daily vitamins and when no one was looking I hid them behind the couch in a neat little row. Nobody suspected a thing. Not even when the vitamins became coated with dust and stuck to the floor. Everyone was too busy watching Bernie tap-dance down the driveway with bottle caps stuck in the soles of his sneakers. I escaped into books where I could become anybody, but eventually I had to come back out again. It didn't matter that I was reading *Don Quixote*. I was invisible next to Bernie.

Our mom started writing down the "Bernie-isms" in a big black journal around the time Bernie started going to special ed because he wasn't reading yet. Bernie-ism 9.9 is my favorite. I remember when he said it, we were eating gingersnaps in the kitchen and we were warm and it was cold outside and I almost *almost* knew what he meant. Like how when you love something so much you think it's inside you, growing in there.

Bernie-ism 9.9:
When I close my eyes, I can see sound.

Of course, I could never actually see sound when I closed my eyes. Apparently he could. Bernie was always saying things like that that made you wonder about the inner workings of his mind.

Our dad didn't quite know what to make of the fact that his son was learning disabled. He got him tutors and specialists and all that,

but it was Professor Lester with the gold-toothed grin who introduced my brother to Coltrane. The tenor sax became Bernie's
shadow. He was good from the moment he took it up. He became
amazing. He could make it sound like our mother's laugh. I remember him at fifteen, practicing in the wee hours out on the garage roof
so we wouldn't wake up. I remember watching him out there one
2:00 AM from my bedroom window, perched like an owl, wailing on
that thing like he thought the sound might lift him up over the trees,
like the sound might resurrect the dead. Butterscotch, the neighbor's
cocker spaniel, was sitting still in our vegetable patch, looking up at
him with her head cocked gently to the side. We watched him, she
and I. We watched my brother seeing sound.

Professor Lester took a special interest in Bernie. He was younger
than our dad, and cooler and didn't have kids of his own. He drove
a Cadillac, had a perfect afro, and always, even in the dead heat of
August, wore three-piece suits. He made several TV talk show ap-
pearances a year as one of a handful of recognized spokesmen for
Black America. He was sexy. During puberty I wrote dozens of Lester
love haikus, folded them into paper cranes and stuffed them under
my mattress.

> Black Man where you walk
> The mountains move in terror
> Me I tremble too

Lester was constantly being pulled over on the NJ turnpike because, he said, police make the automatic assumption that a black
man with a slick ride is a pusher or a pimp. Our dad claimed Lester
sped on purpose just to feel self-satisfied when he got to flash his
Princeton University ID in front of a cop.

Lester was impressed by Bernie-ism 15.2:

> That mess about judging people by the content of
> their character and not the color of their skin
> —that's some bullshit. Nobody has the right to judge
> anybody else. Period. If you ain't been in my skin,
> you ain't *never* gonna understand my character.

and loosely based a lecture series upon it. He came over sometimes just to pick Bernie's brain. He said Bernie reminded him of how he was when he was a kid growing up in the South Bronx and that school wasn't the right thing to feed Bernie's mind. They started hanging out a lot, listening to Coltrane records, going to museums, protest marches, concerts. They called each other "Nigger," which our father couldn't stand. The weird thing was that it wasn't always like Professor Lester was Bernie's mentor. It sometimes sort of seemed the other way around. Our mom was jealous. I was jealous.

When Professor Lester kidnapped Bernie to bring him to the Million Man March down in Washington, our dad had a fit. It was way past midnight when Lester's burgundy Cadillac finally rolled up the driveway that night. Our mom was upstairs pretending to be asleep because she was mad at our dad about something. My dad and I were waiting. I had trouble sleeping when Bernie wasn't home.

They came slinking up to the house. My dad was taking up the whole doorway so it was hard to see. Lester was smoking one of his Kools. Bernie had his so-what look on his face.

"You missed a great day, Brother Bernard," said Lester.

"I will teach my son how to be a black man," said our dad.

"Who's stopping you?" asked Lester.

"Get off my porch."

"All right, man"—he leaned in real close to our dad—"but just so you know, it ain't all in the books." He winked at me over our dad's shoulder before turning to go.

Dad told Bernie to get his ass to bed; it was too late to talk about it now. To me it seemed more like he just hadn't figured out what to say. The lecture on how the saxophone would never pay Bernie's bills didn't fit this situation.

I followed Bernie up to his room. He looked faraway. He set his limited first edition "Coltrane: Ascension Live from Stalingrad" that Lester gave him for his sixteenth birthday low on the flip side and stretched out on his half of our old bunk bed with his hands behind his head. I sat cross-legged on his floor and fingered the frets of his saxophone. The music spilled around us.

"He's pretty mad," I said.

"Him? He's just scared of what he doesn't understand or hasn't already heard."

"So, were there a million men?" I asked him.

"Had to be. At least."

"What did it feel like?"

Bernie didn't say anything for a minute. I thought he was lost riding with Coltrane. I wanted to go lie next to him and close my eyes. Then he started telling me how the march felt like ten million. Each man times ten. Like each man had all the weight of all the men that came before him and behind him only it wasn't heavy like a burden. My brother's voice was so deep I could feel it the way you can feel the amplified vibrations of a bass guitar all the way down in your bones.

"We were light," he told me, "like we weighed nothing, and we were lifting up. I could feel Bernard One there and he was carrying me and his father was carrying him."

Bernie was my we. I didn't like to hear him talk about other people like he belonged to them. If the Bernards were carrying each other all the way back to the slave ship and past the ocean and be-yond the grave, I didn't know where that left me. I didn't know who was carrying me. I felt like crying when he told me about the ten million, but I didn't.

I asked him if there were any women there.

"Some." He looked at me. He looked at me for a long time like he could see behind my face.

"What?" I said.

"You gotta cut that shit out," he told me.

"What shit?"

"You think I don't know what's going on?"

"What?"

"You know what I'm talking about. You better cut that five-finger shit out before you get caught. You're too smart for that mess. Har-vard don't take folks with criminal records." Bernie rolled over so his back was to me. "Wipe your fingerprints off my saxophone and go to sleep. It's late."

I'd been shoplifting, little things mostly, that fit in the palm of my hand. ChapStick, tweezers, spools of thread. The first thing I took was a green Rub Kleen eraser. I walked straight out of Woolworth's with it closed in my fist, then tossed it in a trash can two blocks away. I was euphoric. Nobody had seen me. Nobody could see me. I started shoplifting every day. I took tortoise shell barrettes and leather money clips. Batteries. Bubblegum. Whatever. I was very good.

I kept my booty in a lacquered ballerina jewelry box under my bed. I didn't stop after Bernie talked to me, either. I secretly devised schemes for stealing him the sterling silver saxophone that hung in the window of Farrington's like the letter Z but I only had the guts to steal little things. Not just petty things though—I stole several watches, loads of jewelry, and once I even lifted a $400 pair of plat-inum Cartier cuff links from Hamilton Jewelers while the saleslady was fitting a couple for their wedding bands. I felt bad about taking those, not because they were expensive but because they were beautiful and I knew I would never use them or be able to explain how I got them if I gave them away. I decided to bring them back and leave them on the store's doorstep early one morning while everyone else was still asleep. I put on my gym clothes so that if my mom asked me what I was doing out so early I could tell her I'd been jogging. But when I got back she hadn't even noticed I was gone. She was trying too hard to wake Bernie up for school, promising him she'd make banana pancakes because banana pancakes were Bernie's favorite.

⁂

When people ask me what I am, I want to tell them about Bernie because I grew up in his skin. We were a breed of our own. And now I'm alone. My brother belongs to the vegetable race. He has become the simplest of machines. Food goes in. It comes out changed.

Because I have been in my brother's skin, I can judge him. I wipe the dribble from his third-degree chin and I hate his guts. I hate his fucking guts for being a selfish, self-serving son-of-a-bitch stupid motherfucking bastard. I hate Professor Lester for treating him like a prophet and our mom for treating him like goddamned God his whole life.

*This is not heroic, Bernie. There is nothing romantic about being a vegetable. You look like a monster, Bernie. You are so repulsive I want to vomit when I look at you, so fuck you for leaving me.*

⁂

Six weeks into my first semester at Yale, my mom called me in hysterics.

"Did your father call yet?"

"No."

"Oh God."

"What is it?"

"It's Bernie. It's Bernie. Oh my God."

"Mom?"

"Oh my God, I don't think I can do this. I can't do this."

"Mom, what happened?"

☙

I missed Bernie so bad on the first day of college I felt unreal. I felt like the ghost limb of an amputee. Everything felt wrong. Bernie had dropped me off with my stuff, helped me unpack, then walked away smiling.

"Was that your boyfriend?" my new roommate asked, staring after him. Her name was Fran and her family owned an olive ranch in California. She'd hung pictures of Georgia O'Keefe vagina flowers on three of the four walls and taken the good bed by the window.

"My brother."

"Oh." She looked at me perplexed. "He's gorgeous."

"Yeah." My eyelid was twitching and I couldn't swallow.

She was looking at me funny. "So what are you anyway?"

On the third day of college, a guy came knocking at our door. "Hi, I'm Karim," he said. His eyes were kind of like Bernie's, but not as wide. "I'm looking for Emma."

"Yeah," I smiled. I noticed that he had dimples and a kind round face.

"Is she your roommate or something?"

"No—I'm she. I'm Emma."

Karim looked confused. "Oh. There must be some kind of mistake or something. I'm supposed to be Emma's culture counselor. Through the Af-Am Center?"

"Well, that's me," I said. "I mean, I'm Emma."

He stared at me for a moment. "All right, then. So, I'll see you around." We shook hands and he never spoke to me again. We were in the same James Baldwin seminar and also African-American History: Reconstruction to the Present, where we were assigned Professor Lester's fourth book, the one that was dedicated to Bernie. I wanted to tell Karim that the last chapter "The *New* New Negro" on biracialism was inspired by my brother, especially the paragraph about the liminal space between black and white America where

there can be no life on the hyphen. The "mulatto" cannot be
both black and white just as he cannot be neither black nor white.
These terms are mutually exclusive and mutually imperative. In
the hyphenated psyche, an internal choice must be made to privilege
one of two warring selves. Black-White. Pick one! Or this choice
will be made hard and fast by the external world. (p. 272)

which is all pretty much a drawn-out, sloppy, convoluted paraphrase of Bernie-ism 16.9. I tried wearing make-up and I practiced saying witty things to Karim in case I ran into him on cross-campus. I even spent two hours one morning putting my hair in the tiniest braids but it was like he couldn't see me.

I started writing Bernie letters instead of taking notes in my classes and I wrote cryptic haikus in black felt-tip marker on the back of my closet door.

*I am Raisa*
*Wandering among giants*
*Stuck in a strange land*

I avoided all social interaction. I stole boxes of cereal from the dining hall so I could eat in my room. I heard Fran on the telephone telling someone that I was a snob. I took several naps a day. I liked to imagine that Bernie was missing me back. I was sleeping when my mom called that day.

❧

"Oh God, I can't do this."

"What happened?"

"Your brother's been in an accident."

"What happened?"

"Emma, you have to come home now. I can't do this by myself."

❧

At around four AM that morning, Bernie had climbed to the top of the resting shuttle train down at the Princeton train stop with a bottle of malt liquor and his saxophone. He had gotten drunk and stupid and urinated off the roof of the shuttle train right onto the third rail. A current of electricity had run up his golden stream of piss, burning him from the inside out, ruining his epidermis and dermis, shorting the circuits of his brain, knocking him clear off the train and landing him twenty feet away on the concrete platform. He must have looked like a shooting star.

When I arrive at the hospital, they have him on life support. My father is in the corner standing strange like a scarecrow, standing like he might fall down. They are telling my mother that skin grafts will not help him. That they are going to have to amputate his penis and one of his hands and probably both of his legs. She is lowing like a cow. She has tucked his saxophone next to him under the white sheets as if it is his teddy bear. It is dented in the middle from the impact of flying with him off the train. The mouthpiece is chipped. His hair is gone, his eyebrows and lashes. His lips are gone. His fingers on one hand are twisted like the spokes of a broken umbrella. His skin is raw meat and later it will be leather.

23

He is a monster.

A doctor with a mustache like a broom tells us we have to consider whether or not it is worth it. He does not say what IT is.

"What are you asking me?" says my mother. Her voice is a screaming tenor saxophone. "What the hell are you asking me?" Dad tells her she needs to calm the hell down and I want to slap them both. Instead I tell them to leave. The doctor, my mother, my father. *"Leave,"* I say. At first they don't want to. They want to pat my hair and rub my back or they want me to pat their backs and squeeze their hands. I tell them again. *"Leave. Get out. All of you get out,"* and after a while they do. I sit with Bernie. I poke his arm. He is breathing through a machine. I am scared to touch his face.

֍

We are lying in the wet grass staring at the moon. We are surrounded by gigantic cast-iron bells. I am sixteen and my brother is seventeen. Our dad is the dean and we live in a castle on a hill under a tall bell tower. It is summer and there is a golf course spread out like the train of a bridal gown down at the bottom of the hill. There are old people down there, dancing between the sand traps under paper lanterns. It is their reunion and they have an orchestra and the orchestra is playing a waltz and the violins trill out strings of sound that fly like kites up to us on the hill. The old people are waltzing in their world far away down there between the sand traps.

It is summer and today an enormous crane like a bony arm came to pluck the bells from the bell tower. They are ten-feet, twelve-feet, twenty-feet tall and each of them makes a different sound. They are going to clean them here on the ground because they are old and rusting. Their silhouettes curve like hips in the nighttime. Like skulls. It is summer and I am supposed to be thinking about applying to colleges. I am supposed to be thinking about where I will go.

My brother looks like an Arabian prince. His saxophone is dismembered. The pieces are shining laid out in a circle around us. Bernie is pulling on a joint and holding the smoke in his lungs so long I worry he's not breathing. I am staring at the side of his face. The iron bells are silent and old like black mountains in a dream. Like slumbering giants. The bells are not breathing. My brother is not breathing. The saxophone is in pieces. The moon is watching us. I touch his face and he lets go the smoke and it rolls away slowly.

"I found out what happened to Bernard Number One," he tells me. Our dad's dad is a secret.

"Did Dad tell you?"

"No."

Bernie and my dad don't talk anymore. They made our dad the first black dean and he moved us to this castle overlooking a golf course and he looked around and said what the hell am I doing here, my life is halfway over and look where I am. He told us, "I may be gone for one month, I may be gone for two months, I may be gone forever." Then he ran off with a pretty graduate student and left us in the castle where we don't belong with our mom who turns on the bathwater just so we can't hear her sobbing and begs Bernie to sleep in her room at night.

Bernie-ism 12.6:
Women will do anything not to be alone.

The pretty graduate student is black so our father's leaving makes sense to everybody but Bernie and me, but we're smart enough to know it's forever he'll be gone.

This betrayal has made my brother more beautiful. More beautiful even than anger and rage. I want to touch his face again and see if he is crying. I want to put my hand on his chest so I can feel his voice.

He tells me, "They burned him in a baseball diamond and hung him from a tree."

"What?"

"He was too good at baseball. He was better than all them motherfuckers so they burned him for it and they hung his black ass from a tree." Bernie draws again from his joint. "For everyone to see."

My chest hurts and I am getting heavier and I think I am sinking into the ground. The wind is choking the violins. "Did Dad tell you this?" I whisper.

"Motherfucking violin motherfuckers."

"How did you find out?"

"You think it's a coincidence I'm named for him? There's three of us. That's a triangle. I'm the third point. Understand?"

"No." My brother is so stoned.

"I got put here to finish something. They got Bernard Number One before he could do it. Bernard Number Two has failed in every respect to get it 'cause he's blind. I'm Number Three. Number One came back in me. In us."

"Who told you about our grandfather?"

"I remembered it. I remember. We got put here to do this thing."

"What's that?"

"You think it's a coincidence we chose to descend through the same womb into the world? I wasn't finished yet when I came. I came too fast and I left some of me behind. That was you. So you came afterwards to finish me. I'm the he of you and you're the she of me. Understand?"

"Yes," I say, even though I don't.

"Then don't forget." Bernie sits up and starts fitting together his saxophone. "We were baptized by fire to come back stronger."

We can hear the old people laughing down there in the sand traps. They do not see us up here hiding among the bells. My brother wets the reed and brings the horn to his mouth.

⚜

I've learned that when people ask me what I am, which is not an everyday question, but one I get asked every day, the easiest thing to do is to tell them what color my parents are—just the black and white of it. I *want* to tell them about Bernie. As if he is an answer and not a question himself. As if he made sense to me. As if I knew what I was put here to do any more than anyone else.

When I go down to visit, I tell my mom to take a rest. She is suddenly old. There are liver spots on her hands. She has taken to drinking juice glasses full of sherry and playing solitaire. When Dad comes she goes out to the driveway and sits in her car, staring out the windshield at nothing. I make her tea. I draw her a hot bath. She doesn't want anything from me, except maybe a fourth Bernard. She is not smart enough to know he is in me and not in that bed.

The oxygen tank stands like an atom bomb. Bernie himself is the fallout. There's a tube in his nose, a tube in his throat, a tube in his arm, and, under the thermal blanket, there are more tubes. He has forgotten how to breathe. I think, how would it be if I just flipped off that switch? How would it be if the up down up down just came to a rest and the chest became still? It could be my act. Like shaving a head. Changing a voice. Climbing through a hole.

I don't do it, though.

I just sit there in the living room for hours watching that raceless, faceless thing in that bed, hoping it'll die already so I can start. I do a crossword. I brush my hair. I wait.

# BERNIE'S LUCID DREAM

Behind my eyes I take the shape of an owl. It must be an owl I am. I can see behind my own head and that's the way I go through the dark window there. Behind backwards I fly. See me lifting off the sill on the upswell swoop. So quiet I go forward smooth, back and back. See me. I leave myself there in the bed that flesh-and-bones thing I am and fly back before I was to hunt myself.

The eyes on me now. Whoa. Night has a touch on my eyes. What was shadow now I see sharp through. The little things that crawl, them, worms they call. The worms are dreaming. I see their dreams. I pass the dream shapes of sleepers. The wishes and fear. My eyes can see the shapes they take there in the shadows, let out like kites from their sleeping selves on twitching strings of spider silk. I see a chaser and a chased. An echoing stairwell. A skeleton key on the floor of a lake. A heartbeat with no heart. I leave those nightmare things. I leave them fly go find me back where I was.

In sonar I follow a sound. A crack. The bat to the ball is the crack of a whip. The feet on the ground is the roll of a drum. I hear it before I see it, on the march of the wind. I smell it. I smell myself burning into a different shape. My begging face is burst. My wings are roped gasoline. Around me mob the twisted shapes of spitting faces flickering through flame. I'm trapped in a diamond. It's hot in this blistering skin. In this sin. The diamond is shining. The sun is on fire.

The rope at my neck is a leash. They drag me like a bag to a scarred bark tree and string me to turn in the breeze. See me? My limbs are part of the air now, part of the smoke and the dust they must be. This is the shape of me leaving my body. I would rather be an owl. Here I go steal away, steal away home.

# BERNARD JR.'S UNCLE LUSCIOUS

**W**e don't wanna go," the boys said at the same time. It was the first Saturday of the summer and they were salting a slug under the pecan tree out back.

Nanan Zanobia adjusted her pillbox hat. "What you mean you don't wanna go?" she asked, pointing her eyes at B.J., who was short, serious and round as a sweet potato. "I know I don't have to remind you she's your mother." Then she pointed her eyes at Luscious who was long, pretty and thin as a string bean. "And I know I don't have to remind you she's your sister." Nobody knew just how old Nan Zan was or how many other people's children she'd raised, but everyone agreed she had scary eyes. Her face was dark as a chestnut but her irises were so light blue they were almost white. "Or am I gonna have to remind you with a switch from this tree?"

"No, ma'am," said B.J., looking down at his orthopedic shoe. In his early childhood he'd worn a series of corrective plaster casts to correct his right foot, which was twisted inward at birth, and he still walked with a limp.

"But Nan, I'm supposed to help out Miss Pauline at the Curly-Q today," whined Luscious. He had a slight lisp and was rumored to be a pansy.

"You got a summerful of Sairdays to be Miss Pauline's shampoo boy. Today you're going to visit your sister up at the hospital and stop giving me lip, hear?"

Luscious looked down at the place in front of his bare feet where the salted slug was turning inside out like the wrong side of an eyelid.

"Good Lord. Is that one of God's creatures?"

The boys were silent.

"Is it?"

"Yes, ma'am," answered B.J., pushing up on the bridge of his glasses although they hadn't slipped down his nose. The slug was writhing in the dust like a rabid tongue.

"What I tell you two about tormenting animals?"

"It's just a bug," mumbled Luscious, rolling his eyes.

"What I tell you?"

"Do unto others," they said at the same time.

"That's right. Everybody 'just a bug' to someone else who think they bigger and better. That don't mean they a bug. It mean someone else got a problem with they eyes. Now get in the house, wash up and throw on your Sunday clothes. We got a bus to catch."

"I don't care what she says. A slug is a bug," Luscious said under his breath as they made their way past the chicken coop toward the back of the shotgun shack. "'Sides, she's mighty good at wringing chicken necks to be casting stones. Or ain't a chicken a creature of God?" They trudged up the sagging porch, through the kitchen and into the airless boxcar of a room they shared.

Luscious had lived there since he was a baby when his mama ran off to Chicago to sing in a nightclub and got herself stabbed on

Blackhawk Street. Bernard had lived there since the age of three when his mama finally lost her mind at the five-and-dime after trying twice to drown herself in the Gulf of Mexico and trying once to slice her wrists with the lid of a peach can. People still talked about it. How she'd pushed over one shelf with a half a ton of merchandise onto the one behind it and how all the shelves toppled down in slow motion like a line of dominoes, the last one shattering the storefront window and disfiguring Dudley, the waterhead man, who was sweeping the sidewalk out front. Nobody blamed her after what she'd been through, but everyone agreed with the judge's order when he sent her over to Biloxi to get her head straightened out.

"And if that place is a hospital then my name's Dwight D. Eisenhower."

"Shhh," whispered B.J. "Nan can still hear you."

The boys were twelve and thirteen now. Even though Luscious was only eight months older, he insisted B.J. call him "Uncle."

"Miss Pauline was gonna pay me fitty cents for washing heads too."

"Hush, Uncle Luscious. She'll hear."

"So what if she do? Shoot. That's good hard-earned money I'm losing. How'm I supposed to buy a guitar when I gotta go to the nuthouse on my workday? Look at this thing." He held up a shoebox with rubber bands stretched over the top and plucked at it. It made a twangy sound that rose up at the end like a question getting asked. "You ever see a sorrier instrument than this here?"

B.J. shrugged and struggled into the pants of his hand-me-down baby blue Sunday suit. Luscious had grown out of it the year before. Nan Zan had taken up the cuffs of the jacket and pants and let out the waist to fit over B.J.'s belly. The suit was shiny in the spots where Luscious's elbows and knees had worn it thin, but those spots fell somewhere below B.J.'s elbows and knees.

"That old woman's got it in for me. I swear."

"I dunno."

"What you mean you dunno?"

"I mean she has a point is all."

"No she don't."

"Yes she do."

"No she don't."

"Yes she do."

"What's her point then?"

"How she's your big sister and all."

"Half sister. And she's your crazy mama. So what?" Luscious looked haphazardly through the chest under their bunkbed.

"So we're her family. She's expecting us."

Luscious sucked his teeth. "She don't remember neither one of us. Or Nan. Why can't I find my pants? Didn't Sarah just sit there staring at the floor last time?"

B.J. didn't say anything.

"Here they go. Yes she did. Just sat there shimmying her leg and staring at the floor like a zombie. She didn't even look at those Easter eggs we brung her."

"Don't say that."

"Why not? It's the truth. Besides, you just got done telling Nan you didn't want to go any more than me. Where's my goddamned Sunday shirt?"

"Shhh. In Nan's wardrobe. She ironed it for you."

Luscious strode into the room railroaded behind theirs. B.J. clipped on his tie and followed his uncle. Nan's room was almost entirely taken up by a big brass bed. Above the bed hung a wooden crucifix with a pewter Jesus nailed to it. You could see all of his ribs and the muscles in his stomach. Around the crucifix hung close to two dozen hand-tinted photos of children Nan had brought up.

One of them was a dentist now. One of them was an alderman. One of them was B.J.'s daddy. In the picture he looked to be about eighteen years old. He had posed with a baseball bat, crouched in batting stance, smiling into the sun. The picture was blurry, as if the person snapping the shot had forgotten to focus the lens, but you could still see how white and straight his teeth were.

B.J. sat on the bed and pulled at a loose thread in the patchwork quilt. "I don't mind the nuthouse," he said, which was a bald-faced lie because he was terrified of the nuthouse.

"Bullshit. I don't see it in here." The open wardrobe smelled like mothballs and mildew.

"Hanging next to Nan's raincoat."

"Oh." Luscious stuck his long arms into the sleeves of his starched shirt and buttoned it.

"It's the bus I don't like."

"Don't even get me started on the bus."

"I can't stand that bus."

"You said it."

"Yep."

"Tough tiddy for the both of us."

"I heard that!" Nan Zan called from the kitchen. "God don't like ugly. Shake your monkey tails. We got to go!"

The boys looked at each other. Luscious shook his head and checked himself out in the mirror on the inside of the wardrobe door. The mirror was cloudy and freckled, not because it was dirty, but because it was ancient. "I look gooood, don't I?"

"You look awright."

Luscious whistled at his reflection. "I am one pretty nigger," he said. "Too bad I got to waste it on a bunch of basket cases." He looked at B.J. "Hey, you look nice too."

"Thanks."

"Sorry I called your Mama a crazy zombie."

"That's okay. I know she's crazy." B.J. rubbed his glasses against his baby blue pant leg. "She does remember us, you know. She just don't act like it."

❧

Pretty much all the white folks on the bus were going to Biloxi to visit someone in prison. Nan Zan and the boys boarded and were making their way down the aisle to the back when a little white boy in a straw hat stuck out his foot. B.J. tripped, lost hold of the library book he'd been carrying and fell flat on his face. Several people snickered.

"Jasper John!" said the little boy's mother. She wore so much makeup she looked like a clown. "Did you just do what I think you did?"

Nan stopped to give B.J. a hand.

"Step to the back, auntie," called the bus driver.

"Did you just trip him?"

"No, Ma."

"Don't you fib."

"He fell on his own. See?" He pointed at B.J.'s corrective shoe. "He's a cripple."

"You oughta be ashamed."

"What for?"

"For acting up that's what. If your deddy was here, he'd smack you silly."

B.J. adjusted his glasses, which had slipped off. He blinked his eyes. He saw his library book under a seat and reached for it. A foot kicked it and it slid back under the next seat, too far for him to reach. Someone snickered above him. He crawled toward the book and reached for it again. Another foot stomped down on the back of his hand and twisted, hard, like it was putting out a cigarette. B.J.

yanked his hand free, grabbed his book and pushed himself up. His hand throbbed. So did his chin, from where it had struck the floor of the bus.

"Just say you're sorry to the poor colored boy."

"I'm sorry to the poor fat colored boy," said Jasper John, looking at the ceiling of the bus. "The crippled one."

"I swear, if your deddy was here—"

"Well he ain't," said Jasper John, crossing his arms, "so shut your pie hole."

His mother smacked him.

B.J. sucked in his stomach, limped to the back of the bus and sat next to Nan Zan. *"Cracker trash,"* Luscious said under his breath. "You awright?" he asked. A muscle under his eye twitched.

"Yeah."

Nan Zan straightened B.J.'s jacket. "Lord have mercy, would you look at this," she muttered. Someone's chewing gum had stuck to one of the lapels. She pulled a napkin out of the pail on her lap and dabbed at it. The gum was sticky and had melted in the heat. It stretched out like a tightrope. She scraped at it with her hat pin but a pink spot remained. "I'll get the rest out later with some salt, honey-lamb," she said.

"Okay."

B.J. opened his library book. It was *Oliver Twist* and several pages were missing but he liked it anyway because it was about an orphan. He was only allowed to check one book out of the bookmobile at a time. In one week he had already read *Oliver Twist* twice and another week would pass before the bookmobile came around again on its summer schedule. He stared at what someone had scrawled on the inside cover in crayon. The words blurred up so he couldn't make them out, but he remembered what they said: "Gracie Champlain is a Grade A slut." He turned to the first page. His hands were shaking and his face was hot.

"Look at me, Bernard Jr." Nan Zan took his chin in her hand. She wet her thumb with her tongue and rubbed away the streak of filth on his cheek. She looked at his face. "I'm *so* proud of you."

"I know," he said.

◦◉◦

It smelled like a zoo in the east wing. Most of the patients were tied to their bed frames. One of them screamed somewhere and the sound reverberated against the mint green walls. Then someone else screamed. This reminded B.J. of birdcall. He couldn't tell where exactly the screaming was coming from.

There were four patients to a room and none of the rooms had doors. B.J. tried not to look but Luscious was staring. It was difficult to tell the men from the women except for a couple of individuals who were naked. Everyone else wore standard-issue white cotton pajamas and white ankle socks. Some of the patients were bleeding at the ankles and wrists where their restraints had rubbed them raw and some of them had soiled themselves and some of them had shaved heads and some of them were veterans who had lost limbs or eyes in the War.

One man was missing both his legs. They'd been amputated above his hips. He was propped up against his headboard sitting on his pillow, and when the boys passed his room he stretched out his arms and pretended to shoot bullets at them through his pointer fingers. Luscious told B.J. he bet they cut off that man's pecker judging from where his body ended and he probably wore a garbage bag for underpants to catch his mess.

"Maybe so," said B.J.

They were lagging behind Nan and the Assistant Director, who led them down the long hallway.

"Pardon me, why did you move her to this wing?" Nan asked.

"She had an episode, and we thought she'd be better off here," said the Assistant Director. He carried a clipboard and wore a white coat and a smile. His face was covered with acne.

"What happened?" asked Nan.

"We took care of it, and she's doing much better now."

"Well, when do you expect to move her back to the north wing?"

"That depends."

"On what?"

"Well, on several factors." The young man's smile stretched like taffy. "Here we are." He looked at his clipboard, stepped into the doorway and called to the woman in the second bed from the left, "Sarah, your folks are here."

The woman turned her head to them. She was thirty-one years old, and her hair was completely white. The bed sheet was pulled up to her armpits. It was also white. Her face was pretty and looked a little like both of the boys' although neither one of them resembled the other. There was a bandage on the side of her neck. She turned her head away again.

"Good Lord," said Nan. "What happened to her neck?"

"That's self-inflicted. Please try not to excite her and don't undo the restraints. That's just a precaution so she won't hurt herself again."

Nan and the boys stepped over to her bed. There weren't any chairs in the room so they stood there. The room smelled vaguely antiseptic.

"I just don't understand this," said Nan.

"Remember to sign out at the front on your way out," called the Assistant Director. Then he was gone.

Nan handed her pail to Luscious. "Hey there, Sarah," she said sitting at the top of the bed. "These bother you?" She started to untie the restraints.

"Don't," blurted B.J. "She might hurt herself."

"I'll just loosen them a little to make her more comfortable. Look, Sarah. I brought your baby brother. Say hello, Luscious."

"Hey, Sarah. How you makin' it?"

"And here's your son. Give your mama a kiss, Bernard Jr."

"In a minute."

"Look how much he's grown since Easter. Everybody says he's the spitting image of his daddy. Just a little more hefty. Tell her your good news, sugar."

"You tell her."

"Bernard Jr. here won himself a scholarship to a fancy boys' school up in N'Awlins. He'll be moving up there end of August so he can start come September. This the last time you'll see him before he shoves off. It's a Catholic boarding school. They say he's so smart they gon' skip him two grades and put him in the high school. They took up a collection for him at St. Rose de Lima too, for the school uniform and all those books he's gonna need."

"And I got a job at the Curly-Q," added Luscious.

Nan Zan stroked Sarah's hair. "When's the last time they combed your hair, sugarpie? I should have brought my comb."

A dry noise came from Sarah's throat.

"What's that, Sarah? Is there something you need, honey? Bring me that pail, Luscious."

Luscious stepped forward with the pail.

"You got a appetite? If you're hungry, I brought you some fried shrimp and some pound cake and some sweet peas from my garden. If you're thirsty, I have lemonade. Bernard Jr. squeezed the lemons for me."

"I'm hungry!" announced the woman in the first bed. "I'm *starving.*"

She had two depressions in her forehead, as if someone had scooped two spoonfuls out of a mound of dough. Her head was covered with gray stubble and she had whiskers on her chin.

"Well, we got plenty to go around," said Nan, standing up and smoothing her dress. "I'm gonna go see if I can't talk to the Director about all this and get some new dressing for that neck wound. Luscious, bring the lady some shrimp. I'll be back soon."

"Her hands are tied," said Luscious.

"You can feed me," the woman said. "I won't bite."

Luscious went over with the pail. Nan went to find the director. B.J. sat where Nan had been at the head of the bed and looked at the side of his mother's face, which was turned away from him. He looked at her ear. It was filled with rust colored wax. He looked at the bandage on her neck. It was dirty.

"Hey, Mama," he said.

"Just drop it in my mouth, boy," instructed the woman in the first bed. "I still have all my teeth. See?" She bared her teeth. They were pointy and coffee-stained.

Luscious started feeding her shrimp.

"You have hands like a girl," she said with her mouth full.

Luscious inspected his hand.

"More please."

He gave her more.

"Delicious," she said with her mouth full. "Much obliged."

"Nan made it. She's a good cook."

"I'll say. She your granny?"

"Nan? Naw, she's my—she's just Nan."

"*My Granny was a hooker in New Orleans. . . .*" sang the woman. "You know that little ditty?"

"Never did hear that one."

"That's 'cause I just now made it up."

"Too bad I didn't bring my guitar," said Luscious. "We could have played a duet. More shrimp?"

"You bet, sonny."

"Peas?"

"Mmmhmm." She smacked her lips. "I notice you're staring at my noggin."

"Oh—beg pardon."

"No need for apologies. You wanna know why it look the way it do?"

"Okay."

She lowered her voice. "They interfered with my brain and took out my memory."

Luscious looked at B.J. B.J. looked at Luscious. Luscious looked back at the woman. "Did it hurt much?"

"I can't remember."

"I'm sorry."

"Don't be. Worse things have happened. They could have taken my heart. Or my intestines. Oh, they take any old body part they please and run scientific experiments on 'em. Liver, kidneys, stomach, what-have-you. I've seen it done more times than I care to speak of. More shrimp please."

"I think I better save the rest for Sarah," Luscious said, although B.J. wound up wolfing down the remaining shrimp on the long bus ride home, one after the other.

"Suit yourself. It's real good of you to come visit your mama."

"She's not my mama. She's my half sister. We got the same daddy."

"I see. She's a awright roommate for a colored girl. She's better than them two chowderheads," she said, referring to the women in beds three and four, both of whom appeared comatose and were drooling. "I like your sister, but she don't say much."

"Oh, she don't talk at all. She stopped speaking altogether when she lost her mind at the five-and-dime."

"That ain't true. She said something just last night."

"What'd she say?" B.J. piped in.

The old woman looked over at B.J. "You want me to tell you what she said, boy?"

"Yes."

"Tell this one here to give me a piece of pound cake first. I got me a sweet tooth."

"Give her a piece of pound cake, Uncle Luscious."

Luscious broke off a little corner of pound cake and brought it to the woman's mouth. "OWWWWW!" he yelled, jumping back. "She bit me!" He shook his hand. "I'm bleeding!"

"I'm sorry!" sobbed the woman. "I'm so ashamed."

"Why'd you bite me?"

"I can't help it," she cried. "I'm crazy."

Nan rushed in with a ribbon of gauze streaming behind her. "What's going on in here?"

"That lady almost bit my finger off!"

"These are alligator tears," said the woman. She stopped crying.

"He gave you the cake," B.J. bargained, "so you tell me what my mother said."

"No, I'm too ashamed."

"You promised."

"Will you tell your brother I'm sorry?"

"Yes."

"Tell him now."

"She's sorry."

"We're not brothers," said Luscious.

"Tell him I'm sorry for *biting* him."

"She's sorry for biting you. What'd she say?"

The woman sighed.

"What'd she say?"

"Sounded like she said, 'Steal home.'"

"Steal home?" asked B.J.

"I believe that's what she said. She won't say it again, though. They went in and took her throat."

"What did you mean, Mama?"

"Doesn't anyone care at all that I'm *bleeding*?"

"Simmer down, boy," Nan said, wrapping his finger in gauze.

"Look at me, Mama," said B.J.

Sarah arched her back then and screamed. It was a long scream that echoed off the walls and was promptly answered by someone down the hall.

❖

That night at 9:30, they turned on the kitchen radio.

*Who knows what evil lurks in the hearts of men?*

"The shadow knows!" cried the boys at the same time. The shutters were closed against the night but a mosquito had found its way in and was hovering at their ankles, poised to prey.

❖

"What do you think she meant?" asked B.J. They were lying in the shade of the pecan tree. B.J. was finishing *Oliver Twist* for the third time. He had a bruise on his chin and on the back of his hand. Luscious was picking out a song on his shoebox guitar. He had a cut on his finger. The sun was going down but it was still hot.

"Huh?"

"Steal home."

"Oh. Can't say."

"I figure she might have been talking 'bout my daddy."

"Since he played baseball and all?"

"That's what I figure."

"Could be."

Almost everything B.J. knew about his daddy was from the old men at Benoit's Barbershop. Those men still talked about Bernard Boudreaux's potential batting average like it was legend. From what B.J. had gathered, his daddy had everything going for him before he died. He had just married Sarah, worked a good job night-managing the icehouse and had been visited by a scout from the Negro American League when he was killed. Nobody would talk about how it happened.

"That story's too ugly to pass on," Nan Zan would say, "but it had a happy ending, and that's you." B.J. had been born premature, two weeks on the heels of his daddy's death.

He tried to assemble snatches of information about his parents in an order that would explain what had gone wrong. He couldn't remember much about his mama except talcum powder on her chest and hiding under her skirt. People said she was a remarkable beauty, that a white traveling insurance salesman from San Francisco had proposed to her when she was just sixteen years old. So had Moe Haskell, who ran the colored funeral home, but she only had eyes for his daddy, they said. B.J. always imagined that something bad had gone down at the icehouse, that his daddy had been killed in that place, possibly crushed by a block of ice, as by an elephant's foot, although he couldn't be sure.

The barbershop stories pricked his ears. King Benoit would start while conking somebody's head to look like Nat King Cole. "Your daddy was some strongman slugger. Coulda been the next Turkey Stearnes."

"He coulda been better than Turkey Stearnes. He coulda been the next Josh Gibson," Oscar Brown, or somebody else playing checkers in the corner would add. "When he was in high school, your daddy batted .351."

"One year your daddy hit fifty-four home runs."

"Fifty-nine."

"And he was fast."

"Lord Almighty, he was fast."

"We called him the Iceman."

"Your daddy could go from first to third on a bunt."

"He could steal two bases on one pitch."

"Once he hit a single and got hit by the same ball he batted when he slid into second."

"Your daddy was so fast he could cut off the light and hop into bed before the room went dark."

Then they would start running off stories from the barnstorming days about Cool Papa Bell and Smokey Joe Williams and especially Satchell Paige—Satchell's jump-ball, his bee-ball, his trouble ball; how once Satchel threw thirty straight pitches over a chewing gum wrapper being used for home plate; how his fastball burst into flames between his arm and the catcher's mitt. B.J. would get these stories confused in his mind. He'd look up at the picture of Jackie Robinson over the barbershop sink and halfway think it was his daddy.

"It's a shame what happened to your daddy," someone would finish, picking up the *Jet* magazine he'd left off reading to gab about baseball. The room would grow reverently silent then, until the man in the barber chair would clear his throat and complain about the job King was doing on his head.

"This don't look a thing like Nat King Cole, now."

"I hear he sprays it with shellac," someone might joke. They'd all chuckle then and the checker game in the corner would resume.

These stories made B.J. sadder than proud. He had no aptitude for sports on account of his foot and could never follow in his father's shoes. He sensed he was a disappointment to the old men.

He thought about what his mama meant by "Steal home." If it was a message or a clue. Through the leaves of the pecan tree, the sky was now the color of the inside of a peach. The katydids were singing in the grass. *Katy-did, Katy-didn't, Katy-did.*

"I'm bored," said Luscious, wiggling his toes so the hot dust squished through. "Let's go gig a frog or somethin'."

※

The summer wore on. The sun was browning out the grass. The days spun out like one long endless day. On Sundays they sat through mass at St. Rose de Lima and lit candles for Sarah. On Saturdays Luscious washed heads at the Curly-Q. Every other Friday the bookmobile rolled around and B.J. borrowed a book. They listened to the radio. They helped Nan weed her vegetable garden, bordered by sun-bleached seashells. There were green onions, butter beans, snap peas, mustard greens, carrots, tomatoes, radishes, okra, hot peppers, and summer squash as large as catchers' mitts. Some nights, Luscious's snore would wake B.J. out of a nightmare into a terrible hunger pang. He'd sneak out to raid the raw vegetable patch in the moonlight with his blood rising like sap in his veins.

As a result, Nan announced there was a jackrabbit thief on the loose. Luscious told her not to worry, they would catch him. They set traps. They continued to torture small animals and insects. They drowned garter snakes and tiny terrapins in the rain barrels at the corners of the house. They stole bird's nests and stashed them under the steps. They pilfered the wire from Nan's broom so Luscious could make a make a diddly-bo and received a beating with the broomstick. They swam in the bay. They avoided talking about how B.J. was going to leave when the summer was up.

One day in July they were lying out back when a cricket jumped from Nan's bed of black-eyed Susans and landed near B.J.'s head. He quickly cupped his hand over it. It tickled his palm.

"I got a cricket," said B.J.

Luscious sat up. "Where?"

"Right here." He pinched its wings between his finger and his thumb so it couldn't get away. It kicked its jumping legs in the air.

"Rip off his wings."

"It's a girl cricket."

"Rip off her wings and legs. No! How 'bout leave one leg on her and set her down."

"Awright." B.J. was methodical about yanking her apart. He lined up her wings and legs on top of his library book, *Walden*. Then he dropped her in the dirt where she twitched around in a circle with her one remaining leg.

"Go, Fat Sally, go," cheered Luscious. The boys leaned on their elbows and watched. Eventually she stopped moving.

"She dead?"

"Naw, she's just playing possum. Gimme your glasses," said Luscious.

"Awright." B.J. wiped them on the bib of his denim overalls. The overalls were hand-me-downs from Luscious. Nan Zan had adjusted the buttons on the sides so they'd fit over his belly. "Here."

Luscious caught the sun in one of the lenses and aimed it at the bug. She began to struggle in the hot pinpoint of light.

"Time me."

"One Miss'ippi, two Miss'ippi, three Miss'ippi, four Miss'ippi, five Miss'ippi, six Miss'ippi, seven Miss'ippi, eight Miss'ippi, nine

Miss'ippi"—B.J. thought again about the words "steal home," how when you put the two words together it meant running into base when the other team wasn't looking and probably sliding and getting dirt on your pants and cheering and pats on the back from your teammates if you made it, but also how in another way it could mean robbing someone of their house or their land, stealing it from them and making it yours and sending them packing like those Indians on the trail of tears, and how in a third way it sounded like *steel* home, a house made of steel, a bulletproof place for a superman to live—"forty-two Miss'ippi, forty-three Miss'ippi, forty-four Miss'ippi, forty-five Miss'ippi, forty-six Miss'ippi, forty-seven Miss'ippi, forty-eight Miss'ippi—"

"She's fried," said Luscious. The cricket's body had blackened and shrunk.

"What's the time?"

"Forty-eight seconds."

"Almost beat my record."

"That's funny."

"What's funny?"

"I'm leaving in forty-eight days exactly."

Lucious's expression changed. B.J. offered him the cricket legs.

"What I want them for, dummy? It's the wings make the song."

"I'm keeping her wings. I'm the one what caught her."

"Suit yourself, Professor," said Luscious, chucking the glasses back at his nephew unnecessarily hard. They landed in the dirt next to the shriveled insect. B.J. picked them up, wiped them off on the bib of his overalls and put them back on.

"Don't call me that."

"Okay, 'Fess."

"You mad or somethin'?"

"I'm bored." Luscious lay down like a corpse with his arms folded over his chest and closed his eyes. "Bored, bored, bored."

B.J. picked up the wings. They were impossibly light and veined like leaves. He stepped over his uncle and limped over to the back porch, under which the boys kept two cigar boxes full of feathers, claws, fur, shells, beaks, and headless dragonflies. He added the wings to the box marked "B.J." He was hungry.

He could hear Nan Zan snoring inside, even though she had her bedroom shutters closed to keep cool for her afternoon nap. Stepping as lightly as he could, he made his way up the porch steps and into the kitchen. He crept over to the icebox, snuck out the stick of butter, dipped it in the sugar bowl, and bit into it like it was a Mars bar.

"B.J?" called Nan Zan from two rooms down. "That you in the butter?"

B.J. froze in his tracks and waited for the old woman's breathing to become regular again. Instead, she padded into the kitchen in her mules.

"I knew it. Keep your monkey paws off the butter, chile!" She swiped it out of his hand and stuck it back in the icebox. "I'm expecting company tomorrow. I might just need that butter to bake me a cake. Don't you think a piece of cake on a plate would taste better than a stick of stolen butter?"

"Yes, ma'am."

"Now let a old lady catch a nap in peace."

"Nan?"

"What is it?"

"What do you think she meant?"

"Who?"

B.J.'s stomach growled. "Never mind."

Outside, Luscious was stretched out in the shade of the pecan tree, looking up and contemplating its leaves. B.J. rejoined him.

"I'm bored," said Luscious.

"Want me to read to you?"

"Nope."

"Want to chuck rocks at the beehive?"

"What beehive?"

"That one in Miz Mary's quince tree."

"Nope. Let's go hunt for that jack rabbit. The one ate Nan's beans."

"With what?"

"We could set a trap."

"It's too hot to be going to all that trouble." B.J. scratched his head. "I wish it was Friday already." The bookmobile was coming around that Friday. "I guess we could go down to the beach and watch the shrimp boats. Maybe take a dip."

"Awright. Ain't nothing better to do," said Luscious. "Grab our slingshots and let's go."

They walked along the train tracks in the direction of the bay.

"Hurry up, slowpoke," said Luscious.

"I'm looking for skipping stones," said B.J. He was out of breath. Soon they came upon the old icehouse. It had been unused for a few years, now that everyone had refrigerated iceboxes and was now in a sorry state of disrepair. Some of the planks had been stolen for lumber. Part of the roof had caved in. There were weeds and blackberry bushes growing out front like unkempt hair.

"There's the old icehouse," said Luscious.

"Yep," said B.J., looking down at his corrective shoe. The icehouse made him uneasy. He squatted down and picked up a round brown stone that wasn't at all fit for skipping and put it in his pocket.

"Looks like someone's movin' in."

"What?"

"Look." There were several large wooden packing crates piled out-side. Some of them were as tall as six feet. "Those look like coffins."

"Huh."

"C'mon, let's go peek."

"Naw."

"Don't you wanna know who's movin' in?"

"Not really."

"That place still give you the heebie-jeebies?"

"I guess so."

"Awright then. You just wait here a minute. I'm fixing to go see what's what."

B.J. squatted down on the far side of the tracks with his back to the icehouse. It was high noon and he was squatting on top of his own shadow. The heat was lying low on the ground, making witch-water up and down the train tracks. He wrapped his arms around his knees and wished he'd brought his library book and wished he had some ice cream and wished his uncle would hurry up. He couldn't help imagining the inside of the icehouse, although he tried not to. He tried to think about *Walden* and the uniform he was going to wear to school in September, but his mind kept wandering to the icehouse behind him, not as it was now, decrepit and chewed on by termites, and not as he had ever known it to be, but as he imagined it was when his father had worked inside hauling the bricks of ice and cutting off chunks of them with a pickax. Since he had only seen his daddy in the one photograph, the man he imagined was an amalga-mation of men from movies and comic books and the barbershop stories, a man who strutted like Jackie Robinson.

The icehouse in his mind was cool and damp inside, dark like St. Rose at nighttime. It sounded like a dripping faucet. The blocks of ice shone as if illuminated from within. They were heavy and his father was tremendously strong to be able to lift them onto his shoulders. He imagined his father's muscles bulge as he picked at the ice with a motion of his arm like a blacksmith hammering steel. The Iceman. The ghost. With each blow, sparks of ice flew out like little filaments of fire, although there could not have been enough light in the windowless icehouse to reflect how brilliant these sparks were in B.J.'s mind.

"Here," said Luscious. He thrust a handful of blackberries at B.J. "Nobody's there right now, but there's a cot up against the wall and a broom. Somebody's movin' in, that's for sure. I'll have another look-see on our way back."

The blackberries were overripe and their juice looked like blood. B.J. tasted one. It was both too sour and too sweet at the same time. A needle of pain shot up through a small cavity in one of his molars and carried through his jaw to his ear canal. He spat it into the dust between his knees, dropped the rest of the berries and stood up.

"What'd you go and do that for?" asked Luscious.

"I dunno."

"Ain't you hungry? You always hungry."

"Didn't want 'em. Let's go."

"Look!" said Luscious.

"What?"

"A inchworm." It was crawling out of one of the berries B.J. had dropped. It was the color of a new blade of grass.

"It's a tiny baby," B.J. reached out his hand to touch it.

Luscious slapped it away. "Nuh-uh. He's mine. I saw him first." The inchworm lifted its front half and looked around to get its bearings. Then it started inching back in the direction of the icehouse.

"What you gon' do to him?"

"Let's see if he don't turn into two inchworms when I cut him in half."

"Awright."

Luscious dissected the inchworm with his thumbnail. Neither half moved or was consequential enough to keep.

"Guess he's dead," said B.J.

"Yep. Dead as a doorknob."

They kept going, keeping to the shade of the live oak trees that lined the way to the bay. Even in their shade it was over one hundred degrees. The air was humid and salty and sat on their skin. On the way, they almost caught a little orange lizard, but it was too fast and darted under a rock.

They came to the road by the water, which was dark blue and spotted with foam. There were a few white people splashing there and a few more scattered on beach chairs under umbrellas to keep from getting sunburned. The sand was white and fine as sugar.

"Would you look at that," said Luscious. "They take up the whole beach and then don't hardly use it."

They turned left on the beach road and walked three-quarters of a mile to the colored beach. It was rocky and packed with children. There were no wastebaskets. Farther out, where the bay opened into the gulf, a fleet of shrimp boats bobbed in the water, dragging their nets beneath them.

The boys stripped down to their drawers and raced into the water, up to their necks. They dog paddled past some little kids playing Marco Polo.

"Feels good, don't it?" said Luscious.

"Yep."

"I'm gonna take a leak."

"That's nasty."

"I don't care. I'm giving a lagniappe to the sea. Ahhhhhhhhhhh."

"Let's swim to the end of the dock and watch the boats."

They dog-paddled toward the dock.

"Looks kinda crowded," said B.J. They came closer.

Gracie Champlain was sitting on the edge of the dock in her polka dot two-piece, kicking her long brown legs. Purnell Jackson and the gang surrounded her like buzzards, trying to convince her to jump in and take off her top underwater for a buffalo nickel. One of them hooked his finger under the strap across her back and snapped it. He had a hard-on.

"Hey," called Gracie, pointing at Luscious and B.J. "It's the little piggy and the big sissy." The boys on the dock laughed and slapped their thighs. Gracie heard them laughing and kept going. "We'd make room for y'all up here, but you stink." She wrinkled her nose.

"Shut up, Gracie," said Luscious.

"You gon' make me?"

"Let's go back," urged B.J. He was getting tired of treading water.

"You a pansy right? Ain't it true you don't like females?" Gracie asked.

"Oh no she didn't," Purnell laughed.

"He likes girls," panted B.J. "Just not your kind."

Gracie squinted. "What you mean, Porky Pig?"

"Word on the street is, you're a grade-A slut."

The gang laughed even harder at that.

Gracie stuck out her jaw. "What's so funny, Purnell?"

"Well, it's just"—he looked at his friends—"you gotta admit that's kinda true."

Gracie's face crumpled up. She stood and thumped down the dock toward the shore. The salt wind carried their laughter behind her.

"First one to that buoy there gets my buffalo nickel," said Purnell and they all cannonballed into the water like hydrogen bombs.

Luscious and B.J. climbed up onto the dock.

B.J. covered his bad bare foot with his good one, lay on his back and looked at the clouds. He thought of his mother's hair. He was breathing heavily. Luscious sat at the edge where Gracie had been and looked out at the shrimp boats on the horizon. "She just jealous 'cause you're smarter than she is," he said. "And I'm prettier."

B.J. fell asleep for what felt like a long time but when he woke up everything was the same. The little boys were still calling, "Marco!" "Polo." Luscious was still looking out at the boats. The clouds still looked like his mother's hair. Everything was a little blurry without his glasses and the sun hurt his eyes. He closed them. "Uncle Luscious," he started, "when I go up to New Orleans—" then he heard a splash and a spray of water hit him. He opened his eyes and saw that his uncle had vanished.

❧

"Look," said Luscious on the way back. There was a red pickup parked outside the icehouse and all of the crates had been brought inside where it sounded like someone was hammering. "Someone's here."

"Looks like it."

"How'm I supposed to see inside? They shut the door."

"You could knock."

"Are you crazy? That could be a ax murderer in there."

"You could peek through the cracks."

"No way, I wanna get a good look. Help me up on the roof. I'm gon' peek in that hole."

B.J. looked up to the roof. There was a large crow sitting in the rain scuttle watching them. "I dunno about this."

"C'mon. Don't you wanna know who's in there?" Luscious crept around to the back of the icehouse. B.J. followed. "Lock your fingers together and gimme a boost. Yeah, like that. That's good." He grabbed the lip of the roof and lifted himself up. It wasn't difficult since the icehouse was partly submerged underground and the roof was low. As he started crawling toward the hole, the crow walked over from the other side of the roof. It opened its wings and started squawking. With its wings open like that it looked big as a dog.

"Shoo," said Luscious.

"Caaaaw," said the crow. It stepped toward him and started pecking at his leg. "Owww! Get off me." He shook his leg but the crow was on attack. It pecked and slapped him with its wings.

"Caw, Caaaaw!"

"Help!" Luscious called. "Get him off me!" He curled up into a ball like a pillbug. "Get him off me!"

B.J. pulled his slingshot out of his back pocket and the unused skipping stone out of his front pocket. He closed one eye, aimed for the crow's head and shot just as the door to the icehouse opened. Luscious and the crow came tumbling off the roof and landed in a heap.

"Owww," moaned Luscious.

"You killed Jim," announced a light-skinned black man wearing yellow suspenders, an undershirt, and a mustache. He looked to be about fifty.

"That's your bird?" asked B.J.

"That was my bird. Looks like you clipped him in the head."

"I'm sorry, Mister. Really sorry."

"Owww, my *shoulder*."

"You called him Jim?" B.J. asked.

"Yes. That was Jim Crow."

"If I hadda known he belonged to you I wouldna shot him. It's just, he was beating on my uncle."

"Your uncle was spying, I gather."

"Well . . . yes."

"And trespassing."

"I just wanted to see who was inside," said Luscious, rubbing his shoulder.

The man went over and stood above Luscious with his fists on his hips. His shadow fell over the boy. "Me," he said. "That's who. Now that you know, you can bury Jim."

"With what?" asked Luscious.

"Your bare hands will do. Start digging."

Luscious spat in the dirt and started digging.

"Where do you two live?"

"We stay at the end of Saw Log Lane," said B.J.

Slowly, the man grinned. "In a pink shotgun shack?"

Luscious looked up with wide eyes.

"How'd you know that?" B.J. asked.

The man turned around and walked back into the icehouse. "When you're done with Jim, come inside," he called. "I'm not finished with you."

The boys plucked and pocketed two of Jim's tail feathers. Then they took their sweet time burying him.

"What do you think he's gonna do to us?" whispered Luscious.

"Can't say."

"I don't think we should go in."

"We did kill his crow, Uncle Luscious."

"What kind of loonytoon keeps a crow for a pet? 'Sides, *you* kilt his crow."

"*You* snuck up on his roof."

"*You* put me up to it."

"*What?*"

"I just say we get while the gettin's good."

57

"He knows where we live. Remember?"

"You shouldna told him."

"We better just go on and get what we got coming."

They stepped down into the icehouse. The man was up on a stool, brandishing a saw.

"Sweet Jesus," said Luscious.

The man looked up at the hole in the ceiling. "This is going to make a fine skylight when I'm through," he said.

B.J. was surprised at how cramped it was inside. In his mind, the icehouse had always been deep, like a cave, but this looked more like a little barn.

"One of you can take that broom there and sweep up. The other can start opening those." He pointed at the wooden crates that were lined up against the wall opposite the door. Then he started ripping at the ceiling. Luscious went for the broom. B.J. walked up to one of the bigger crates. He pried off its side and was flooded in an avalanche of newspaper confetti. A face looked down at him.

"It's a stone lady," he gasped.

"It's a sculpture," the man said, laughing. "That's what I do."

⚜

The next day they went into town to the candy store. B.J. bought a penny wand of rock candy while his uncle took his sweet time staring into the dirty brine of the dill pickle barrel, trying to choose the biggest one. With their treats in hand, they crossed the street to the pawnshop to look through the window at the guitar Luscious was saving to buy with his shampoo money.

"C'mon," Luscious said when they finished eating. "I wanna get a closer look." Dudley, the waterhead man, was inside polishing the knickknacks. His face was badly scarred.

"Ain't she fine?" said Luscious. The guitar had no strings but was so shiny you could see your face in it. There was a five-dollar price tag around its neck.

"Don't be putting your grubby fingers on that guitar, boy," said the junkman behind the counter. He was chewing on a toothpick.

"I'm saving to buy it."

"Git out and come back when you got the money."

Dudley dropped a china figurine. It was a bride and she broke in half at the waist when she hit the floor. "Uh-oh, uh-oh," said Dudley, holding his head.

"That's it, Frankenniggerstein," said the junkman, "you can just forget about getting paid this week."

They passed by Miz Mary's house on the way back. She was out on her front porch reading the newspaper with her bifocals.

"Hey, Miz Mary," called the boys at the same time.

"Hey, boys"—she waved. "You getting ready to go up to N'Awlins, B.J.?"

"Yes, ma'am."

"Never thought I'd see the day. We're all so proud of you, son."

"Thank you."

Luscious spun on his heel and started walking.

"Wait up," called B.J. "I can't go that fast."

At home, Nan and the man from the icehouse were sitting in the front parlor with plates of German chocolate cake balanced on their laps. She had polished the furniture with pine oil, beat out the hook rug and laid out all of her little lace doilies.

"Speak of the devils!" she said, when the boys came in.

"We just wanted to see who was inside!" Luscious protested.

"We didn't mean any harm," added B.J.

"What are you going on about?" asked Nan. "I'd like you to meet Roland Favré. This is Luscious and Bernard Jr., B.J. for short."

"Pleased to meet you," said the man from the icehouse.

"Mr. Favré's been in Europe. He used to stay under my roof a long time ago. Now he's a world-famous artist."

"I wouldn't say that."

"That's why I did. I don't raise duds."

"Pleased to meet you," said Luscious and B.J. at the same time.

"Are you on Nan's wall?" asked B.J.

"I'm the one in the sailor suit," said Roland Favré.

"Bernard Jr. here reminds me of you when you were small, Roland. He goes through books like nobody's business. Matter fact, he just won himself a scholarship to a fancy boys school up in N'Awlins. He's gon' be a professor."

"Is that so."

"Yessir," said B.J.

"He's the first colored boy they ever admitted."

"You must be very proud, Zanobia."

"I'm saving to buy a guitar," Luscious interrupted.

❧

On the first Saturday in August while Luscious was helping Miss Pauline at the beauty parlor, B.J sat on a stool in the center of the old icehouse rereading another library book while Roland sculpted his head.

"How do you like the book?" Roland asked.

"I like it but it's sad."

"In what way?"

"How they make her wear a *A* on her chest everywhere she goes and how they look at her."

"Hold still."

"How they treat her like she's just nothing."

"Can you take off your glasses, Bernard?"

"But then I can't read."

"We can talk instead."

The icehouse had transformed. Roland Favré had cleared away the weeds and installed two windows in each wall in addition to the one in the ceiling. The place was flooded with light.

"Hold your chin up a little more."

"Is that Gabriel?" asked B.J., referring to a bronze bust with three-foot wings.

"No. That's just a regular angel without a name."

"Oh. I guess he's my favorite out of all of them." His eyes roved around the studio and stopped on the plaster head of a man with a rope around his neck. "Who's that one?" he asked. The face was contorted in pain.

"That's the angel's head."

"But—they don't look like they go together."

"All my sculptures go together. They're all different parts of the same being. Yours will be part of it too when I'm done."

B.J. thought about that for a little while. Then he asked, "Are you a communist?"

Roland grinned. "Who told you that?"

"My uncle said they were talking about you at the Curly-Q. They were calling you a Red."

"That's probably the only piece of gossip those old hens had halfway right."

"You mean you are a communist?"

"Let me put it this way. They used to swear the priest was sneaking out at night in a dinghy to supply a U-boat full of Germans with cans of Campbell's soup. They also used to say Zanobia was a witch. Yes, I'm a communist. Hold still."

B.J. held still for a long time. His butt started to go numb. A freight train rolled by, shaking the studio with the tail of its wind. "Mr. Favré?"

"Yes, son."

"Why'd you move back here?"

"I missed home. Try to hold your head steady. I thought I'd come back for a spell when I heard this place was for sale."

"My father used to work here when it was a icehouse. He was a baseball player too."

"Is that right?"

"He was going to play for the Birmingham Black Barons."

"Hold still."

"I *hate* it here. When I leave I'm never coming back."

"That's how I used to feel." Roland dipped his right hand in a bucket of water at his feet and smoothed his palm over the ball of clay. "You know what I missed when I was gone?"

"What?"

"The way the bay smells. And the Spanish moss in the trees. Turn clockwise."

"Like this?"

"Not that far."

"Like this?"

"That's good. Stay like that. Hold your chin up." He started shaving off the excess clay with his knife. "This place is beautiful and ugly at the same time. Just like a human being."

❧

A slight woman in a droopy yellow hat stood on the front porch holding her son's hand. He was so skinny his wrist bones were poking out. Nan answered the door.

"Sorry to bother you," said the woman.

"You're not bothering me, Ophelia," said Nan. "I'm happy to see you. It's been awhile. My, my, is this your little boy?"

"Yes."

"He sure has grown, hasn't he?"

"Like crabgrass. Say hello to Miz Zanobia, Willie."

"H-h-h-hey," said Willie. His two front teeth were missing.

"Would you two like to come in?"

"No thank you. We can't stay; we just come by to ask—I'm heading to Detroit next month to see about a job and I heard one of your boys was moving out."

"I see."

"So I was wondering if Willie here could stay with you for a while."

"Sure," Nan said. She put her hand on the boy's head and tilted it back slightly so he was looking up at her. "Sure he can."

"Just till I get settled up there and can save up enough to send for him."

❧

"Ain't That a Shame," was playing full volume on the radio. B.J. was watching Luscious dance with Nan in the lamplight of the kitchen. The shutters were open to let in the night air. "Shake your hips, Nan!" shouted Luscious. "Pretend you're wearing a red satin dress!" He twirled her around and dipped her.

She laughed. "Let me go, chile, I can't breathe."

Luscious picked up his brand-new secondhand guitar and started playing along with the song. B.J. put his head down on the table and started to cry. He was leaving in three days.

"Bernard Jr.?" Nan came over and put her hand on his back. "Shut that off, Luscious. What is it?"

B.J.'s shoulders shook.

"What's troubling you, brown sugar? Luscious, bring your nephew another piece of pecan pie."

"I don't want it," B.J. choked.

"Good Lord, something must be truly the matter. Come on, let's go sit on the porch. You can tell me all about it and I can smoke my pipe. Luscious, cut that noise and finish the dishes."

B.J. slumped down on the steps. Nan eased into her rocking chair. "I think that fool broke my back." She started filling her pipe with tobacco. The cicadas were buzzing a blanket of sound over them. A sphinx moth hovered in the gypsum weed growing by the steps. Beyond that it was blackness. There was no moon and you couldn't see as far as the pecan tree. B.J.'s eyes stung. He removed his glasses and pushed against his eyes with his fist. Nan held a match to the bowl of her pipe and drew in several quick little kisses to light the tobacco. They sat like that for a long time.

"Out of all the children I've raised, your daddy was the cockiest," she said.

"He was?"

"Mmmhmm. Used to roll up his sleeves and strut around here like a peacock. He was pretty and he knew it. Kind of like your Uncle Luscious." She laughed. "All the girls was sweet on him and he broke every one of their hearts when he married your mama. But they was a perfect match. You couldn't find a better-looking pair than them two."

Nan exhaled a series of smoke rings. They dilated and dissolved, one after the other. "The only thing he loved more than your mama was baseball. You heard about that I guess."

B.J. nodded.

"When your daddy was six or seven he asked me for a baseball bat. I got him one for Christmas—he must have been six 'cause he couldn't read yet. We come out back here so I could throw him some pitches. Let me tell you, that bat was bigger than he was, so I pitched the ball real slow. Underhand. He swung at it and he missed and he got this real mad look on his face. So I pitched to him again and the same thing happened again. I threw the ball for him twenty times and he missed twenty times. Then he said, 'Throw it like they do for real.' So I pitched overhand and he whacked that ball so hard it broke the window behind you."

B.J. turned his head and looked at the window. He could see Luscious inside, scrubbing the supper dishes.

Nan's voice slowed down. "Some people was jealous of your daddy. It looked like he was gonna make a success of himself and they called him uppity. He wasn't uppity; he was headstrong and proud. But they didn't see it like that. So they made a example of him."

B.J. started shimmying his leg on the porch step. "What they do to him?"

"A bunch of them got liquored up and ambushed him over at the icehouse one night. He used to work the midnight shift and then cart the ice around starting when the sun came up. Sleep in the morning. Wake up in the afternoon."

"What they do to him?"

"They kilt him."

"How?"

Nan lowered her pipe then raised it again and took a puff. "They lit him on fire."

B.J.'s leg stopped shimmying. He sat very still.

"Next afternoon Sarah came over here all upset. They were renting a little place on Hickama Street at the time and they were gettin' ready to leave for Birmingham after you was born. It wasn't nothing but a fixed-up lean-to really, but Sarah made it cozy in there. She came over here saying Bernard never came home and she had a bad feeling. So we went knocking on doors asking folks if he delivered their ice that morning and they all said no.

"We went by the icehouse and asked Dollar Hemply if he knew anything. Dollar said when he come to work, the door was wide open and some of the ice was melting where the sunshine was coming in. When he said that I felt real cold and I knew something was wrong."

Indoors, Luscious started plucking his new guitar. The notes flew out at them like bats.

"The last place I could think to look was the baseball field. I told Sarah he probably went over there to practice some with his friends. I was trying to calm her down, even though I knew. I knew. Dollar hitched the cart up to his bony mule and rode us over there. What we saw—it looked like someone had a bonfire in the middle of the baseball diamond, right where the pitcher's mound was, and it was still smoking."

Nan cleared her throat.

"Bernard wasn't there though. Just a heap of ashes. Then I saw him—what was left—hanging up in a oak tree over to the side of the field. Sarah said it wasn't him but I knew it was. I just knew. They strung up your daddy like that for a warning sign. After the funeral Sarah went back with a ax to chop down that tree. Broke her water trying. That's how you come into the world."

B.J. didn't know what to say so he didn't say anything. He hugged his shoulders with his arms and looked between his knees. He felt seasick and his mouth was dry.

"Hate works like a circle if you don't stop it somewhere. I didn't tell you all this before now 'cause I didn't want you hating God and hating them. If you thought that—if you came up hating them 'cause of what they did, you couldn't come so far. But look at you. Look how you been blessed by God. I'm *so* proud of you."

Out in the blackness a screech-owl cried. The porch seemed to tilt then. B.J. stretched his neck out like a turtle and vomited over the steps.

❧

"I don't wanna go," said Luscious. It was raining. He was up in the pecan tree and all you could see were his legs. Nan was standing below him in her lavender dress and white gloves, holding an umbrella. B.J. and his suitcase were waiting out front in Roland Favré's truck.

"What you mean you don't wanna go?"

"I'm staying."

"Don't make me climb that tree, Luscious."

"I don't have to go if I don't feel like it. You can't make me."

"You get your monkeytail down here right now."

"No."

"You gon' make him miss his train."

"I don't care. It ain't like we brothers."

"If you don't come down this second—"

"Noooooo!" Luscious wailed. The word cracked in the middle.

Two minutes later Nan slid into the cab of Roland's truck and shut the door.

"Your uncle can't bear to see you go, honey," she told B.J. "He wanted me to give you this." She handed him a cigar box that said "Loshis" on it. The windshield wiper was swinging back and forth making a hush-swish sound. "Better step on it, Roland. That train won't wait for us."

B.J. turned his head and watched the pink shack getting smaller through a wash of rain.

When they pulled up to the depot, everyone was there to see him off, close to a hundred of them, gathered under a forest of black umbrellas. B.J.'s glasses had fogged up. He couldn't see all of their faces, but he recognized King Benoit and Miz Mary and Father Jacques at the front of the crowd. Gracie Champlain was there too with her whole family, and there was Dudley, without an umbrella, getting sopping wet.

"You gotta hurry, honey, they're boarding already," said Nan, and before he knew it he was rushing by them and Roland was squeezing his shoulder and wishing him luck and Nan was telling him to be careful and they were pushing him up onto the platform and the doors closed behind him. He had to find a seat.

"Two cars back, nigger!" the ticket taker barked.

The train began to roll and he could see them through the window, one big black mass raising up its hands. They didn't know what he would find when he got there.

# WHITE BUFFALO WOMAN

**W**hen I was fifteen years old, Professor Lester got married and I fell in love for the first time, with his wife. She was the loneliest woman I had ever seen. She was also, by far, the most beautiful. It wasn't her beauty that attracted me, but a profound sadness that drew her into the corners of rooms full of people, and that I felt I understood. I'd place myself next to her at dinner parties and model my movements after hers. These movements were extremely subtle as most of her gestures were made with her langorous eyes.

There were things I wanted to confide in her. It seemed to me our town was a stifling trap, my teachers were ignorant, my father was keeping secrets, and my mother was telling lies. I was an adolescent coming into the awareness of the hypocrisy of adults. But she was not a hypocrite. Being a foreigner, she stood apart from the others, as I felt I did. She alone escaped my scorn. I was a painfully angry girl.

That year, I was particularly incensed by a barbarous deer hunt sanctioned by our town. Officially, it was an effort to thin a herd that had grown out of control, but to me, it exemplified the cruelty of those with power and the helplessness of those without. And what could I do to fight it? I wasn't even old enough to vote. All I could do was pray for justice.

My prayers were answered when the hunt was brought to an abrupt finish on the fourth night of its execution. An article in the *Princeton Packet* attributed the cessation to a driveling of funds. That was a lie. Maybe the taxes would have been better spent on road repair, as they argued in the paper, but that wasn't the actual reason the hunt was stopped. This is the true account of the events leading up to that night.

❀

Professor Wright's new wife couldn't sleep at night because the White Buffalo were creeping. She believed she heard them, even with the silencers on their rifles and the lush hushing snow laid one foot deep and two days old and the slackening blackening cover of darkness. Under Lester's snore and the breathing stars through the window off in the hoary woods and veering roads in the strange, strange landscape, she heard them creeping. It was the fourth night of the hunt.

The deer were an infestation. They were said to number in the hundreds of thousands. In two-inch type, the *Princeton Packet* designated them THE NEW JERSEY PLAGUE. In Princeton, where the professor had brought his new wife to live, the deer had been spotted walking in pairs across campus in broad daylight. They'd been seen peering into dining rooms at dinnertime. They'd been caught, frozen in the headlights of one too many cars on Route 206. It wasn't uncommon to hear the squeal of breaking tires on snapping bone, or to find a windshield smashed into a million stars. There were stories of hoof prints on rooftops and razor sharp antlers. There were stories of deer rooting through garbage cans—both the ones on the rims of driveways and the ones stashed under kitchen sinks. There were stories of venomous child-biting, deer-eating deer.

Professor Wright's wife had often been compared to an animal of prey because she was graceful, delicately boned, long-necked, big-eyed, soft-spoken, and Ethiopian. So, not without reason, she identified with the deer. On one of her midwinter walks she stood motionless for twenty minutes, clutching her shawl beneath her chin, watching a trembling rib-thin herd of them crossing Carnegie Lake on their spindly legs. She held her breath and the ice did not crack. After the last deer had lit on the opposite shore and the white tails were no longer visible flickering like candlewicks between the trees, she let loose her pent-up breath and picked her way home, still unused to wearing boots and walking in snow.

When she got home that afternoon she had one of her crying fits in the kitchen. It was set off by the brand-new Cuisinart perched on the kitchen counter, which seemed to be scolding her. It had been a wedding present. It had stainless steel blades and there were two others just like it stored in the basement along with heaps of other stuff.

"What is it?" her husband asked when he happened upon her, crumpled on the kitchen floor. He jerked up his pants at the knee, and squatted beside her. "What's going on?"

Although her fits were frequent, they hadn't stopped surprising him. He couldn't understand why her eyes remained dry when she cried or why her body emitted no sound when heaving with sobs. He tried taking her to the movies. He took care to tell her at least once a day how beautiful she was. He massaged every inch of her from the tips of her long brown toes to the nape of her long brown neck, describing circles over her breasts and shoulders with aromatic oil. He offered to send her to a therapist. None of these things seemed to lift the weight from her heart. Her sadness was intolerable to him because he adored her. In his mind they were Solomon and

Sheba. When he looked at her, he felt he was remembering something from a long time ago.

"She'll adjust," he told himself, but they'd been married for almost six months now. He stopped attributing her unhappiness to culture shock and started blaming himself. He thought it might help if she got involved with something so he encouraged her to enroll in a class at the university for the coming semester. Any class. Any subject. Astronomy. Modern Drama. Drawing. Anything she wanted. She wasn't interested. It occurred to him that she might feel like the last Ethiopian on earth; that for her, the earth's balance had tilted with her feet in this place and the universe had turned its large cold shoulders, leaving her profoundly alone. But what could he do?

"Meteke?" He took her hand. "Talk to me."

Later that day, he tried enticing her with soul food. He attempted his grandmother's Alabama collard greens, but while they sizzled in a hot pan of bacon fat, he got sidetracked scribbling notes in the margins of a new biography on Toussant Louverture. By the time he turned off the flame, the greens were dry as hair. Lester undid his apron, presented the dish to his wife with flair and studied her as she daintily forked his gift into her mouth.

"Very good," Meteke told him, but her eyes were far off as Africa and he knew his comfort food had failed to comfort.

He sat across from her at the kitchen table. Meteke hardly resembled the lighthearted woman he married. "Do you want some tea?" he asked her.

"No thank you."

"How 'bout a foot massage?"

"No."

"Would you like to go for a walk?"

"I already did."

"Do you feel like reading?" Reading always made him feel better.

"Okay," she sighed. He gave her the newspaper.

In the *Princeton Packet* a buck was accused by a housewife of tearing through a screen door, biting into a cactus plant and destroying a newly redecorated living room in its raging effort to remove the needles from its nose and tongue. Meteke began to read the paper daily for its reportage on the deer.

The mayor contracted a team of hunters from somewhere up north. They were to hunt between midnight and dawn, when the residents of Princeton would be asleep. That way the people could dream in peace without seeing the carcasses riddled with buckshot, blooming blood pools in their snowswept backyards.

The sharpshooters barreled down in a fleet of flatbed trucks. Hard-jawed New Englanders. Brawny men said to be lumberjacks' sons. They called themselves the White Buffalo. On the side of each truck was affixed a decal of a great albino buffalo with nostrils the size of fists and haunches as big as Christmas hams. The town officials decided the venison should go to the local soup kitchen. All of this was diligently reported by the *Princeton Packet*. The editor promised to print a running death toll of the thinning herd.

Meteke clipped the article about the hunters. She brought it to her husband in his study one afternoon at the end of the semester. He was behind his messy desk correcting a stack of term papers. She said, "I'm sorry to disturb you."

"You're not disturbing me," he said, eagerly. He smiled.

She did not smile back. "I want to know why these hunters are called white buffalo." It seemed an inappropriate name to her. Why would a buffalo kill a deer? A lion or a tiger, yes, but a buffalo? Buffalo did not hunt. She held out the clipping. The hunters had been photographed standing in a line with their arms folded over their chests and their legs spread wide. There were twelve of them.

This was the first time in a long time she'd shown an interest, not just in civics, but in anything. Lester studied the article. "Son of a bitch," he said.

"What does it mean?" she asked.

"It's a Native American legend," he explained, jumping to his feet. "You'll be interested in this, baby, it will appeal to your sense of the miraculous. I've got a book on it somewhere up in here."

Most of the walls in their house were lined with shelves sagging from the load of his books. Sometimes Meteke had nightmares about being buried beneath them with the corpse of her brother Meles. Lester's books on Africa took up two walls in the living room and wrapped around into the dining room. They were broadly cross-referenced under History, Anthropology, Music, Fiction, Slave Trade, Religion, Colonial, Revolution, Postcolonial, Sub-Saharan, North, East, West, South, and Calamity.

The Calamity books fell under all categories and were generally about AIDS, illiteracy, famine, war, depleted resources, debt, or a combination of the above. They had grandiose titles like *The Problem of Africa, Rape of the Motherland,* and *African Apocalypse.* They were written by colleagues of her husband, men she had met at dinner parties and faculty functions. These were people to whom her nation conjured images of the walking dead. Wasting half-naked women too tired to flick the flies from their faces, broods of children with air-bloated bellies, skeletal men practicing unprotected sex (*lots* of it), then blowing each other to bits in the hills over borders and civil feuds. And of course—the land. The dry, dry land, the hunger, the nothing crops shriveling under that great red ball of a sun, that indifferent bloodshot eye.

The professors were right to think about those things, but they were also mostly wrong. In the presence of these men, black and white, she felt naked and misunderstood—no matter how many layers of clothing she wore, no matter how perfect her English. They thought they owned the world because they wrote about it. She preferred to stand among their wives, who clucked over her clothing, her impeccable posture, the way she prepared lamb and the black kohl with which she rimmed her eyes.

"The White Buffalo Woman is the dominant sacred figure for the Sioux," said Lester, scanning his shelves for the book he wanted to show her. "She's their Jesus."

Her husband's books were different from those of his colleagues. He didn't try to write about Africa except in comparison with the Americas. He liked to read about the past, before the calamity, when there were kings. On the night they met at an outdoor café in the foothills of the Entotto Mountains, she served him a glass of tej by lantern light, neglecting her other customers for three-quarters of an hour while telling him the legend of King Lalibela. She thought Lester dashing. He wore a three-piece suit in the stifling summer heat. He reminded her of Fred Astaire. He had confidence, charm, and money.

"I can't get over how beautiful your country is," he had said, lighting a cigarette.

"You're American?"

"African American." His smile showed a golden tooth.

"What did you come for? To hunt big game?"

"No! Lord no." He laughed. "To research your monarchs."

"Why?"

"I'm interested in comparing them to black militant leaders in the New World."

"Haile Selassie?"

"Him, and the ones who came before."

"Ah!" She clapped. "Then you must go to Lalibela. My mother's family is from there." She talked with her hands. "You will not believe the churches. They are under the ground. King Lalibela built them eight hundred years ago with the help of angels. It was God's command."

"Yes, it's a beautiful story," he'd said, ashing his cigarette.

"You already know it?"

"I read about it in a book."

"It's not a story"—she pointed a long finger at him—"this is what happened."

"Mmmhmm." He sipped from his glass of tej. A soft breeze carried the scent of eucalyptus from the nearby forest and mingled with the scent of her sweat. He breathed this in, intoxicated. "I feel like I've met you somewhere before."

"No," she sized him up. She'd never met anyone with a money clip before. "If we met before I would remember you. You don't believe what I told you about Lalibela is true?"

"I believe you believe it and that's enough to make it real."

"Lazy girl!" hollered the café manager in Amharic. "You're good to look at but not fit to wait tables. Don't say I didn't warn you, lazy girl!"

"What's he saying?" Lester asked.

"You're fired!" spat the manager.

"My boss. He tells me I'm fired." She rolled her eyes.

"In that case, may I hire you to be my guide? Say yes."

She hesitated.

"Say yes. I'll pay you well."

"Yes."

They made love that night in his room at the Addis Ababa Sheraton, violently exploring the landscape of each other's bodies. She scratched his back like a lioness when she came and afterwards, put on his jacket and tie and danced around. He lit a cigarette and inhaled. His lungs were full. He felt complete.

She brought him to Lalibela where he was properly amazed by the underground churches, hewn out of rock.

Later, he showed her the manuscript resulting from the research conducted on that trip. *"For Meteke,"* read the dedication, *"my sister, my wife, my queen; the bridge to my past, the bridge to my future."* When she read this, she instantly imagined her body in grotesque giantess proportions, strapped to an enormous rusty torture rack, stretched a thousand miles and more, over the roiling ocean and into the dark sky, her spine curved over the hip of the globe, turgid and ready to snap. "It's lovely," she had told him. The book was published right before their wedding. The honeymoon was piggybacked on top of his whirlwind lecture tour. She got to see Niagara Falls and the Grand Canyon and the man she married, preaching to crowds. They respected him. It was all a marvel, but off-putting in a way she hadn't expected.

✥

"The white buffalo symbolizes rebirth," he said, still hunting for the book. "They do exist but they're rare."

Lester said his great grandmother was a Hopi Indian and that's why his skin was halfway between the color of lentils and injera. He kept his books on Native Americans cross-referenced under Spirituality and Genocide. He plucked a dog-eared paperback from a high shelf. "Here it is. Hold on a minute. Yup, here we go—chapter five, 'White Buffalo Woman according to John Crying Bear.'"

"But I don't understand why these men in the newspaper say *they* are white buffalo."

"Well that's no new thing, see, the hunting company usurping the name. Ever heard of the Jeep Grand Cherokee?"

"No. What is that?"

"A car. A cultural appropriation. We've also got the Mazda Navajo, the Cleveland Indians, the Atlanta Braves, the Washington Redskins . . . what else?" Lester was animated. "There must be a thousand consumer products stereotyping Indians. Everybody wants to be a warrior." He passed her the book.

"Thank you," Meteke said. She sat in his leather recliner and read the legend. It began with a famine.

The people were starving. The earth was dry. There was no game. Two young men decided to go hunting. On the way, they met a beautiful woman, all dressed in white, who floated instead of walking on her feet. Her dark eyes shone with a great power. This beautiful woman was Ptesan Wi, White Buffalo Woman. The first young man desired her. He reached out to touch her body, but this woman was most sacred. For his disrespect, he was eaten by a dark cloud until he was nothing but a pile of steaming bones. The woman turned to the second young man, who had behaved. She told him to go tell his people she was coming. After four days, she arrived, bringing a holy pipe. She taught the people how to pray with it. She said, "The pipe makes your body a living bridge between what is beneath and what is above." Before she left, she promised to return. Then she transformed into a white buffalo calf and disappeared over the prairie horizon. After that, great herds of buffalo appeared, allowing themselves to be killed so that the people might survive. They were plentiful until the white men came.

Lester stood behind Meteke, and cupped her breasts in his hands.

"Don't touch," said Meteke. "I'm reading."

She finished the legend. The last line read: "We are waiting for her second coming." She closed the book and sat very still for a long, long time. A new blanket of snow was falling outside the window. Under cover of darkness, the hunt was about to begin.

## NIGHT ONE—DEATH TOLL: 36

On that night, the first night of the White Buffalo hunt, Meteke woke with a start from a nightmare she couldn't remember except for the feeling of falling through water. She didn't feel relieved to be awake. Lester was asleep beside her with a fountain pen poking from his afro and his glasses on. In the crook of his arm was a volume of the *Encyclopedia of the Orisha*. His snore sounded like pages being ripped from a book. He did not look like her husband. He looked like a foreigner. She reached toward his face to remove his glasses. At the touch of her fingertips to their frames there was a burst of gunfire.

Meteke leapt back and screamed.

"What? What happened?" Lester asked.

"Guns! Someone is shooting. Can't you hear it?"

He took off his glasses and listened. "No." He put his glasses back on to look at her. He placed the fingertips of one hand against the fingertips of the other. "My guess is that you had another bad dream. Do you want to tell me about it?"

"I was awake. I am awake."

Lester looked at his stunning stunned wife sitting ramrod straight against the headboard of their bed.

"Can't you hear it?" She flinched.

"It's just a dream, baby."

Her face was wet.

"I know what I'll do," Lester said, snapping his fingers. "I'll make you some tea."

Meteke had a series of recurring nightmares, many of which she'd shared with him. Sometimes she dreamt of being raped by the teeth and tongue of the Lion of Judah. Usually the dreams were less figurative and featured her younger brother. He had joined the army at sixteen and disappeared in an Eritrean battlefield never to be heard from again. Sometimes he was floating along the bottom of the Red Sea looking like an angel. Sometimes his face was half gone and the contents of his head were spilling like pomegranate innards down the front of his fatigues or black flies swarmed from the empty sockets of his eyes. What made these dreams nightmares wasn't that he was a corpse, but that when he tried to speak she could not understand. He did not speak Amharic. He did not speak English. Words passed through his cracked lips in the form of rocks dropping soundlessly to the dust. He spoke a language of stones.

Lester made his way to the kitchen. He assumed his wife was dreaming such a dream. He'd already forgotten about the White Buffalo hunters. On his way to the cabinet where the tea was stored he remembered the title of a book he had on dream interpretation and decided to look for it. While rifling through the shelves he came across a volume of Chekhov stories he'd adored as an undergraduate and became distracted by it before falling asleep with the best of intentions at an odd angle on the leather recliner in his study. Upstairs, Meteke had dressed in her white shemma and moved slowly to the bedroom window. Any townsperson who saw her standing there would have compared her to a gazelle. She was listening to the silent sound of gunfire and she was terrified.

### NIGHT TWO—DEATH TOLL: 79

On the second night of the White Buffalo hunt, the professor brought his wife to a holiday party at which Professor Levine's wife mistook her for the help. "Take that cheese tray off the piano and put it on the little table in the bay window, would you? By the menorah."

"No."

"Excuse me? Oh—oh my God! You're Lester's wife! Oh, Meteke,

how embarrassing. I'm so sorry. I didn't recognize you in those slacks. Not that that's an excuse. Would you like a drink? I'm *so* sorry. Let's have a drink."

As the night wore on, everyone became steadily drunk on chardonnay and egg nog. Meteke circulated the rooms without attaching herself to anyone for long. I shadowed her in my stiff green taffeta dress. I wondered where she had gotten the fine gold bangles she wore on her wrists, how she kept the embroidered shawl on her head from falling to her shoulders, and what was the name of her smoky perfume, but I was too shy to ask her any of these things. In fact, I never spoke a word to Meteke. Years later, I smelled her on a sidewalk in Brooklyn and my heart stopped. The incense man told me the scent was Arabian musk, and I bought ten sticks. To me, it was the smell of mystery.

In the den the men drank to the end of the semester. In the parlor, someone hammered out "White Christmas" on a baby grand piano, accompanied by Bernie on sax. In the pantry, there was food enough to feed a small army. In the kitchen, the women complained about the deer. "One of them gave birth on my back porch last spring." "They're like cockroaches." "More like rodents." "They're worse than rodents, they're as big as horses." "Horses with Lyme disease!" "*They're* not the problem, *we're* the problem," my mother interjected as she dabbed at a tomato-juice stain on her blouse with a seltzer-soaked cocktail napkin. "It's suburban sprawl—all those eyesore developments encroaching on their territory."

By the cheese tray in the bay window Professor Levine had loosened his tie and was arguing with my father. "I'm sorry, Bernard, but I don't understand how you can stand there as a man with a son and tell me you admire Daedalus. I don't care about all his other inventions and I don't care that he warned Icarus! You just don't give a teenager wax wings and send him flying headlong into the sky." Professor Levine's sweater vest was inside out with its tag sticking from the back of his neck. Outside the bay window, a sugary flurry of snow began to descend.

Meteke looked for her husband. She found him flirting in the foyer with a group of female grad students. They clustered around him. He radiated in their midst like the sun. His afro was combed out like a halo. He pulled a dollar bill from behind one girl's ear, waved it in the air and began explaining its symbols. The pyramid and its capstone with the all-seeing eye! The bald eagle with the olive branch in its talons! The scales of balance! The girls leaned toward him and nodded their heads. They flipped their hair. He slipped the dollar bill in the vest pocket of his three-piece suit and grinned.

A lost memory came to Meteke—one of Meles, shirtless in the lamplight, counting piles of gun money, big green 100-birr notes that smelled like diesel fuel and body odor, while their mother wailed and tore at her hair over her son who was still a boy, who was fighting in the forest even though his chest and arms hadn't yet developed muscles. With his back to them, bent over the money like that, they could count the knobs of his spine. Meles had been whistling something then. A song with no melody. Meteke approached her husband. "There's my queen!" he cried with tipsy pride, raising his glass. "I'm ready to leave," she said, focusing her gaze on his gold tooth. She went upstairs to get their coats. The time was rounding midnight and the second hunt was about to begin.

That night in bed when Lester reached for her she clamped her legs shut. She turned her tortured face to the wall. "What is it?" he pleaded. "What am I doing wrong?"

"It's not you," she said.

"Then what is it?"

It was the brand-new Cuisinart and the overstocked pantry at the Levines'. It was the dollar bill. It was the deer hunt. Mainly that. How could she explain her mental telepathy with the deer? He might consider her a madwoman. How could she tell him that just then she was feeling the White Buffalo worming on their stomachs through the snow with their rifles slung over their backs?

"I'm tired," she whispered.

"You didn't sleep well last night, baby," Lester reminded her, stroking her hair.

"No. I heard guns." How could she tell him she could hear the buckshot now, tearing through flesh, and sense life draining from the animals as they weaved and dropped and were dragged through the snow, when these sounds were silent to the rest of the town?

"Okay," he said. "Let's get some rest then." But she could not. He fell asleep fast with his arm across her shoulders, white wine and tooth-paste thick on his breath. She was wide awake. She sought to distract herself. She stopped up her ears with cotton balls to deafen the thundering guns. She polished Lester's shoes until they shone like the blackest pupils of the angriest eyes. It was cold in the house so she tried to recall the dry heat of Ethiopia. She walked from room to room. They had too many rooms. A sun room, a guest room, a laundry room, a den. This was America. They had too many things. An exercise bike, a Dustbuster, a leaf blower, a wok. She tiptoed down the cold stairs to the study to reread the legend. This time it read like a terrible warning.

She went to the kitchen for a glass of water. The Cuisinart leered at her from the countertop. She tried to ignore the sound of the guns, but her mind was with the deer. The snow was wheeling down now beyond the kitchen window, but not fast enough to hide their tracks. To distract herself she dusted the bookshelves with an oven mitt. She couldn't sleep.

Time ticked into the afternoon of the next day. Meteke bundled up in her shawl and took one of her walks. The neighborhood children were out in droves, laughing and building snowmen with sticks for arms and carrots for noses. I was not among them. The snowmen reminded Meteke of scarecrows. She remembered how the children in Lalibela planted themselves on platforms in the millet fields where they stood all day long, hollering and throwing stones at the birds. One summer, when they visited their mother's family, Meles had wanted to try it but got frightened by the crickets in the millet and begged to come down. Meteke watched two boys shoveling a driveway. In one spot, the snow was pink with blood.

## NIGHT THREE—DEATH TOLL: 111

On the third night of the White Buffalo hunt, Lester took Meteke to a movie called *Mojo-Cops* in hope of cheering her up. It was a buddy flick with endless chase scenes and predictable jokes. There was an aging, disillusioned white cop who was down and out until his new partner, a smart-mouthed, young, bug-eyed black cop, helped him nab the bad guys and win his mojo back.

"I'm sorry," apologized Lester on the drive home. "That was some offensive drivel." Then, in the middle of a tirade about shucking and jiving minstrels in Hollywood, he almost skidded into a deer. He braked three feet from the animal. "God*damn*!" he yelled at the deer. It stood frozen in the headlights, staring through the windshield at Meteke as if it recognized her. "Get your punk ass off the road!" Lester pressed the horn. "What's up? You brain damaged?" The deer didn't budge.

"He's scared," said Meteke.

"I'll give you something to be scared of! You damn near killed us!"

"Lester."

"*And* you damn near wrecked my Cadillac." He opened the car door and started to climb out.

"No, let me." She left the car and went to the deer. It was a young buck. His head came to the level of her chest. His eyes were blacker than black. Meteke saw herself reflected in them. She saw that he was trembling and that one of his antlers was broken. Slowly, she reached out to pet him. Before her hand made contact, he lowered his head and a molar dropped from his mouth into the snow.

Lester honked the horn again, breaking the spell between his wife and the animal. The buck ran away. His white tail was swallowed in the darkness as he sprang off the road. "That's right, you *better* run!" Lester shouted after him. Meteke bent down to pick up the molar and rubbed it between her fingers and thumb. Its surface was as smooth as moss. "That thing was about to head-butt you," Lester said when she climbed back into the car. "Are you okay?" The dashboard clock read 11:55. The third hunt was about to start. She turned to her husband.

"We need to stop them."

"Who? The deer?"

"The hunters. Look." She held out the tooth. "This fell from his mouth."

"What is that?"

"He gave it to me as a sign to stop them."

"Is that a tooth?"

"Yes. It's a sign."

Lester looked at his wife, dumbstruck. "Did you get any sleep last night?"

"I'm serious. Those White Buffalo are evil."

"I'm not sure I agree with you. I'm not too big on head-on collisions."

Meteke sighed and put the tooth in her pocket. Lester put the car in drive and they continued home, now creeping at fifteen miles an hour, deep in individual thought. She brought it up again in bed, sipping from a cup of hot oolong tea he'd prepared in the hopes of calming her down.

"It's not right to kill them."

"I'm glad you're concerned, baby, but your concern is misplaced. Consider how the deer meat's going to feed hungry people. Doesn't that strike you as moral?"

"I'm telling you I received a sign to stop the hunters." The mug was shaking slightly in her long hands.

"Mmmhmm. But look here, the way I see it, there's just too much *human* suffering to get sidetracked by animal rights. If you really want to get involved, why don't you volunteer at the soup kitchen and help them cook that stew so it's actually edible?" He raised one eyebrow and attempted a joke. "Just don't add too much berbere, most people can't take the heat!"

Meteke flung the cup of tea across the room. It shattered against the wall above the dresser. The tea ran down like fast tears.

"Don't patronize me. You don't own me. I am not your trophy wife for cooking and looking lovely only. I am not a baby. You won't help me stop the White Buffalo. Fine. So I will go myself."

"Hold on now, Meteke, I—"

"Don't touch me!" She pulled the covers over her head. The gunshots began again.

Bewildered, Lester stared at the shape in his bed and then stood to clean up the teacup mess. He wiped the splatter mark from the wall with his handkerchief. Under the covers like that, Meteke looked like a mountain range. "I'm sorry," he said, but the mountains didn't move.

❧

When the sun rose on the next morning the White Buffalo wrapped up a hard night's work. They were out there ax-hacking antlers from skulls, spitting tobacco into the snow as they heave-hoed their game from their hulking shoulders onto the flatbeds of their trucks. They saved the most impressive heads to stuff and mount. They stacked the bodies with reckless care. Hoof. Mouth. Tail. Hoof. The herd was beginning to dwindle. The border between civilized and wild was being restored. Between the yards, the hedgerows were straight. Inside kitchens across the town, pancakes were being eaten, orange juice was being squeezed. The paperboy trudged through the snow with his load. "My footprints are the first," he thought, but then he saw a haphazard track of them, small and shaped like valentine hearts. He felt a twinge of disappointment. A truck rumbled past him down the unplowed road toward the butcher shop, coughing exhaust, dripping something as dark and viscous as maple syrup. The paperboy rubbed his eyes. Their lashes were crusted with sleep.

At the *Princeton Packet* the first day passed in weeks without the phones ringing off their hooks with tall tales of the deer. The reporters were relieved. They could focus on other leads. The retirement of the high school librarian! The parking meter vandals! The new snow plow! The lighting of the Christmas tree in Palmer Square, which was to occur that night, the fourth night of the hunt.

That afternoon, Lester received a congratulatory call in his office at the university. He'd won another Guggenheim. He chose to celebrate with my father, my brother Bernie, and a plateful of oysters at the Peacock Inn. The maître d' asked to see their money before he brought the food.

"I have a Ph.D.," my father said, loudly. "And this man has two Guggenheims. Do you even know what a Guggenheim is?"

The champagne was on the house, to keep the gentleman quiet.

"Chill out, Brother Bernard." Lester grinned. "Don't let them see they're getting to you. Isn't that right, Bernie?"

"That's right, Lester," Bernie said. "Chill out, Dad."

My father glared at his son. The cork popped like a gunshot.

Lester, who enjoyed this brand of drama but was worried about

Meteke, drank the entire bottle while his friend brooded darkly across the table. "Meteke says she hears guns at night," he confessed.

"I hear them too," said Bernie.

"You do?" asked Lester.

"Yeah. Can we get more oysters?"

"No," my father said. He looked at his wristwatch. It was getting late. Down went the sun on the fourth night of the hunt. In Palmer Square the tree was lit with five thousand watts to "Silent Night," attempted in three-part harmony by the atonal choir of St. Paul's Church. The carolers' faces were resplendent, as was the Christmas tree, three stories high, ablaze like the Milky Way.

Lester came home without his overcoat and with a bent bouquet of tiger lilies for his wife. She received them silently in her white shemma, dropped them in a monstrous crystal vase on the mantelpiece, and wrenched herself from her husband's embrace. He passed out on the sofa singing the chorus of "When a Man Loves a Woman," by Percy Sledge. As Meteke removed his galoshes and untied his shoes, he slipped into a troubled sleep. In his dream he watched helplessly from an ivory tower as his wife struggled below him, slowly metamorphosing into a deer.

## NIGHT FOUR—DEATH TOLL: 142
## DEER HUNTER MISSING

Meanwhile, outdoors, the White Buffalo scratched their balls and steeled themselves for the slaughter. The town was tucked in, sleeping soundly. All but Meteke, who stood in her new living room, rubbing the buck's mossy tooth between her palms. Off in the hoary woods and the veering roads, into the big backyards under the breathing stars, the White Buffalo were beginning to creep. She could hear them, even with the silencers on their rifles and the lush hushing snow laid one foot deep and two days old and the slackening blackening cover of darkness. In the strange strange landscape she heard them sneaking. Under Lester's snore she heard the frantic beating of a hunted heart. She heard the drumming beat of running hooves and she was terrified.

She decided to go back to the legend for guidance. By now she had almost committed it to memory. This time, as she sat reading it on the arm of the sofa by her husband's head, the story filled her like a pitcher with hope. She closed the book and put it back on the shelf. Something miraculous happened then. For the first time since the hunt began, the professor's wife finally fell asleep, in a ribbon of moonlight on the Persian rug.

◦🎚◦

This is how I see it:

When she wakes up on the fourth night, there is a doe standing in the living room. The front door is blown open and a drift of snow is powdering the entryway. The doe is too big. She is easily as long as the sofa and as tall as the bookshelves. She is standing perfectly still and she is watching Meteke with liquid eyes. Her breath comes through her nostrils in gentle puffs of smoke. The room is as cold as if its walls have been lifted away. Meteke has gooseflesh on her arms and legs but she is not afraid. She decides to climb onto the deer's back. She assumes this is what she is supposed to do. She is ready to fight, like her brother fought. As Meteke rises from the floor, the doe bows her head and bends her front legs, lowering her entire front half to the floor.

Lester is sleeping the sleep of the dead. He doesn't see his wife stroke the giant doe's face and straddle her shoulders to settle between their blades. He doesn't see her look back at him as they step out of the house, nor does he hear the front door bang shut behind them with a great gust of backdrafted wind.

Off they ride with Meteke's arms tight as a sash around the doe's neck, past the shuttered houses, down Nassau Street, past the Catholic church, the sleeping shops, the shoe store, the pancake house, the jeweler's, the gate to campus with its crouching stone eagles. Off they race down Witherspoon Street, past the public library with its dark windows, behind the elementary school and through the baseball field whose stretch of snow looks through Meteke's squinting eyes not unlike the desert sands at night—an optical illusion, a trick of the reflected moon. Off they run under the silent thunder of guns. Off they ride into the woods with Meteke's hair streaming behind her, along with the vapor trail of her breath. They arrive at a clearing in a thicket of bullet-marked birch trees. Their branches are ensconced in ice. She dismounts there and the doe leaves. She is surrounded by dozens of hiding eyes. She stands barefoot in the snow amid the watching deer and waits. A vision in white. A trap.

She feels the hunters coming closer, tracking, scratching themselves, tromping in their boots over the roots of the icicled trees. She sees them before they see her—two of them, clutching their rifles in their oversized hands. She smells the tobacco wet wool stink of them. One of them has a beard. The other does not.

"White Buffalo!" she commands.

The men stop in their tracks, forty feet from the clearing.

"What the hell was that?" says the one with the beard.

"Look," whispers the other, pointing at the figure in white with the tip of his rifle. The hackles at the back of his neck have raised and he has an uneasy feeling in his stomach.

His partner whistles. "Well I'll be damned." He moves toward her.

"Wait!"

"What?"

"Let's turn around."

"What's the matter with you?"

The beardless hunter suspects she is a ghost. "I just think we should turn around."

"What are you talking about? That lady might need our help." He removes his hat and slinks into the clearing. His partner follows reluctantly, a few steps behind. "You lost, ma'am?"

Meteke stares at him, ice-faced.

"You know, you shouldn't be out here at night. A pretty thing like you." He gestures at the trees with his rifle. "There's a hunt going on."

"I'm here to stop you."

"That so?" His lips curl up in a smile. He holds his gun like an erection.

"Yes."

"Get a load a this. You believe this?" He glances at his partner, but his partner is looking down at his boots. "You must be pretty cold in that little nightgown." He digs his fingers in his beard. Then he makes a terrible mistake. "I'll warm you up, honey," he says and reaches out to grab her.

What happens next is so revolting the beardless hunter defecates into his longjohns and drops to his knees to pray for God's mercy. In a matter of seconds, he sees his partner skinned before his eyes. The man's beard and hair drop like pencil shavings. His clothes turn to dust. His eyes turn to jelly and bleed from their sockets. His lips and testicles are chewed off by an unseen force. A league of invisible maggots worm through his skin and fatty tissue. His blood is sucked by the air, exposing a network of veins that are likewise consumed. The muscles are wasted. The kidneys, the liver, and the snaking intestines are digested. In the jail of his rib cage, the heart shrinks from the size of a fist to the size of a raisin and drops through the pelvis. The ligament and bone of him stands teetering for a moment longer.

Then the skeleton is sucked dry of its marrow and the bones are suddenly wrenched apart—mandible from the skull, shin from femur, hand from the wrist of outstretched arm. The bones pop apart and land in a heap. They blacken and smolder like a dying campfire at the woman's feet. Her eyes shine with a great power.

"Go and tell the others," she warns. "This hunt must end."

⚜

Later, it will. Later, the White Buffalo will pack their gear and drive up 206 like bats out of hell with their mouths clamped shut. Investigators from the missing persons bureau will be called in and they will find nothing but chewing tobacco and hoofprints in snow. The *Princeton Packet* will run the story on the front page. There will be no mention of a woman. The headline will be splashy. The paperboy will read it on his route countless times as he pitches the *Packet* at door after door. Lester will wake up later and his wife will be sleeping on her side on the Persian rug. Her hip will be curved like the globe. He will lift her tenderly and carry her up to their bed where she will open her eyes halfway and smile at him for the first time in weeks. He will ask her if she's having a good dream without noticing the twigs in her hair and the dirt under her fingernails. Later, the snow will melt. Christmas will come and go. There will be more presents than anybody needs. These presents will go unused. Those things will happen later.

Right now the beardless hunter is terrified and something else. He is humbled. He squats in his own waste marveling at the spectacle before him, the ruined body of his partner and the destroyer above him. She resembles an angel in her white robe. Her face is beautiful to him in its righteous anger. He feels she is watching him with a hundred eyes. In this awful moment, he thinks simply, "How wretched I am. How small."

# SYNESTHESIA

KKKKKKKKKKKKKKKKKKKKKKKKKKKKKKKKKKKKKKK
KKKKKKKKKK.

I see a sound. KKKKKKKKKKKKKKKKKKKKKKKKK
KKKKKKKKKKKKKKKKKKKKKKKKKKKKKKKKKKKKKK.
It looks like KKKKKKKKKKKKKKKKKKKKKKKKKKKK.
It looks like gravity ripping. It looks like the jets on a spaceship.

I catch the sound and it takes me into the cold. One light year, two
light years, three light years, and Earth is a marble. I'm past the tenth
planet without a map. The Milky Way went. There are strange suns
and knuckleball moons thrown backward. That galaxy is a tin pan.
Someone lost their rocking chair. It's rocking there in the ring around
a world with no oceans. I can't stay and sit, I have to look.

Where will I find you, where will I find you.

It's so cold I can't feel my hands. I have no hands to count these
universes. Where are you in this vast? I feel the sand of blasted mete-
ors. Does that wormhole lead to you? Are you in that quiet black? I
slow. I float silent at the mouth of the hole. It's too dark to see into

and I forgot my flashlight. I want to look for you in there. I call your name and it echoes my voice back to me cracked. KKKKKKKKK KKKKKKKKK. The sound gets louder and pulls me away like a magnet. KKKKKKKKKKKKKKKKKKKKKKKKK. That sound. It looks like the tail on a shooting star. It catches me. I look back and the black hole where maybe you are shrinks to a dot, a nothing.

KKKKKKKKKKKKKKKKKKKKKKKKKKKKKKKKKKKK KKKKKKKKKKKKKKKKKKKKKKKKKKKKKKKKKKKK KKKKKKKKKKKKKKKKKKKKKKKKKKKKKKKKKKKK KKKKKKKKKKKKKKKKKKKKKKKKKKKKKKKKKKKK KKKKKKK. I come back down like rain. The globe grows. I see Africa. I see the United States. I see my state and my town and my block and my roof where I land. I have my hands again, but I'm still cold.

# RASH

It's better to share a rash with someone else than to endure one on your own. My brother Bernie and I had a mutual rash on two occasions. The first time was from the shoe polish we used to black up our faces in the middle of the night and go vandalize Mrs. Turner's lawn jockeys. The second time was from the quiche we ate on the night our father left. In between those two outbreaks, I suffered the rash over fifty times by myself.

I am not exaggerating the number. I have documentation.

The rash was unattractive and uncomfortable but inveterate and therefore familiar. That's why when I woke up with the rash before dawn on the morning I was supposed to go home for winter break, I wasn't alarmed. I didn't even have to look in the mirror to know it was there, but I did. This time it was as if someone had painted a half-line down the middle of my face, beginning at my widow's peak and ending at my chin. The right side was perfectly normal. The left side was red and swollen as a catcher's mitt. I could barely open that eye. I looked like I'd been the victim of a stroke, or sucker-punched, or stung by a squad of wasps. I smiled. I frowned. Only the right side of my mouth obeyed. The bells of Harkness Tower were tolling five.

I pulled the rash journal from my bookshelf, walked into the blue computer light of the common room and sunk into the Papasan chair across from my roommate, Fran. She was pulling an all-nighter in order to finish her final paper for the History of Modern China. I wasn't under the same sort of pressure, having been granted a note by our dean that allowed me unlimited extensions. He'd called it my "get out of jail free card," and I hadn't laughed at the joke.

Fran was the only freshman on the Yale women's varsity lacrosse team. She was from Sonoma, where her stepfather owned an olive orchard. She told me that when she was a child her hair had been white-blond but that at the age of seven, when it began to darken, her mother had wet it with lemon juice and forced her to sit outside in the sun. She was an only child and it showed.

"Hey," I said.

She jumped. "Jesus, Emma! I didn't see you."

"Sorry."

Fran had been eating a Cup-a-Noodles with a plastic spoon. She spilled some of it on her bare stomach when I startled her. She wore nothing but a purple bra and matching panties. All of her bras and panties matched.

"How's the paper going?"

"Not good, I can't stay awake," she complained, wiping the broth from her skin. "Oh my *God*! What happened to your face?"

"Voodoo," I told her.

"No, seriously. What happened?"

"It's my rash," I said. The left side of my face was feverish, taut, and ready to split like the skin of a stewing tomato.

The reason Fran was so scantily dressed was that it was way too hot in our dorm room. We couldn't control the heat. The ancient radiators clanked day and night, as if inhabited by a team of angry, industrious blacksmith elves. Steam belched out from their coils like dragon smoke. We tried opening the flu on the fireplace hoping to catch a draft but the chimney was plugged. Even with the windows cranked open to December in New England, our room felt like the Amazon.

"It's so weird," Fran said, coming closer to inspect the rash. She turned on the halogen lamp behind the Papasan. "You've only got it on the one side. Does it itch?"

I reached back and turned off the lamp. "Yeah," I told her, "it itches like hell." But by this time, I'd learned to refrain from scratching in front of others. It made people uneasy.

"I've never seen a rash like that." She pressed my cheek with her thumb pad like she was testing the ripeness of a peach, then pursed her lips in a way that made her look middle-aged. "Are you allergic to something, or something?" she asked.

"No," I said. "I don't think so."

My mother did. She catalogued each of my childhood rashes in a journal, along with what I'd eaten directly before it appeared, in the hope that a pattern would emerge. She began the journal out of frustration with doctors after I'd already had the rash several times. She persisted in the belief that I had an allergy even after cutting dairy, chocolate, nuts, wheat, and Yellow #5 out of my diet in stages failed to stop my skin from rebelling against itself. She made me bring the rash journal to college to keep up with the entries.

The journal had a red cover, which I thought was appropriate. It was a gift from her sister Patty in Milwaukee. Aunt Patty sent my mother a journal every Christmas and my mother put them all to use, not one at a time, but simultaneously. They had specific designations. There was a gardening journal, for example, a goal journal, a poetry journal, a prayer journal, a dream journal, and a journal of things to be grateful for. She kept a recipe journal in the kitchen. Its contents were culled from cooking shows but seldom put to practical use. All of the other journals were stored in the cabinet of her nightstand, which did not lock. It was obvious she wanted someone to read them, and by someone I mean my father, but I'm sure I'm the only one who ever did.

"But you've had this rash before?" Fran wanted to know.

"Never exactly like this one," I explained. This one was peculiar, my face being perfectly dissected as it was. "But yes, I've had it lots of times."

As I said, the first time I got the rash was from Kiwi shoe polish. Bernie and I used it to black up our faces like cat burglars, then snuck across the street while our parents were sleeping. It was his idea. He painted Mrs. Turner's lawn jockeys white. I suspect it was to please our father, who was offended by them. (Every egregious act Bernie ever committed was to win our father's love.) The next morning, we woke up with an identical rash, and Mrs. Turner suffered a stroke resulting in complications that killed her.

I was only eleven when that happened, but even then I had a sense that the rash was an outer manifestation of my inner state—in this case a bilious guilt. This wasn't the case for my brother. Bernie had no sense of compunction over Mrs. Turner's death. I asked him if he thought our neighbor had the stroke from the shock of her lawn jockeys turning white. He said no, she had the stroke because it was the only way for her to get out of her broken body, and if it did have anything to do with the lawn jockeys, it was only because they served as an example of how that could be done. I didn't get it. He explained that the lawn jockeys were stuck in the way people looked at them, until we released them. The same thing had happened with Mrs. Turner, more or less. According to Bernie, she'd left her body but was still around. He claimed he could smell her. I wasn't convinced. The rash seemed like a punishment.

Our pediatrician's prognosis was poison ivy because we were both scratching. He gave us each a lollipop. "Can I get two more?" Bernie asked him. "I got one but me and myself didn't. The three of us got a sweet tooth."

"The three of us *have* a sweet tooth," our mother corrected.

"No can do, kiddo," said Dr. Cox. "One sucker per patient. That's my policy."

Dr. Cox wore a clown nose. He had the most colorful office in Princeton Professional Park, a complex that also housed our dentist, my orthodontist and Bernie's reading specialist. There were rainbows and balloons painted on his walls. There was a plastic indoor jungle gym for the under-five set. Dr. Cox let you use his stethoscope and filch latex gloves from the cardboard dispenser. But he was not a good listener.

"They haven't had any exposure to poison ivy," our mother informed him.

"I know it when I see it." He winked. She treated our faces with calamine lotion according to his advice. Bernie's rash was gone within a couple of days, but mine spread. It moved down my neck, expanded across my chest, and extended the length of my inner arms where it stopped at my pulse. My mother marched me into my father's study.

"Look at that, Bernard," she said, lifting the hem of my turtleneck to the level of my eyes. "That can't be poison ivy." I couldn't see whether he looked away from his book at the vicious red bumps on my trunk or not.

"So take her back to the doctor," he said.

Dr. Cox told her he still believed it was poison ivy. The fact that my condition hadn't abated in ten days only meant my allergy was severer than most. He made a fist holding the tip of his thumb between two fingers and told me, "I got your nose!" Then he prescribed an antihistamine and handed me a lollipop, which I saved for my brother because he was my best friend.

❧

"You must be allergic to something," Fran said. "Hold on a sec." She went into our bedroom and came back with her medical kit, which was a large Easter basket. Fran's real father was an internist. The basket of meds he'd packed for his daughter included Band-Aids, rubbing alcohol, and a gross assortment of prescription drug samples. If Fran had been entrepreneurial, she could have made a fortune in college, off the Vicodin alone.

She sat on the futon with her goodies. "Let's see," she said, rooting around. "Oooh, ephedrine. That'll wake me up. And I know there's some hydrocortisone somewhere in here for you."

"No thanks," I said. "It won't help."

"But I thought it itched really badly?"

"It does, but that won't work. I've tried it before."

"Oh," said Fran. She set the basket on her lap, rested her chin on its handle, and stared at my face like it was a museum piece. "I don't get it. That half is big as a pumpkin, but if you turned your head sideways, I couldn't even tell."

"It's a mystery." I shrugged. The two prevailing mysteries of my life were my rash and my father.

"Do you think it could be stress related?" Her voice turned maternal. "Because of your brother's accident?"

"No," I stiffened. I opened the rash journal and bent over it.

"I didn't mean—"

"It's okay."

"I was only trying to help."

"I know."

"You should really see a doctor, Emma. It looks pretty bad."

"Right."

Fran swallowed two ephedrine with a sip of Mountain Dew and returned to her desk to conclude her paper. After a while she began pecking at the keyboard. Except for the bluish light emitting from her computer screen, the common room was dark and full of shadows.

I was the shadow of my rash. It had form. I didn't. It was begging to be scratched. That sensation was the only thing that was real. That and the book in my hands. Everything else was a bad joke: Fran's panties, the sweltering heat, the Papasan chair, the gothic leaded windows, the mantelpiece, the mini-fridge with its poetry magnets, the fact of Bernie's preposterous accident, the leopard print futon, the hammering radiator, the phallic cactus plant, Fran's lacrosse stick, and the words "Flip Fitzroy, '39 BOOLA BOOLA," carved in block letters on the wood floor. I examined these items in the dim light and couldn't make sense of them. Fran also struck me as unreal. They were all part of a stage set that could fall apart without a moment's notice. I began to panic and turned on the halogen lamp. The effect was the same, even under illumination. None of it had meaning. The bells of Harkness Tower tolled six. My face itched terribly.

I turned to the rash journal and after a few pages, became absorbed. Each entry was headed by my age in years and months, rather than the date. My mother used this same notation in the big book of Bernie-isms where she recorded all the precocious things my brother ever said from the age of eight to the age of nineteen. Bernie's book was the most meticulous of all her journals; it reads like a hagiography. She stopped writing in it when he fell into the coma. I think the reason our mom used our ages rather than the dates to annotate these journals was that for her, we marked time rather than time marking us. The first entry in the diary of my rash read:

11.11
Emma has the rash again. Seems chronic. Red pinpoint
spots on face, more heavily concentrated on cheeks and forehead.
Eyelids clear. Itchy. Catalysts? Tuna fish with celery, dill pickle,
chocolate pudding, milk. Jergens soap? Insect repellent? The SUN??

I don't remember that rash, but I do remember the next one:

12.3
Raised red bumps on face, backs of knees and inside elbows.
Look like spider bites. Itchy. Hamburger Helper, lima beans,
milk.

The reason I remember that rash is that I still had it on the first day of seventh grade when Vlad Ludlow called me "greasegirl" because he mistook it for acne.

In spite of the name-calling, I didn't really mind. As a matter of fact, I grew to enjoy the attention the rash attracted. There was something magic in it. I normally felt invisible, but the rash made people stare. It lured my mother's attention away from Bernie, who outshone me at everything except for school. It won sympathy from my teachers. It dominated my biracial features, which my classmates found perplexing. Most important, when it was bad enough, the rash demanded my father's compassion.

My rash was often violently itchy, like something live crawled under the skin. I'd attempt to dig it out. One time my mother found me raking my face with two forks, snatched them away and marched me into my father's study.

"Your daughter was scratching her face with silverware!" she informed him.

"Take her to the doctor," he said.

"Look at her! Her face is bleeding. She's crying."

"No I'm not," I pointed out.

"And if you think Dr. Cox can help her, you're wrong. He doesn't know what's what. Last time he gave her antibiotics and even *I* know—"

"So bring her to a dermatologist."

"It's Saturday. Nobody's open on a Saturday."

My father sighed. "Do you want me to take her to the ER? Is that what you want?"

"It's not really an emergency, you guys," I said.

"Your mother seems to think so."

"Don't you put words in my mouth."

"I'm working on a lecture, Lynn. What is it exactly you want me to do?"

"*Help* me for once!" she entreated. "Help her. She's sick."

Later that night after she tucked me in, there was a knock at my door.

I immediately stopped scratching my face and crossed my hands over my chest like Sleeping Beauty. "Come in," I called, sweetly.

My father entered, with two industrial-size rolls of Christmas wrapping paper. One of them had snowmen on a blue background. The other had candy canes on a green background.

"Hello, Emma," he said.

"Hello, Dad."

"I got you these for your rash."

"Thank you," I said, "They're very nice."

He sat down on the side of my bed and held my hand. My heartbeat accelerated. He smelled like bay rum. "They're to go on your arms so you can't scratch your face." He stuck my hand in one of the tubes and pushed it up to my armpit. He sheathed my other arm in the same way. I experienced two simultaneous but contradictory sensations. The first was that my father had made me a present of my own body. The second was that he was forcing me not to open it.

"Try to bend your elbows."

I couldn't.

"See?" he said.

I smiled. "Uh-huh. Thank you."

"You're welcome. Good night."

"Good night." I could have freed my arms easily, but I didn't. I lay inert all night long wearing the Christmas casts while my rash raged.

My mother had plenty of other tricks to keep me from scratching but none of them worked as well as my father's wrapping paper. She clipped my fingernails down to the quick and put mittens on my hands. "Otherwise you'll get scars," she told me, dousing the affected areas with calamine lotion. "Do you want scars?" She drew me oatmeal baths like she did when Bernie and I had chicken pox. I'd soak until the oatmeal clotted and my fingers puckered. Bernie would open the bathroom door and holler, "Is my breakfast done yet?" Sometimes those baths were soothing. But then I'd towel off and be in the same prickly state of irritation as before. I had to scratch. I did it in private. There was something deeply satisfying in it.

"Whatever you do, don't scratch," my mother warned. "It'll make matters worse."

> 13.6
> Red pimply rash confined to face. Some swelling around eyes
> and mouth. Scabby in places where Emma has scratched the
> sores open. Turkey casserole, broccoli, fruit cocktail with
> cottage cheese.

Soon after the night of the wrapping paper, I realized I could manipulate the rash. I couldn't make it go away once I had it, but I could bring it on when it wasn't there and I could make it worse once it came. I began by scratching at a patch of normal skin. If I did this furiously enough, red tracks would rise like zippers, and elongate in a matter of seconds. I was able to chart which way on the map of my body I wanted these tracks to run—east, west, north or south. By the age of thirteen I developed my power to the point where I didn't even have to scratch to bring out the rash. I could just stare at my naked arm with intention until a welt appeared, and then another, and then a family of them.

> 13.10
> Red traveling welts just underneath skin of inner
> thighs, inner arms and stomach. Peanut butter and
> jelly sandwich, orange, Oreo cookies, juice-box.
> Laundry detergent? Deodorant?

Bernie caught me at it once. Our father was away on a research trip or a lecture tour or getting an honorary degree. I was sitting in the broken high chair in the attic staring at my face in a hand mirror.

"What are you doing?" Bernie asked me. He was outside the rear window with his saxophone, standing on the roof of the back porch.

"What are *you* doing?" I asked him.

"Don't worry about it," he said and climbed in, ducking his head so as not to bump it on the eaves. "You're giving yourself the rash, aren't you?"

There was no use lying to him. He would have been able to tell. "Yes," I admitted. I was ashamed.

"I thought so. Why?"

"I'm not sure."

Bernie considered my ability for a minute. "Can you give yourself stigmata?"

"Probably."

"Can you give me the rash?"

"I don't think so."

"Try."

He put down his saxophone and brought his face directly in front of mine. We didn't look too much alike. I always wished I looked like him, but I was only his pale imitation. After the accident he looked like a monster, but before that he had gingerbread skin and movie star eyes. There was a mole under his eye like a tear. I stared hard at that and tried to put the rash on him but it didn't work. Instead, my face grew hot and I began to cry.

"Shhhh, Emma. You're gonna be okay." Bernie hugged me to his chest. His arms were getting stronger from the weights he was using. He rocked me until I quieted down. "Shhhh," he said. I could feel his heart against my cheek.

"I'm sorry," I told him.

"It's all right. I get angry too. That's how we are." He picked up his saxophone and smiled. "Watch this," he said. He blew into it hard. Then he started working his fingers over the keys so wild it sounded like a police siren and a riot all at once.

Our mother shouted from below for him to cut it out. "It's too loud!" Bernie pretended he couldn't hear her. "ENOUGH!" He kept going. "Quiet down! The neighbors!" She climbed the stairs and drew her finger across her neck. Bernie quit his rant. The last note hung in the air like an exclamation point after a curse word.

"What is going on?" she demanded.

"We're mad," Bernie explained. He started taking apart his saxophone.

"You are?"

I nodded my head.

"About what?"

"You wouldn't get it," Bernie said.

"What do you mean? I'm mad."

"It's not the same. You have to look like us."

"I look like you."

"No," Bernie explained. The midsection of his saxophone was dripping saliva. "You have to look like Dad."

"Oh." Our mom looked injured. I felt bad for her, but that's how it was between Bernie and me. We were a club. She touched her hair and said, "Well. It's dinnertime. We're having beef stroganoff."

14.2
Raspberry eruptions on cheeks and chin and palms—look like stigmata. Inflamed. Itchy. Beef stroganoff, tossed salad, iced tea. Radishes?

The bells of Harkness Tower tolled seven but it was still dark outside. I looked at my reflection in the window. My mouth was closed but my lips were so swollen on the left side that the right side had involuntarily parted to show my teeth. I still couldn't open my left eye. Fran was typing furiously, pumping her left leg up and down like a jackhammer and grinding her teeth on account of the ephedrine. I gathered her paper was going well. She was talking to herself. "Oh, this is good. This is really good," she said.

"When's it due?" I asked.

"Nine," she answered. "Don't talk. I'm on a roll."

I kept reading.

14.5
Colony of hives wrap from back to chest, up to neck and face. Baked chicken, brussel sprouts, mashed potatoes, apple juice, rainbow sherbet.

By the time I was fourteen and five months, Dr. Cox had long since referred me to a dermatologist named Dr. Rhinehart, who was equally self-assured and equally at a loss for a cure. Dr. Rhinehart operated a private practice out of a solar-powered house designed by Michael Graves. He was one of the first doctors on the East Coast to specialize in Botox injections. The waiting room outside his office featured a Japanese rock garden and a speaker in each corner that played "The Four Seasons" on a looping soundtrack. It was always a long wait to see him, during which my mother flipped through the parenting magazines fanned on the glass coffee table and said, "That's a laugh."

Dr. Rhinehart's first diagnosis was dermatitis. He prescribed a number of steroid creams, none of which had any effect. I always felt violated after visiting him, in part because he had to scrutinize my chest at the time I was beginning to develop breasts, and in part because he wore a pair of creepy magnifying glasses to see into my pores.

"How's school?" or "How's summer vacation?" he would ask, depending on the season, while studying my skin. His eyes were as large as testicles behind those glasses.

"Fine."

"Does it hurt when I do this?"

"No."

"Does it itch?"

"Yeah."

"Try not to scratch it. Don't fidget. How's your family?"

"Fine."

"You have very smooth skin under this rash."

"Thank you."

Dr. Rhinehart's second diagnosis was psoriasis. He referred me to a tanning salon called Beach Bum in the hope that the ultraviolet lamps would dry out my sores. These treatments were not covered by our health insurance plan and only served to exacerbate the rash. But they did make my color match my brother's and I liked them for that reason.

I saw Dr. Rhinehart until I was fifteen when the journal indicates my mother became fed up with him:

> 15.1
> Blotchy rash on face. Fishsticks. Tartar sauce. Creamed spinach. Ricemilk. Hawaiian Tropic? Dr. Rhinehart is a quack. We will try Eastern medicine.

Dr. Lee operated a sunlit center for herbal healing in New Hope, Pennsylvania. It was decorated with Tibetan flags, spider plants, and sisal mats on the floor. A foot-high figure of a naked man festooned with qi points and meridian lines stood sentinel on her desk. He was not as well defined as the Christ on the crucifix at our church. That is, Dr. Lee's qi doll had no apparent rib cage, belly button, pupils, nor fingernails. His eyes were closed like Buddha's and he didn't have eyelashes. He was made of some white substance like modeling clay or wax and, maybe for that reason, struck me as malleable and unformed, like a fetus.

Dr. Lee herself was of indiscriminate age. She could have been forty and she could have been seventy. She had a wiry gray braid that reached to her waist, no body hair, a gentle manner, and little child hands. The first time I saw her, she made me lie on her massage table, open my mouth and say, "Ahhh." My mother asked what she was doing.

"I'm reading your daughter's tongue," Dr. Lee said.

"What does it say?"

"Her liver is full of toxins."

"It is? How can you tell?"

Dr. Lee consulted a book full of passport-sized color photographs of tongues. She flipped backwards through the pages until she found a tongue resembling mine and showed it to us. It had faint purple spots. The text underneath it was in Chinese. A tongue on that same page had a large black growth. Another was red as blood. Another had plaque as thick as fur. I was mortified. Dr. Lee closed the book.

She checked the pulse points in my wrists and said, "Her energy flow is blocked."

"What's blocking it?" my mom asked.

"The liver is supposed to process what comes into the body and purify it. Her body ingests negative substances—exhaust, lead, pesticides, stress—but her liver isn't flushing them out. It's not able to eliminate the heat and toxins inside her."

"Why not?" asked my mother.

"You see this?" Dr. Lee pointed to my face, which was blistering with the rash. "Your daughter consists entirely of fire."

"Pardon me?"

"She's disharmonious. There is no water element in her character." I didn't enjoy being referred to in this way, especially in the third person. I channeled my anger at the qi doll and tried to topple him off the doctor's desk telekinetically. His face was serene and without character. He didn't budge.

"My goodness." I could tell my mother was enthralled. "What do you suggest we do for that?"

"Aloe leaf to cool the skin. But this is an internal problem, not an external one. She needs to drink a gallon of purified water every day. She should also take milk thistle, dong quai, and dandelion tincture to help the liver function. Artichoke is also good. And, please, no more processed foods."

"No processed foods?"

"That's right. No additives."

"OK, but do you mean *none*?"

"Definitely not."

My mother was mystified. "Then what on earth am I supposed to feed her?"

"Organic vegetables."

15.5
Lava-like rash spread from hands up arms to elbows. Beets, kale, parsnips, garlic, brown rice. Sweet potato, maple syrup. Distilled water with dong quai drops. What am I doing wrong?

It took three-quarters of an hour to drive from Princeton to New Hope in my mother's Toyota. She usually filled the full forty-five minutes discussing the fights between Bernie and my father. These were increasing in both number and intensity during the period I saw Dr. Lee. Bernie was a colossal disappointment. He was failing high school. He was growing weed in the backyard. He was staying out all night. When he got arrested for suspicious behavior, our dad took his saxophone away and accused him of trying to be a statistic.

"Look at this house!" he yelled. "Have you ever wanted for anything? You don't know the meaning of want. You live in one of the best communities, with one of the best school systems in the *country*. I work my ass off to give you everything and you do everything in your power to throw it away."

"I never asked for any of that stuff. That stuff don't mean shit."

"Oh it doesn't? Your great-great-great-great grandfather was a slave so your great-great-great grandfather could be a sharecropper, so your great-great-grandfather could be a farmer so your great-grandfather could be a preacher so I could be a professor so you could be anything you want. Do you mean to say none of what those men did for you mattered? Look at yourself. Are you proud of what you are? I know I'm not."

"You missed one."

"What?"

"You left out my grandfather."

"That's not the point! The point is—all you have to do is take your crown and wear it. But what do you do? You go and get yourself arrested for suspicious behavior."

Bernie claimed he was just running to school because he was late.

"Oh, because you were *late*?"

"That's what I said."

"Last time I checked you weren't too worried about going to school, let alone getting there on time."

"I can run if I want to."

"But you just had to start running when you passed a patrol car? As fast as you could."

"It's a free country."

"You may be a fool, but you're not stupid."

"Last time I checked you said I was."

"Your behavior certainly was stupid."

"I didn't do anything wrong!"

"You were fleeing an officer!"

"You know he only arrested me 'cause I'm black."

"What are you trying to prove?"

"Nothing."

"No, enlighten me. I'd really like to know what you're trying to prove."

Bernie squared his shoulders. He was taller than our father when he stood straight like that, but something about them looked exactly the same. Especially when they fought.

"Maybe it's cursed," Bernie said.

"Excuse me?"

"That crown you were talking about. Maybe it's *cursed*."

My mom's opinion was that Bernie sought negative attention through repeated acts of rebellion. "Dr. Lord says it's because your father never gave him enough positive attention. What do you think?" she asked me on one of our drives to New Hope. Dr. Lord was the psychiatrist she'd just started seeing.

"Could be," I said, concentrating with great effort on the reflection of my face in the side view mirror.

"Boys need their fathers. If their fathers aren't around, it drives them to misbehave. Of course, your father's there in the physical sense. But he's emotionally absent. Sometimes I wonder if he's capable of love." Once she advised me not to marry a black man. "They're too complex," she warned.

> 15.10
> Rash again on face, neck and shoulders. Also in armpits.
> Tofu, tomato, artichoke salad. Vinegar dressing. Soy milk.
> Dr. Lee did acupuncture on liver points starting on top of
> E.'s feet, inside ankles and up inner legs ending at groin.
> Emma skeptical. We will see.

"Are there two *P*'s in happenstanced or one?" asked Fran, surprising me from the rash journal. I'd been unconsciously clawing at the left side of my face. I dropped my hand into my lap.

"What?" I asked. She was talking too fast from the ephedrine and it was hard to understand her.

"HOWDOYOUSPELL 'HAPPENSTANCED'?"

"I don't think that's a word, Fran," I said.

"Sure it's a word. Of course it's a word. It's the past tense of happenstance."

"Use it in a sentence."

"'Rather than dynastically, Mao Zedung happenstanced the modernity of a U.S.-modeled open labor market system whereupon the faltering structural economy of China maintains unabetted.'"

"That's a sentence in your paper?"

"Yeah. How does it sound? I'm wrapping up."

Not one word of it made sense to me. Nothing did. Nothing but the feeling of the rash. And not even the source of that.

I doubted anyone would read her paper anyway. I'd written a violent haiku in the middle of my ancient philosophy midterm and the professor hadn't noticed. "You'll probably get an A," I told Fran.

"I better. What time is it?"

"Twenty to eight." The day was beginning to dawn.

"Shit! Don't talk to me. I have to finish this." She attacked the keyboard and I went back to my mother's entries.

> 16.4
> Outbreak of rash on face. Bernie has it too this time.
> Contagious? Itchy, red, slight swelling around eyes.
> Spinach quiche.

Our father had been inducted as the first black dean of Princeton's Graduate School of Arts and Science. An oil painting was made of him and hung in Nassau Hall. We moved into the gloomy dean's estate. Wyman House was listed in the registry of National Historic Landmarks and situated above a golf course. Among other things, it included a rose garden, a silver safe, a housekeeper, a grand piano, and a gallery showcasing an antique gun from the Revolutionary War.

Our mother was against the move. I know this because I read her most private journal named The Pillow Book, after Sei Shōnagon. She thought the new administrative duties would put too much strain on our father and take up too much of his time. Also, she wasn't keen on the idea of hosting graduate functions and teas. Bernie and I were against the move too. The bedrooms were in separate wings. The floors were cold. We weren't allowed to bring a lot of our things because the house was already furnished.

We didn't belong. Four months after the move, our father told us he was leaving. He didn't say anything about a midlife crisis, or the pressure he was under, or the pretensions of suburbia, or the hollowness of academia, or the politics of power, or the neediness of us, or the woman he was seeing on the side. These were all topics my mother wrote about in great detail in The Pillow Book. What he did say was: "I may be gone for one month, I may be gone for two months, I may be gone forever." Then, he got up from the dinner table and walked out the door.

"Did you see that coming?" Bernie asked.

"No," I hiccupped.

"Did you?" he asked our mom.

She looked like a used tissue. "It's something we've been discussing," she said.

"Do we have to stay here?" I asked. I hiccupped again.

"Yes. Until we can get the old house back."

"Where's he going?" Bernie wanted to know.

"He got an apartment."

Bernie began hiccupping too. Nobody said anything else for a little while. Then our mother mentioned that the quiche was getting cold and we should eat.

"I'm not hungry," I said. My hiccups were very bad.

"Me neither," said Bernie. His hiccups were Herculean.

"Well, if nobody's hungry, I guess I'll go to bed," our mother said. It was seven o'clock. She rose and went upstairs.

"Stop hiccupping," Bernie said.

"You stop."

"I can't."

"Me neither." My stomach felt like a squeeze toy being squeezed.

Bernie picked up the quiche and brought it over to me like he meant to serve me a piece.

"No thanks. I'm really not hungry," I managed to say between hiccups.

He force-fed me a forkful. I immediately stopped hiccupping.

"Now do it to me," he said.

After I gave him a bite we went and stole a golf cart to go for a ride. Bernie had a mini-key that fit into the mini-ignition. I asked him where he got it.

"Don't worry about it," he said.

It was December. There was frost on the green so the grass crunched under the wheels. We drove past the naked weeping willows along the banks of the man-made creek and up to the ninth hole where Bernie parked by a sand trap. He got out and lay down on the sand with his hands behind his head, like he was at the beach.

"It's cold," I complained, but I joined him anyway. I watched the cloud of breath vaporizing from my brother's mouth. I tried to match my breath to his but my teeth were chattering. "Look. There's Orion." I pointed. "See his belt?"

Bernie scratched at his jaw.

"On the other side of the equator he's upside down."

"How do you know he isn't upside down here and right-side up there?"

"Good point."

"No it ain't. Do you really give a fuck about Orion?"

I didn't know what to say.

"Do you?"

"I guess not."

"How come you don't ever say what's really on your mind?"

"What do you mean?" I bristled. My goose bumps grew larger.

"I mean you're just like him. How come you always gotta talk about something faraway instead of what's close to you?"

"I don't know," I said. I felt like crying. "Maybe I don't know what I think."

"Bullshit, Emma. All you do is think."

"Then I guess I'm just shy."

"That's a bullshit word. 'Shy.' That just a pretty word for selfish."

I thought about that for a while until I understood what he meant. "Did you see it coming?" I said softly.

"Don't matter. He was already gone anyway. The true part of him was never there."

"Where do you think it was? I mean, what do you think happened to him?"

"I think he killed it."

"Why?"

"To protect himself."

"From what?" I shuddered. But when Bernie was getting ready to answer, I saw something out of the corner of my eye. "Look!" I pointed. A flashlight beam was slowly sweeping the eighth hole.

"Lie back down," Bernie said. "That guy won't find us."

"But—"

"He can't see us. We're invisible."

I could feel the rash coming out on my face. No, it was more like my face was falling away to reveal the rash and the rash was my natural state. I lay very still and didn't scratch it. We could hear the groundskeeper's boots crunching the ground, coming closer. When the beam of his flashlight compassed our sand trap it lighted on my brother's face, then crossed it, then kept on sweeping the course. In the instant Bernie's face was illuminated, I saw he had the rash too.

"I'm furious," I admitted.

"No shit," Bernie said. "If it was you and Orion in the ring, I'd put my money on you."

16.5
Full body rash.
I don't remember what she ate.

The bells of Harkness Tower chimed eight.

"Shit!" said Fran.

"Almost done?" I asked.

"Almost."

I closed the rash journal and got up to look out the window. The day was castle gray. The buildings were castle gray. Old Campus was empty except for the statue of Nathan Hale and a lone black maintenance man, spearing plastic cups and beer cans into a garbage bag.

"I guess I better pack," I said.

Fran didn't stop typing. "Uh-huh. What?"

"I'm going to pack."

"Good idea!"

I went back into our bedroom and checked my face in the long-view mirror on the back of Fran's closet door. The rash was unchanged except that it looked worse in the daylight. The left eye was still swollen tight as a clam. I turned this way and that to see myself in profile. It was true—I looked like two different people. I pulled my duffel bag out from under my bed. Just as I finished filling it and zipping it closed I heard Fran's printer start whining.

She ran in and started throwing on clothes. "What time is it?"

"Eight twenty-eight."

"Good. I'll make it."

"Listen, I won't be here when you get back," I said.

"What do you mean? Aren't you going to University Health to see about your rash?"

"No. I'm going home. There's a train at 9:07. If I walk down with you and set out now, I should just make it."

Fran looked exasperated. "You're going to walk to the train station?"

"Yeah."

"But it's dangerous!"

"It's only a mile away. I'll be fine." I set my duffel bag on my shoulder.

"Wait!" she yelled, like she thought I was going to disappear. "Sit down. I have something for you!" She opened her closet and took out a tastefully wrapped gift. "Merry Christmas!"

"Oh," I said. "Oh."

"Open it!"

The weight of her affection made the left side of my head hang. "I didn't get anything for you."

"I don't care"—she pressed—"open it."

I opened it. It was a jar of olives.

"They're Manzanillos! From our ranch." Fran sat next to me on my bed, bouncing it a little. "And the offer still stands." She and her parents had invited me to visit them during winter break in order to regroup. That was the word she'd used—"regroup," and it had put me in mind of a sanitarium boot camp. "Sure you won't reconsider?"

"Yeah," I said. "But thank you." At that time, before I realized he'd left his body, I just wanted to be near my brother.

"I understand. You've been through a lot this semester." She turned solemn all of a sudden, as if she'd crashed off the drug, or was sobered by my tears, or both. "I think you're really brave, Emma," she said.

I wiped my nose and rolled my eye. "What, because I'm walking to the train station?"

"You know that's not what I mean."

"Yeah, but I'm not brave. I can't even—"

"Just say thank you."

The jar of olives felt good and solid in my lap. "Thank you." I unzipped my duffel bag and settled them next to my rash journal. "Oh," I said, seeing the *nkisi* nestled on top of my underwear. "I do have something for you." I handed it to her. "Merry Christmas."

"What is it?" asked Fran.

"It's a good luck charm. I made it yesterday." Actually, I had made it for Bernie after reading a chapter on vodun in a book called *Hunger of the Gods* for my Haitian anthropology class, but she didn't need to know that. I'd ripped off the pocket from my red wool toggle coat, filled it with dirt I'd pilfered from the grave of a man named Hezekiah Gilbert interred at Grove Street Cemetery, stuck in a white feather from a Long Wharf seagull, tied it closed with one of my hair bands, and glued on a silver-plated earring. I had crafted it out of desperate need for a miracle, knowing that it would fail.

"We better get going," I said.

We parted ways at Phelps Gate. Fran galloped across Old Campus to turn in her paper. I passed under the gateway, and within a matter of seconds was transported into an alternate world. It was like stepping through the looking glass. On this side, everybody was black and seemed to be waiting at one bus stop or another for buses that weren't coming any time soon. There was no grass, no green, just gray. The garbage cans were overflowing. Stores were burnt out, or bankrupt, or gated shut and vandalized with graffiti. The air had a harder, clearer edge. It seemed impossible for the two worlds to exist on the same plane. I looked behind me over the New Haven Green to check. My suspicions were confirmed. My school was a stage set, a cardboard fortress. Harkness Tower was a fake. Its hands said 8:40. I turned right on Church Street and hurried along. The sidewalk was blowing with litter. It was bitter cold and I wasn't wearing gloves. I tried shoving my hands in my coat pockets, but one of my pockets was gone. I felt cockeyed and schizophrenic. I crossed a traffic bridge and kept on going. I scratched my face. Then, before I knew it, I was lost. I heard the whistle of a train, but I couldn't tell what direction it was coming from. I took an educated guess. I turned left into a housing development. The pigeon-gray buildings were low and grimy and so was the sky. This was a stage set too, but for a different play. I stopped by a dumpster that smelled like rot. I scratched my face again.

*"Don't move,"* someone said behind me. He had a male voice, but it cracked, like he wasn't a man yet. "I got a gun, bitch."

I'm not sure why, but I didn't believe him.

"Don't turn around. Just set your bag on the ground and keep walking."

I turned around.

"I *said* don't—" He gasped when he saw my face. He was wearing a puffy black jacket and a yellow wool hat with a kangaroo on it. He held a bottle of Gatorade but not a gun. He wasn't any taller than I was. I guessed he was about fourteen.

"I'm trying to get to the train station," I said.

"Somebody smacked you? I mean, why your face look like that?"

"Voodoo," I told him.

"Word?"

I smiled with the right side of my mouth.

"That's fucked up."

I unzipped my duffel bag. "I'll give you this if you tell me where the train station is."

"What is it?"

"Olives. They should be really good. They're from California." I held the jar out to him.

The boy shrugged and accepted the offering. "I like olives all right." He struggled to unscrew the lid then tried one. "Spicy," he said. "You want one?"

"Yes, please." I took an olive. "That is good."

We spat our seeds on the ground.

He smiled. "You know who you remind me of?"

"No."

"Two-Face. From Batman? You know, 'cause your face all split in half."

"I hadn't thought of that. The bad guy."

"I ain't saying you a bad guy or nothing."

"I'm not saying you are." We laughed. "What's your name?"

"Shorty."

"Nice to meet you, Shorty."

"What's yours?"

"Bernie."

"C'mon, Miss Bernie. I'll walk you. Train station's right this way." The ground was covered with broken glass. He took me by the arm. "My real name's Curtis," he said.

"My real name's Emma."

"You got a boyfriend, Emma?"

"Don't flirt with me. I'm old enough to be your mother."

"I'm twenty-one."

"I'm Miss America."

We laughed again. We came to the edge of the projects. Union Station was across the street, but the traffic light was against us. Curtis popped another olive in his mouth.

"Sorry 'bout how I tried to rob you before," he said.

"Don't worry about it. We get angry sometimes. That's just how we are. Watch this." I threw back my head and yelled at the top of my lungs. Curtis was so surprised he dropped the olive jar. It smashed on the concrete.

"Damn, girl," he said. "You crazy like Two-Face too. I should smack you up the other side your head for getting olive juice on my Nikes." We laughed real hard at that.

"So long, sister," he said.

"So long, brother." I never saw him again.

I made it onto the 9:07 to New York just before the doors closed. There were a few businesspeople in the car and all of them stared at me choosing my seat. As the train pulled out of the station, I took the rash journal out of my duffel bag. I turned to the page after my mother's last entry and began to write.

Dear Bernie,

My rash is back but I didn't give it to myself this time. It came on its own. I have two faces.

Imagine a butterfly with one wing as thin as tissue paper and the other as bulbous as a human ear. That's what I look like. Imagine a one-legged man with no crutch. That's how I am with you gone. Not like the man, like the missing leg. You made me symmetrical. How do I stand now? How do I withstand it?

Show me a dictionary, Bernie. Nothing makes sense. Not even language. A "dromedary" and a "pinecone" are the same thing. Shapes to fill. Voids. "Trapezoid," "hunger," "pogo-stick," "black," "white," "God." A pogo stick is the same thing as happenstance until you balance your feet on it and bounce. Where is God in this? What is the word for me now? I was your sister. You used to say we were the same thing. What does your absence make me? An empty shape. A two-faced shape shifter. A fire.

Did it hurt when you burned? Did you do it on purpose? Are you dead?

---

Mom thinks you can hear us talking. She believes you are straddling this life and the next. I walked through two worlds today on my way to the train. If there are two worlds, one on top of the other, why not three, or four, or one million? And if one million, which are you in? Show me the bridge. All I want is for this train to take me there.

Love,
Emma

At Grand Central Station, I craned my neck to stargaze at the ceiling. I scratched my face. "There's Orion, the hunter," I said out loud.

"Where?" said a pregnant woman in a Yankee jacket. Her head was thrown back like mine. Her belly was big as a globe. Her hands were at the small of her back. "I don't see it."

I pointed. "See his belt?" He was five stories above us, far away but near, mesmerizing and just out of reach.

"Oh yeah," she whispered. "That's him all right."

I left her standing in reverie. The crowd orbited around her at a furious pace. They were late. They had somewhere to be.

I took a cab to Penn Station and hopped a New Jersey Transit Train to Princeton Junction where my father was to pick me up. Normally I would have taken the shuttle train directly into Princeton, but it had been the site of Bernie's accident and I couldn't stomach it.

He was standing down in the parking lot with one hand in the pocket of his overcoat and the other on his cane. I saw him from the platform before he saw me. His hair had more white in it than I remembered.

"Hello, Dad," I said, approaching him.

He took one look at my face and said, "Have you been messing with goofer dust?"

"What?"

"Tell me the truth. Did you touch graveyard dirt?"

"Yes," I admitted. "How did you know?"

"Get in the car," he said.

We buckled our seatbelts. "That's the punishment when you mess with a bigger power than yourself," he explained.

"It is?"

"Swelling of the face. On one side."

I considered Hezekiah Gilbert, exacting revenge on my face for disturbing his place of rest. "Really?"

"My godmother taught me about it when I was a boy."

"Nanan Zanobia?" He almost never talked about her.

"That's right."

"Did it ever happen to you?"

"Did what ever happen to me?" We drove past the frozen soccer fields along Washington Road, where Bernie had played as a goalie.

"This," I said, meaning my face.

"Once."

"How?"

He was squeezing the steering wheel so hard his knuckles were white.

"Whose graveyard dirt did you touch?" I pressed.

"My father's." He flicked on the windshield wipers. It had begun to rain.

When we were still living at Wyman House, Bernie told me that our grandfather, the first Bernard, was lynched. Dad didn't tell Bernie this. He claimed to have remembered it in a dream. Now I wanted to ask my father whether or not it was true, but I was afraid. Instead I asked what he did with Granddad's goofer dust.

He cleared his throat and said, "I ate it."

We stopped at the light on Faculty Road and sat in silence. When the light turned green he said, "I'll drop you off at your mother's house. I've got some papers to grade."

"Okay," I said.

We drove past the university, the Woodrow Wilson School with its plantation white pillars. I saw that it was cardboard too. I would have liked to ask him if he felt schizophrenic, but something held my tongue. I was relieved for the moment just to know the rash was larger than I was. We drove by the eating clubs with their manicured lawns. He stopped in front of the house Bernie and I grew up in, minus all of his things. There was no Christmas tree in the living room window. My mother's Toyota wasn't in the driveway, which meant she was at the hospital, sitting with my brother. My father didn't notice. Later (after the doctors told her there was nothing more they could do for my brother, that he would never wake up, that he was brain dead), she would bring Bernie home and set him up with his respirator where the Christmas tree used to go. She would arrange his limbs in the most optimal position for circulation, rearrange him to prevent bedsores, rub salve into his skin, and talk to him about her day. I would snoop through her journals and read what she had come to decide about doctors: "Ultimately, they are ignorant concerning the human heart."

I unbuckled my seatbelt. "Well, thanks for the ride," I said. I repressed the urge to scratch my face.

Without looking at me, he reached over and laid his hand on my head. It rested there for a full eight seconds, during which I felt my heartbeat roaring in my ears.

# SINGING FOR THE CARDINAL

The boy's choir of St. Ignatius Prep was in the chapel rehearsing Fauré's Requiem in preparation for their trip to Rome. Pinky St. Pierre had been elected to do the solo, which was something of a controversy among the boys, who were all in agreement that Ned Drake had the better voice. Since Ned's voice was changing and he really couldn't be depended on to hold a high C longer than two bars without it suddenly cracking in the middle like an egg and dropping three octaves, this idea probably had more to do with the fact that he was much better liked than Pinky. Adding to Ned's popularity were the facts that he kept a library of mint condition Mexican porn under his bed, was liberal with his stolen Marlboros, and had a bounty hunter for a father.

Pinky St. Pierre, on the other hand, was practically an albino. He could be counted on to get sunstroke during shot put, he was a day student rather than a boarder, and his face was pretty as a girl's. Also, his father was only a bank teller. Pinky was really only one rung above the colored kid on the social ladder.

"What does your father do?" Pinky had squeaked at the colored kid from across the reject's table in the dining hall during the first week at lunchtime.

The colored kid couldn't be sure if this was an attempt on Pinky's part to be polite or a setup for more ridicule. He pushed his glasses up the flat bridge of his nose and leveled his eyes at the smaller boy, who had made a bib of his napkin and was taking miniature bites of his rice pudding to make it last longer. Pinky St. Pierre looked guileless enough. His white-blond hair made a cowlicky cornsilk halo around his head.

"He's a sculptor," the colored kid answered. "In Europe." This was one in a string of lies that had started from his mouth after the golf club incident on the day he arrived at St. Ignatius. "He makes sculptures out of ice."

"You mean like those swans they got at the fancy weddings?" Pinky squeaked, licking the rice pudding from his spoon.

"Exactly," the colored kid answered. He was starving for conversation.

"I sure do like rice pudding when they make it like this. With the cinnamon on top."

"Who doesn't?"

"It's yummy."

"I agree."

"Do you like dragons?" Pinky asked.

"Sure do," the colored kid answered. He'd never considered how he felt about dragons before.

"I hate them," Pinky shuddered. "With all my heart."

"Oh."

Pinky hadn't said anything else after that, as if the disagreement about dragons was an unbreachable chasm. He continued to eat his rice pudding in silence. The colored kid searched for something else to say.

After a moment he began, "The thing about sculpting ice is, only a handful of people in the whole world know how to do it. That puts my dad in high demand."

"Uh-huh." Pinky savored his last bite of rice pudding.

"Matter fact, a Siberian count just hired him to make his youngest daughter a playhouse all from ice, including the furniture and a itty-bitty tea set. My dad told them it would hold through the winter but come next spring the whole thing's bound to melt into a big old puddle. The count said that was okay by him; he can just hire a Japanese and turn it into a goldfish pond."

Pinky St. Pierre wasn't exactly listening. Instead, he was looking forlornly into his empty bowl.

"Here," the colored kid offered, "eat mine. I don't want it." He was trying to lose weight. He was trying to make a friend.

Pinky hesitated.

"Go on. I don't mind."

"That's okay," Pinky said. His face registered a brief pale look of disgust.

"Go on," the colored kid tempted, pushing his bowl of rice pudding across the table.

"No thanks," Pinky chirped, jumping back from the table so quickly he overturned his chair. In the moment before the chair toppled, its legs screeched against the floor. The sound shot through a small cavity in one of the colored kid's molars, sprung up his jaw and stung his ear canal. He cradled his chubby cheek in his hand as if he'd been slapped. The chair clattered to the floor. Pinky darted off with his lunch tray like a startled starling. He had forgotten to remove his bib.

The colored kid continued to sit, looking into his bowl of rice pudding for clues. "I didn't touch it," he said to no one in particular. His dessert was beginning to congeal.

Now Pinky St. Pierre was standing next to the organ, holding his choir-folder at the level of his heart in preparation for his solo. He was practically swimming in his white choir robe. The sleeves belled over his hands and the red collar around his neck brought out the unearthly paleness in his skin so that he resembled a Christmas card angel. Except for the colored kid, who was late for rehearsal, the rest of the choirboys were standing in neat rows on the risers, according to height. They looked cleaner in their white robes than it is ever possible for adults to look, despite the fact that most of them had rings of dirt behind their ears. An outsider happening upon them might have described the group of boys as "reverent" or "serene." Inside their ranks there was no such sense of harmony, but rather a dangerous and complex energy of the sort one might find in a beehive without a queen.

The colored kid entered the chapel by way of the sacristy, where he picked up the last hanging choir robe. He limped up to the treble section and took his place between Wendell "Win" Picquet and Percy "Droopy" Drury, both of whom gave him a wide berth, as if he stank.

It wasn't his fault he was late. There'd been an incident with the emergency eye wash faucet at the hands of the older boys in chemistry class. He'd had to go back to the dorm to change out of his wet pants into his spare pair. The eyewash incident was unpleasant, but relatively speaking, couldn't hold a candle to the golf club incident. The clubbing had become a barometer for the colored kid, against which he measured the other bad things that happened.

He tried not to think about it now, hoping to lose himself in the requiem. That happened sometimes in choir when their voices harmonized in the right way. At a certain frequency, he would just lose himself and liberate into a vibration. But they weren't singing yet and it was hard not to think about it, especially with Brick Griffin standing behind him and to the right on the risers. He opened his choir folder but couldn't read the music without his glasses.

"Take off your glasses," Brick Griffin had said the first night, not impolitely, just as a matter of course. He'd been taught never to hit a kid with glasses by his father, Millard Griffin, M.D. The good doctor was in attendance at the front gates, expectorating with the rest of the crowd when the colored kid stepped up to the campus. Well, limped up really, because there was something wrong with his leg. Millard Griffin, M.D., had also taught his son Brick never to hit a cripple, but apparently that rule didn't apply. He'd given his boy the golf clubs as a confirmation present. There were woods and irons enough for each initiate who bedded in the second dorm. Tiny Brunet had been reluctant to participate.

"Do you want to be a dragon or don't you, sissyfuck?" Brick jeered.

"Of course," Tiny answered.

"Of course, *what?*"

"Of course, sir!"

"Just make sure you don't bend it," Brick instructed, handing him a driver. "Use it more like a cattle prod."

The colored kid made believe he was reading the music. Without the glasses to aid his vision, his other senses were more alert. He was awake to the smell of lemon oil in the pews, the sounds of whispering, cracking gum, the creaking of the risers under shifting feet. A bead of sweat ran from his underarm to his belt. He was acutely aware of which boy stood where and how far and who was watching him.

When the clubbing was finished the janitor had found him alone, curled in the fetal position against his own reflection on the polished floor of the cloisters, with his glasses in one hand and a torn piece of fabric in the other. Mercifully, he led the boy into his closet and sat him on a stepping stool. "Never let them see you cry, son," said the old man as he attended to the boy's cuts with iodine and a clean rag. The janitor's fingernails were stained yellow and ridged like clamshells.

"I wasn't crying," the boy lied. (That was the first.)

"Sure," said the janitor. "That's what you let them believe." He capped the iodine and placed it next to a box of Borax. "Now let's see if I don't have a needle and thread somewhere up in here."

The boy stiffened. "I don't need stitches!" he said, although he really could have used three or four to close the skin at his temple which had been cut in a backwards letter C by Brick Griffin's pitching wedge and later turned into a liver-colored scar.

"Not for you," the janitor reassured him. "You gonna be just fine. For your jacket there."

August Dupree, the one they called Skunk, had torn off the school seal patched on the left breast of the colored kid's new red St. Ignatius jacket. The boy was clenching it now in one hand. The patch bore the school's insignia, which could also be seen on the iron gate at the entrance, painted on the floor in the gymnasium, and decorating a mustard-colored banner that hung above the doorway of every classroom in St. Ignatius, alongside the American flag. To the amusement of St. Ignatius's rival, Holy Cross, this insignia depicted the holy spirit as a dove with an olive branch in its mouth, for which the football team was named the Mighty Doves. Holy Cross's team had the unfair advantage of a secular name: the Ragin' Cajuns.

The school seal was damp from the boy's sweaty palm. He thought to wipe his glasses clean with it. When he put them on, the closet came into focus. So did his pain, which was duller somehow when he couldn't see straight.

"Where'd you put it?" the janitor asked himself. "Think."

The boy fingered his arm and then his kidney. They were just bruised. Nothing was broken. For once he was glad he was hefty. His extra weight had served as padding.

"Here we go," the janitor said, producing a spool of white thread and a needle from a small toolbox on a low shelf. "I'm not much of a hand at sewing," he warned, "but I'll do my best." He held the needle up to the naked lightbulb and attempted to thread it. The boy examined the old man's face. He was somewhere in the indistinguishable range of fifty to seventy. His cheeks and neck were covered with razor bumps like a field of peppercorns. His left eye was made of glass. The white of the glass eye was pristine, whereas the real eye was bloodshot. He was having trouble getting the thread in the hole, which reminded the boy of a line of scripture his Nan liked to quote when she was thinking on retribution.

"It's easier for a camel to pass through the eye of a needle than for a rich man to enter into the kingdom of God," he recited, matter-of-factly. The words sounded funny through his puffed lip.

"That's for damn sure," said the janitor. He squinted his working eye as if to see better with the false one. This trick seemed to work. The thread slid through. "Popped the cherry," he said.

"Beg pardon?"

"Never mind." The janitor overturned his mop bucket, sat with the threaded needle and said, "Hand me your jacket."

The boy did so.

The janitor lay it over his knees.

"That too."

The boy passed him the torn-off patch. The old man held it in place on the left breast of the jacket approximately where it was supposed to go. Then he stabbed the needle through the dove's wing and began an uneven stitch.

"Thanks . . ." searched the boy.

"Don't mention it."

"I don't know your name."

"Samson. The Sexton."

"Thanks, Mr. Samson."

"No 'Mister.' Just Samson."

"Pleased to meet you. My name's Bernard Boudreaux."

"I know." Samson grinned. "You're a celebrity around here." He started whistling something happy. It sounded like "The Yellow Rose of Texas."

After awhile Bernard asked, "What happened to your eye?"

Samson smiled. Instead of answering, he asked how Bernard was feeling.

"Fine," Bernard told him. (That was the second lie.) There was a terrible pain in his side.

⚜

Four long weeks had passed since that night. Bernard tried to shake it from his mind. He focused on Pinky, who tipped back his head, formed a perfect O with his pink lips, inhaled for the first note of his solo, and was disrupted by a farting sound from the risers. Ned Drake yanked his hand from his armpit.

"Who did that?" asked the choir director. Mr. Wainright was also resident adviser in the second dorm. He was a sensitive young man from New Hampshire who hated his job. The boys called him "Yankee Chinless" behind his back on account of his weak jaw. He tried to disguise the defect with a beard that only served to call more attention to it. He looked at Ned. Ned met his gaze with Bambi eyes.

"Let's focus, *please,* gentlemen?" Mr. Wainright said. He turned to the sheet music and placed his fingers on the organ. "I'm sorry Pinky. Let's take it from the top. *Lento.*"

The fart noise trumpeted again, twice as loud as the first.

"Who's doing that?" Mr. Wainright repeated. His face flushed from the recessed hairline to the recessed chin. He was not a talented disciplinarian.

"Bernard, can you tell me who's making that obnoxious noise?"

"No, sir," lied Bernard. Deep down, he wanted to be just like the others.

"I see." Mr. Wainright scanned the risers. He folded his arms, then unfolded them. "Could someone be telling me he's not mature enough to visit Rome?"

"I'm mature enough," Skunk volunteered.

"Me too," said Buzz.

"Me too," said Eugene "Genius" Goubert with a stupid grin on his pimple-pocked face.

"I'm more mature than anyone here," said Ned. "I shave."

"Me too," said Win. "I'm already a man. Just ask the girls at Immaculate Conception."

"Take a look at this," piped Tiny, rolling up a sleeve of his choir robe to brandish an anthill bicep, "and tell me I'm not a man." He swiveled his head to see whether anyone laughed at his joke.

"That's enough, now!" Mr. Wainright interjected, but it came out more like a question than a command, and it was too late anyway. Order was unraveling.

Bernard felt a spitball sting the back of his neck. His hackles were raised. He pretended to read the sheet music, but the notes were swimming hatefully off the staff. No progress was made on the Requiem that day. When the bell rang, Mr. Wainright called Bernard to the organ.

"I'm sorry I was late," Bernard began.

"That's not why I wanted to speak with you. Monsignor Malcon asked me to send you to the rectory after choir rehearsal."

"Now? But I've got catechism."

"He wants to see you just the same."

Bernard hesitated. "May I ask why, sir?"

The Monsignor had a reputation for being insane. Visits to his office were reserved for the severest disciplinary cases. Usually when a boy acted out he was cracked on the head with a ruler and barked at. If he really acted out he was sent to Penance Hall where he had to stand on one leg with his arms at ninety degree angles in the posture of Christ with a volume of the Encyclopedia Britannica in each hand, books *S* and *P* more often than not, because they were heaviest. If he really, *really* acted out (say he drank holy water on a bet), he was sent to be guilted by Principal Father Pierce. The Principal would end a long lecture citing all Ten Commandments plus the Jesuit dictum—"Give us a boy and we will return you a man, a citizen of his country and a child of God"—with a tense call to the boy's parents on a big black telephone so ancient its numbers had been rubbed away. If the boy really, really, *really* acted out (like Kenny Crepas, who'd done the unthinkable and socked Father Eymard in the windpipe) he was sent to the Monsignor, who had the supreme power to expel him to public school, excommunicate him from the Catholic Church and consign him to hell. As far as he knew, Bernard hadn't done anything wrong. He'd only been the victim of acting out.

"I don't know why he wants to see you." Mr. Wainright busied himself with the sheet music at his organ and avoided Bernard's gaze. He was ashamed of himself for losing control of his class. His students brought him back to the perdition of preadolescence. Instead of being a twenty-five-year-old Jesuit scholastic with an advanced degree in sacred music, he was once again a twelve-year-old reject put upon by bullies.

"Chickenlegs," they used to call him when he was their age. And "Virgin Irwin." If you had a gentle spirit they would hunt it out of you.

The bell rang in the next period. Bernard trailed his fingers along the wall of the empty corridor, favoring his left leg as he went. He turned down the Hall of Honors, passing a row of display cases crammed with trophies and photographs of St. Ignatius sports teams from years past. The pea-sized faces in the photos were grave, and without exception, white. The jersey of the boy who'd gone and won the bronze for pole vaulting in the 1928 Olympics was also on display. There was a spiderweb in the jersey's armpit. Bernard's footsteps echoed down the hall, which, thanks to Samson, gleamed with floor wax like a dark mirror. Step drag step drag step.

❀

"Believe me, I'm not satisfied with the arrangement," Monsignor Malcon explained in his trademark stentorian drawl, "and I promise it's a temporary one." The turkey wattle at his neck wagged over his clerical collar as he shook his head back and forth. He was a great hulk of a man. His varicose hands were set squarely in the center of the ink blotter on his office desk. The desk was jacaranda, and big as a door. The boys called him Cannonhead. The nickname was a referent to his head, which had taken an odd shape at birth from the pinch of the forceps, but also to the oxlike stubbornness and iron will the head contained. As happens more often than not with public personae, he'd grown into a caricature of himself.

"On the surface it may seem you are being punished for the misdeeds of the others. But for the sake of your safety, and until their consciences catch up with them, I'm afraid this is the best solution."

To begin with, there had been the violent episode with the golf clubs. Also during Welcome Week, there was an incident with a baseball bat, and another with a bar of Ivory soap in a pillowcase. Father Pierce had enumerated these misdeeds and others, counting them out on his arthritic fingers as he requested the Monsignor's assistance. He didn't like to be a bother, but it *had* been the Monsignor's progressive notion to admit a Negro against the wishes of the parents, many of whom were distinguished alumni. Bede Adams had chosen to withdraw Little Bede in light of what he deemed "the contaminant." Others had threatened to do the same, complaining of their alma mater's downfall.

"They're *cruc*ifying him," Principal Father Pierce exclaimed, his wrist limp with frustration. He didn't stoop to say, "I told you so," although he had. He had thought desegregation the right thing at the wrong time, something for the public schools to tackle first. "Now what are we to do?" he pressed.

"I'll talk to them," Cannonhead promised. Bernard was here at his behest. He felt responsible. On the second Monday of the semester, he put aside his diocesan duties to call a mandatory assembly in the Little Chapel of the Martyrs on gentlemanly comportment. He proclaimed it not only illegal but un-Christian to antagonize the colored boy in their midst.

"Persecutors are bound to be punished," he'd cautioned the boys, "not in the corporeal sense, but the spiritual one, which is the worser of the two." Principal Father Pierce sat behind him in a high-backed chair with his toupee askew, nodding his head in agreement, although privately the two men agreed on very little.

Swift on the heels of Cannonhead's speech came the episode with the tennis rackets. Father Pierce responded with a threat. He would suspend offenders from sports of all kind for a period of two to four weeks, depending on the nature of the crime against the colored boy.

To prove he meant what he said, he'd made an example of Stumpy Jackel, St. Ignatius's track star in the fifty-meter dash. Stumpy's participation in the tennis matter was indisputable, as his racket had been discovered in the rec room, rimmed with blood.

Cannonhead thought Father Pierce soft. He argued for more exacting punishments. The principal explained that he couldn't be expected to accurately discipline the students when their parents absolved their behavior. If only a few more chose to withdraw their boys, the loss in tuition would mean ruination for the school. He was running a business. His hands were tied.

Then there was the affair with tooth powder and another with a coat rack that went unpunished. These crimes were reported by Irwin Wainright, who was distraught and at a loss for how to handle the boys. Certainly more incidents went unreported.

Bernard was a stoic. He never once complained. He just kept winding up, tight-lipped, in the infirmary.

The school days piled up like a car wreck into weeks until, after a disgusting incident with dung in the dormitory, Cannonhead superseded Principal Father Pierce by opting to move the colored boy to the supply closet.

"It's a decision I hope you'll agree is in your best interest," Monsignor Malcon finished. He rapped his knuckles on the desk two times like a gavel.

Bernard didn't know what to say. Faintly, he could hear the boys of the junior cadet corps practicing their precision march out on the quadrangle. He tried to make out the Monsignor's foreign coin collection. The coins were showcased in a custom-made frame that hung on the wall behind the enormous desk. Bernard's glasses had gone missing that morning and another three days would pass before Violet, one of the housekeepers, would find them stuffed in a gym sock in Happy Hebert's laundry bag, with the frames bent but the lenses miraculously intact. Without his glasses, the coins looked dull and undifferentiated. He may as well have been underwater. Nothing had edges: including Canonhead, who was an intimidating bald blur, including the monumental desk between them, including his own corrective shoe when he looked down at the floor. He wasn't sure the foot belonged to him. It was fuzzy and unfamiliar.

He hadn't been at St. Ignatius a month, but he felt he wasn't the same Bernard he was before he came. He shared a body with that Bernard. That was all.

The drums of the military drill grew louder.

"I've asked Samson to clear out the space and remove the shelving to make it as comfortable as possible for you," Cannonhead added. The fact remained that there was no window.

The boy didn't say anything. Monsignor Malcon had the uneasy feeling the child was looking straight through him. His mouth slowly filled with the taste of bile.

"Pardon me." He uncapped the bottle of aspirin next to the paperweight on his desk, shook two pills into his palm, chewed and swallowed them without aid of water. He grimaced. A memory he'd suppressed for fifty years had come alive in his stomach, where it rooted itself and was slowly spreading its rot. He suspected he was dying.

"You're a very brave young man," he offered, but he felt the gaze penetrate that offering like a dart.

Actually, Bernard was only trying to focus his eyes.

Monsignor Malcon cleared his throat. "Don't worry too much about the others. They'll come to tolerate you in time. Meanwhile, you ought to pray for them as Christ prayed for his assailants on Calvary, and ask the Lord to forgive them, for they know not what they do."

"Yes, Father," answered the boy.

A poison snail uncurled in the Monsignor's belly.

"I've kept you long enough. Have you got history now?"

"Catechism."

Bernard sang with the boys from the lower school who were his age, but took classes with the boys in the high school. It didn't help his standing with the others that he was preternaturally smart.

"All right, then, you're dismissed."

The boy didn't move. The poison snail began its slow toxic dance, sliming the inner lining of the Monsignor's stomach.

"Is there something on your mind, Bernard?"

"Yes. I've been wondering about the choir trip."

"What of it?"

"The money," he whispered.

"Ah yes," said the Monsignor, pinching the wattle at his neck to distract himself from the other pain.

"It's not included in my scholarship, is it?"

"No."

The snail was feeling with its little horns now, burrowing its snout with as much insistence as a fingertip picking a nostril. Then it bit. It pinched a fold of his stomach in its toothless, gumming vise. This boy was watching him. The boy and the pain were linked now. Cannonhead was sure of it. He could read it in the grip of the boy's eyes.

"Are you okay, Father?" asked Bernard. The Monsignor was grabbing at his middle.

"Yes. I'll pay it," he answered. There was a tremor in his voice. His head was slick with sweat. "I'll pay it out of my own pocket," he begged.

Bernard was taken aback by the generous offer. He hadn't expected it. "Actually, I was hoping I could work it off some kind of way," he began. "The others—they call me a charity case. I don't care whatever else they call me. I'm nobody's charity case."

So it was arranged that Bernard Boudreaux would work off the cost of the trip to Rome by doing yard work in the rectory garden for Monsignor Malcon. When he had his office back to himself, Cannonhead reached again for the aspirin. After eating two more of these to relieve the bilious cancer, he closed his eyes. The backs of his eyelids were bright yellow. Terrified, he opened them again.

๛

"Guess this makes us neighbors," Samson said later that evening as he helped Bernard set up house. The supply room was next to the janitor's closet. It was the size of a horse stall. The boy didn't have much in the way of belongings: just a second set of pants, another shirt, a crucifix, a cigar box of mementos, his schoolbooks, and a picture of Jackie Robinson ripped out of *Life* magazine.

"You like baseball?" Samson asked, unfolding a rusty cot that left only a ribbon of space in the room.

"Yeah," lied Bernard. He was holding one of his schoolbooks to his chest like a plate of armor.

"Well, it ain't much to look at, but it's yours. Sorry about the smell. I did what I could." The closet smelled of mothballs and must. Bernard didn't mind. It reminded him of home. A dim bulb with a dangling pull chain was the only source of light. There were studs in the walls from the screws that had held up the shelving. They looked like bullet holes from machine gunfire. Bernard put his finger over one of these spots and left it there, as if plugging a hole in a dike to keep away the floodwaters.

"I'll fill those in with some spackle tomorrow morning and slap some fresh paint on the walls. I figure I better rig you up a lock on the door too. Oh—and Violet said she's gonna crochet you a pillow sham to brighten up the spot. What you think?"

The fact remained that there was no window. "It'll do."

"That's right. Maybe Violet can fix you a paper shade for that light after I find a higher watt bulb. I'll ask her."

"Samson?"

"What's up?"

"I gotta ask you another favor."

"Shoot."

"We're supposed to read chapter three for history class tomorrow. It's about the Holy Crusades?"

"Can't say I know much about that business."

"That's okay. Problem is, someone took my glasses and I can't make out the words. Can I trouble you to read it to me?"

Samson massaged the back of his neck. "Ain't no trouble 'cept I only made it to the fourth grade. I don't expect I'll know half the words in that book."

"Oh," said Bernard. He looked crestfallen. There was going to be a quiz.

"Hand me the book, son," said Samson. "I'll spell out the big words and we'll figure it out together. What chapter you say it was?"

"Three." Bernard smiled.

They sat next to each other on the cot and the bedsprings me-owed. Samson cleared his throat and hunched over the book. He squinted his good eye and, curiously, seemed to focus on the text with the one made of glass. He cleared his throat again.

"Let's see. Uh. First word starts with a *D. I-V-I-N-E.*"

"Divine."

"Second word: *P-R-O-V—*"

"Must be providence."

It took them close to two hours to get through the chapter in this manner. Bernard thanked the janitor when they were finished.

"Don't mention it," Samson said. He stood to go. "I figure I should lock you in tonight. Just for tonight till I can fix you a lock on the inside."

"Okay," said Bernard.

"I'll be by six o'clock tomorrow morning to let you out."

"Okay."

Samson lay his hand on Bernard's head. He seemed reluctant to remove it. "You gonna be awright?"

"Yep."

After the lock was in place Bernard stretched out on the cot with his cigar box balanced on his round stomach. He opened the box, felt inside, pulled out an oily black feather, and held it in front of his mouth. He inhaled a deep breath and exhaled it slowly. The feather bowed. The room was a coffin.

*Breathe in. The feather stands up. Breathe out. The feather bows down.*

He imagined a breath so strong it blew down the walls.

⚘

In the middle of the night, an unsyncopated banging incorporated itself into Mr. Wainright's dream. BAM! BAM! BAM! Ned Drake was pummeling him in the back with a music stand while the others stood cheering in the chapel risers. The boys were hysterical and solemn at the same time, like fans at a football game. He was certain his spinal cord was broken. BAM! The sound opened his eyes. He lay there for a minute shifting from the dread of the nightmare to the dread of being awake. The banging continued. He hopped out of bed and scuttled down the hall in his nightshirt and slippers in pursuit of the noise.

"What are you doing?" he demanded, flicking on the hallway light.

Four of the boys were gathered outside the door of the supply closet in their pajamas. They looked like cornered foxes with matching crew cuts. The blacks of their eyes began to shrink.

"Damn Yankee Chinless," mouthed Tiny, nudging Skunk.

"What?" Mr. Wainright asked.

"Nothing," Tiny pipped.

Mr. Wainright was painfully aware of his calfless bowlegs under his cotton nightshirt. "I asked what you're doing."

"Nothing." Ned blinked.

Chinless detected the unmistakable smell of sulfur.

"We were worried about the colored kid," suggested Win.

"That's right," said Skunk, snaking his hands behind his back in the same posture that had lost his father, Assemblyman Dupree, the last mayoral election. People said it made the man look dishonest. "We just wanted to make sure he's doing all right in there, is all." Skunk smiled, winningly.

A book of matches fell out of the cuff of Tiny's pajama pant leg.

"Hand me those," said Mr. Wainright. "Thank you. Go to bed, please. Leave him alone now. Seriously, guys. Lights out."

"But we were only trying to be good Samaritans!" Ned objected.

"Please," the choir director said weakly, "just leave him alone. Lights out." The boys scuttled off to their rooms. Win whooped out a spontaneous Indian war cry as they went, clapping his palm against his mouth. Then his arm shot out like a lever in a pinball machine and shoved Tiny into the wall. Tiny lost his feet, hit the floor and sprung back up like a jack-in-the-box. "Go Dragons!" he screamed.

"Shut up, faggot," ordered Ned.

"Hey!" Mr. Wainright called after them, almost as an afterthought. "Guys!" Tiny was the only one to look back. "I'm afraid Principal Father Pierce will hear about this in the morning."

Later, on a drinking tear after his first wife left him, Tiny would remember this night. Nobody would call him Tiny anymore, but that is how he would feel. With a chorus line of vodka shots in him, each shot coupled to a beer back, this was the regret that would bother him the most, more than cheating on his wife even, with her own half sister.

"I'm not a good guy," he would say to the bartender, thumping his chest. "I admit it."

"I've seen worse," the bartender would say.

"That's right," Tiny would agree. "Lend me a pen, Jack." He would start to write Bernard an apology note. He would get three cocktail napkins down before demanding a postage stamp and falling off his stool.

❧

"What do I care?" called Tiny, racing after the others.

"Bernard?" Mr. Wainwright asked delicately. "Are you all right?"

There was only the two inches of door between them. Bernard was crouching on his heels in the dark on the other side. Scattered at his feet was the ash of a dozen half-burnt paper matches. When the boys couldn't open the door to get at him, they'd tried kicking it in. When that failed, they'd tried to smoke him out.

"Bernard?" The priest knocked, but not with intention. It was a knock like a weak handshake.

One by one, Bernard had blown out the matches as they slid under the crack. He blew them out methodically, like going at trick birthday candles. Deep down he'd wanted to be just like them. He wanted a father who was a businessman and gave him a weekly allowance. He wanted a mother who baked Bundt cakes for the church bake sale. He wanted to wear his uniform like they did, with the tie loose like he didn't care. He wanted a best buddy to invite

146

him home for Thanksgiving or sailing on Lake Pontchartrain. He wanted to draw a cartoon of Cannonhead doing it with a naked lady and pass it around Latin class. He wanted to leave his tray in the dining hall without wondering about who had to wash his plate and where the food scraps were going to go. He wanted to be white. He wanted to pay the price of admission to their secret society. But when the little sparks of fire kept coming, he saw himself illuminated as the ghastly thing he was. He was the price. Those things he wanted would never come. One by one he blew them out like wishes going dark.

Mr. Wainright jiggled the door handle ineffectually. "Bernard? They're gone," he coaxed. "It's over now."

Bernard disagreed. It wasn't over. They wanted to burn him alive. He crouched there, imagining himself on fire, his limbs ablaze. He imagined Nanan Zanobia coming on the train in her pillbox Sunday hat to collect his charred bones, her heart crushed like a tin can. All the folks would come out to the depot for his homecoming. Their hope returned in a cardboard box. The same who saw him off with a prayer would receive him again with a moan. Or, maybe they never moved from the platform the day he left for New Orleans. It had been raining that day. Maybe they never shut their hundred umbrellas but were froze in a fairy-tale spell he alone could break.

"Bernard Boudreaux," pleaded Mr. Wainright. He despised himself. "I'm sorry," he said.

Bernard made a choice then and there. Did he want to be a Bernard whose life was a series of lessons in cruelty or a Bernard who schooled other people? If he couldn't be like them, he would be better than them. He would be untouchable.

"I'm sorry," the priest was repeating, on the other side. "I'm sorry." He knocked like he believed there was a way Bernard could open the door.

*"I'm sorry."*

"Don't be!" Bernard suddenly blurted. The sound of his own voice surprised him, as he'd halfway convinced himself he was dead and locked in his coffin. But he was glad he said it. It proved he was alive. The other Bernard was dead—the one who could be pitied. "Go away," he snapped.

Mr. Wainright hesitated, then retreated like a dog with its tail between his legs. He shut the hallway switch, taking with him the strip of light under the supply room door. With that gone, the room went double black. Bernard couldn't see his own hand in front of his face. He felt his way to the cot and sang Fauré's Requiem to himself to prove he was alive until he fell asleep.

❧

When Samson unlocked the supply room and opened the door at six on the dot the next morning, it was onto a slightly altered universe. Strange things started taking course at St. Ignatius.

"You look different," said Samson.

That was the first thing. Bernard's face was now an ice-hard mask. He began bearing assaults from the other boys so soundlessly they started to be slightly afraid of him. That was the second thing. Bernard remained a pariah, but they no longer hunted him out. After a time, they left him alone, then ignored him entirely.

The third thing was, once his glasses were returned, he swiftly accelerated to the top of his class and was placed on the honor roll. He took the coveted Brother Barnabus Prize in freshman composition for his essay, "Suffering and Salvation: The Passion of Christ." By mid-October he was star of the debate club. With deadpan delivery, he snared his opponents with irrefutable turns of phrase and used their rebuttals to corroborate his own arguments. He raked in the highest marks on midterm examinations and seemed to do it without effort.

Fourth, Cannonhead took him on as a kind of pet. Bernard spent countless afternoons with him in the rectory and attended him at the altar during high mass. Fifth, right before Halloween, which they were not allowed to celebrate because of its pagan roots, Bernard was unceremoniously switched from the supply room back into the dorms. When he was given the choicest single bed by the only bay window on the floor, displacing Ned Drake and his stash of mint condition Mexican porn to an unoccupied upper bunk smelling faintly of urine, the boys presumed (incorrectly) it was because of his privileged position with the Monsignor.

Almost simultaneously, the sixth and most unthinkable thing happened. Bernard replaced Pinky St. Pierre as soloist in Fauré's Requiem.

"I just don't get it," Skunk said after Chinless made the announcement. Nobody did. It was a risky move not only because the boys choir was precipitously close to departing for Rome where they would perform for an estimable audience, an organ of the Curia Romana, but because the soloist was supposed to be ambassador for the choir, the school, and the nation. While Pinky was a "dweeb" and a borderline "retard," you couldn't deny his Shirley Temple lollipop appeal. Bernard was, well, colored. And a crippled one, don't forget. On their semiannual Ixthus retreat, the usual debate over who was easiest: Marian Mercy girls, Little Flower girls, or the girls from Immaculate Conception, was supplanted by a heated debate over the reasons for Bernard Boudreaux's newfound distinction.

"Just drop it, why don't you," said Ned, though he was clearly as disturbed as the others. He took a furious drag on his cigarette. "Why do you care?"

Pinky claimed he was suddenly too shy to sing in front of a cardinal but nobody believed him. It was easier to believe Bernard was blessed. Why else had he come into such sudden and unprecedented fortune? Why else was he impervious to pain? Why else did Cannonhead smile upon him as a son? Why else did he score one hundred percent on every single test he took? They began to refer to him as Saint Bernard.

❧

These events were inexplicably strange to the white boys of St. Ignatius. Mysteries were abounding, that was for sure. Whether or not they were the ways of God, as the Jesuits claimed, Bernard was undecided. He was learning that very little was as it seemed.

For example, when he went to the rectory to do yard work for his choir trip money, Monsignor Malcon directed him to an enclosed garden.

"Samson's out there composting," the Monsignor said, "He'll show you what to do."

But the man shoveling in the compost heap behind the St. Ignatius statue was not Samson. He looked something like the janitor, but clearly wasn't the same man. The gardener was much younger for one thing—somewhere in the indistinguishable range of thirty to forty years old. He was also taller, by several inches, and lighter-skinned.

"You're not Samson," Bernard said.

"Sure I am," the gardener replied.

"No you're not."

"I swear on my old man's grave."

"But you don't have a glass eye!"

"Calm down, son."

"The *real* Samson has a glass eye."

"Hush now," said the gardener, gripping Bernard's wrist.

"Let go of me. You're not Samson."

"Let me clear things up." The gardener checked to make sure Cannonhead wasn't watching. He leaned in conspiratorially and lowered his voice. "I'm Samson's baby brother. We're both called Samson."

"What?" Bernard knitted his eyebrows. "I don't get it. Why?"

"'Cause our daddy's name was Sam. He had five sons in all and we all got the same name. Me and Samson's the only ones left. Samson and Samson got killed in the war. Samson drowned when he was your age. How old are you?"

"Twelve."

"Samson was eleven, rest his little soul. We got a sister too. That's Sammy. She makes wigs."

"Doesn't it get confusing?"

"Sure, but it's better for me and Samson that way. They can't tell us apart, see. Means less work. Say I feel like going home and take a catnap in the middle of the day. I just tell Monsignor I got to clean the toilets over at the school. Then if he feel like checking up on me, why looky there! It's good old *Samson* with the toilet brush."

Samson sucked his teeth. "We all look just alike to them."

Bernard considered what he'd just been told, then remembered his manners. "Well, pleased to meet you, Samson. I'm here to help with some yard work. My name's Bernard Boudreaux."

"I know that already. You're a celebrity around here. Go on into the shed and pull out the gardening shears. You can start by pruning that hedge."

How strange not to be able to tell them apart, thought Bernard. Except for a slight resemblance, the Samsons weren't alike at all. The older one only talked when he had to. The younger talked just to hear the sound of his voice.

Another mysterious thing was how Cannonhead watched him when he came to the garden. He'd be raking or weeding and all of a sudden he'd get a creepy feeling. That was when he knew Cannonhead was at the little rosetta window, hiding behind the stained-glass petals.

"Don't look now but Bats in the Belfry watching you," Samson whispered once, as he dug out the dandelions.

Bernard wanted to know if Cannonhead really was crazy or if that was just a rumor.

"Lemme put it like this. What's the Easter flower?"

"Lily."

"Sides the lily."

"Daffodil?"

"Daffodil. That first year after they hired me and Samson, I noticed they didn't have no daffodils growing. Now that's strange, I thought. I couldn't figure why. So next year, when it came time to make the order from the Burpee book, I picked some daffodil bulbs, thinking wouldn't that be nice."

Cannonhead moved behind the rosetta window. His face was distorted by the fragmented glass.

Samson lowered his voice. "I put those bulbs down there all around Iggy's feet," Samson pointed at the marble statue of St. Ignatius. "Some in front of the church, and all up and down the front gate to the school. Come March, those flowers shot up like I don't know what. Yes, I do—like popcorn. They just up and popped out like popcorn one day. Bright yellow. Pretty as you please. I'm thinking how happy everyone gonna be when they see those. First thing to bloom after the crocuses. But do you know what that old fool did?" Samson gestured at the rosetta window with his dandelion fork.

Bernard shook his head and studied the rose bush he was de-beetling.

"He tore out here without no shirt and gone at them daffodils like a bloodhound on a coon. Swear to God. Ripped 'em all to pieces with his bare hands. All them daffodils all over the ground looking like the battle of Normandy. Cryin' shame. This was first thing in the morning, just after the sun come up, so the only one to witness it was me. *No yellow flowers,* he told me."

Bernard dropped a beetle into his coffee can of vinegar.

"Look around, Bernard. You see any *yellow* flowers up in this here pretty garden?"

Bernard looked around the garden. It was true. There were no yellow flowers.

Samson picked up his pile of dandelion roots and carried them over to the compost heap. He swaggered back and wiped his hands off on his pants. "So. You tell me. Crazy?"

"Sounds like."

"Damn straight. I'm fixin' to go home and take a nap. He asks where I'm at, just tell him Samson's over at the school, mopping up in the gymnasium."

Bernard shook his can of drowned beetles. He thought about his mother, who was interred at a mental hospital in Biloxi. When a black lady was crazy, they put her away and tied her to her bed. When a white man was crazy, they made him a monsignor. One of the beetles was still alive. Bernard watched it climb onto the back of another, to keep from drowning in the vinegar.

One week after Bernard started working off his choir trip in the garden, the Monsignor asked him to come in out of the sun. "You must be tired," he said. They sat in his office, same as before, Cannonhead at his jacaranda desk and Bernard opposite him—only this time, the Monsignor seemed somewhat smaller. Bernard waited for the Monsignor to speak. To distract himself from his discomfort he counted how many foreign coins there were on each side of the custom-made frame on the wall behind the priest. Forty-eight multiplied by thirty-six made what? One thousand, five hundred and thirty-six.

"Do you know why I collect coins?" Cannonhead asked

Bernard shook his head and waited for the answer. It never came. Cannonhead just inspected him with a pained look. After ten minutes or so, Bernard excused himself to go finish raking up under the Rose of Sharon.

By the following week, the Monsignor was paying Bernard to sit with him in the rectory rather than working in the garden. Sometimes he talked. Sometimes he just surveyed Bernard's face.

"Cannonhead's got a soft spot for you," Samson smiled, drinking from the garden hose.

"Don't ask me why," Bernard said rolling his eyes, but secretly, he was glad for the attention.

He'd noticed another peculiarity. Cannonhead was shrinking. Every time Bernard was made to pay him a visit, the Monsignor was the littlest bit smaller than he was the time before. His clerical collar grew looser and looser around his neck. It was obvious he wasn't well. He held himself bent in the middle. Sometimes he got confused and called Bernard Shine. During mass he made embarrassing mistakes, mixing Cajun and Latin words, and once spilling the blood of Christ across the mantle. On one of his more lucid days, he said he had a confession to make.

"I'm not a priest," Bernard pointed out.

"That's right. You're an act of contrition."

"What do you mean?"

"My father was a portrait photographer," the Monsignor started, by way of explanation. "He had a mean sinning streak in him. He liked to drink and abuse my mother and myself. She died. My mother did."

"I'm sorry," Bernard offered.

"Of the scarlet fever. Lots of people got that in those days, but not the way she did. He had a studio set up in our front parlor and a sign painted in the window. He was good at what he did and people respected him for that. Rich people. The studio was very elegant, but if you went into the back rooms or upstairs, you'd have been shocked to find them almost entirely bare. He drank up all our money, you see. The front room was merely a show, when in reality, we were practically starving."

Cannonhead lay his hand on his stomach and rubbed it with his thumb.

"People used to come from far and wide to be photographed in costume. That was his specialty. My mother sewed the costumes and he would photograph the well-to-do families dressed as famous figures. There was a Marie Antoinette costume, Antony and Cleopatra, and Venus, with a little harp. Alexander the Great and such. People like to play at being kings and gods. Do you know why, my boy?"

"No," said Bernard.

"They can't help it!" The priest laughed, then stopped abruptly. "I'm no exception. It's a very seductive illusion."

He studied Bernard. "You know what I'm referring to, don't you?"

"I couldn't say."

"Then guess. Go on."

"I don't know."

"Oh, I think you do. You're a smart boy."

Bernard pushed his glasses up his nose. "You're talking about power."

"Yes," said the priest, wrapping his knuckles on his desk. "That's it." His eyes filled with tears. "I think my father wanted to destroy himself with drink, but only after he destroyed us first. What do you think?"

"I didn't know him."

"No. He was a brute. He didn't think I had any guts. I was a sensitive boy so he thought I was soft. A lot of people mistake the two. Do you know what he did?"

Bernard shook his head.

Cannonhead coughed. "I'll tell you. One day after church he told my mother we were going to a picnic. She was to stay home and mind the house. He brought a jug of moonshine and had me tote his Hawkeye. He told me I was a man now and had to prove it. This was my birthday, but it wasn't any picnic. When we got there, there was a large crowd of angry men. They had a colored man . . ."

Bernard bristled.

". . . with a rope around his neck. I knew that man. He was named Po Penbro and I used to go fishing with his boy, Shine, when I was hungry. They were there to kill him, but don't ask me why. My father pushed up to the front and I followed on his heels. I didn't think I had a choice, you see. Not even when my father aimed the shutter blade on the Hawkeye. He told me to shoot and I did it. I didn't think I had a choice.

"This was my birthday. I was thirteen years old." He coughed. "I was a child. But when I looked through the lens at the hangman and exposed him on a glass plate, I was struck by something. I've carried it with me till this day. Do you know what it was?"

Bernard didn't say anything.

"How Po Penbro looked like Christ on the crucifix."

Monsignor Malcon stopped to eat two aspirin and closed his eyes. He remembered how his father had rode him into town afterwards to buy his mother a bolt of silk. "You pick the color," his father said, slapping him on the back. He chose yellow. Yellow like ripe corn. It was cursed. When she touched it to turn it into a costume, she grew sick and died.

"It's not your fault," Bernard whispered.

Monsignor Malcon opened his eyes. "Thank you. That's kind of you to say. Thank you, Bernard." He coughed.

After awhile, Bernard said he had some studying to do.

"Do you know why I wanted you?" the priest stalled.

"What do you mean?" said Bernard.

"Do you know why you're here?"

"No." Bernard was itching to go.

Cannonhead tapped his temple. "I know what became of your father."

"I don't know what you mean," lied Bernard.

The priest leaned forward. He planted his arms on his desk like it was propping him up. The poison snail was trailing his stomach walls. "We don't have to become our fathers, do we?"

"What do you mean? He's a sculptor," Bernard protested. "In Europe."

Monsignor Malcon started coughing again. It was a hard wet cough. He grew red in the face.

"Do you want some water?" Bernard asked.

The Monsignor wagged his head no, although the cough was getting worse. Something seemed to be trying to jump out of his mouth onto the jacaranda desk. Maybe a lung. Bernard wasn't sure what to do so he sat very still.

The Monsignor tried to seize back his speech. The poison snail had cracked out of its shell and was expanding. The boy had his soul in a stranglehold. "What"—he coughed—"what do you want"—he coughed—"from me?" His eyes were wet and behind their film they were pleading.

"I want to go to Rome," Bernard answered. He didn't understand the question but he could hear it wasn't rhetorical and knew he ought to say something.

ᴥ

There was one Samson who was really two. There was a frightening monsignor who was really afraid. There was something else in the litany of things that weren't as they appeared.

To Bernard's surprise, he found Ned Drake fucking Pinky St. Pierre underneath the bleachers in the football field. This was a quiet spot he liked to go to be alone during his free period, after catechism, before lunch. He'd never run into them before, but it was obvious this wasn't their first time. The remarkable thing, more than the act itself, was the gentleness with which it was being executed.

The boys had spread their red St. Ignatius jackets below them to keep from getting dirty or to soften the packed ground. Their eyes were closed and they were lightly moaning. Pinky was on all fours like a kitten, stripped naked. Ned was behind him on his knees, still clothed but with his pants undone so that the backs of his nubile thighs showed underneath his shirttail. His left hand was at Pinky's waist. His right was stroking Pinky's smooth white back. His rhythm was slow and tame. It stirred a light wind that lifted his shirttail like a sail each time he pushed into Pinky's rear, revealing his hairless testicles. There was a wet smacking noise, like small kisses, and the jingle of Ned's belt buckle. Ned was biting his lower lip. Otherwise, his face was in utter repose. Pinky's neck was straining forward and he was whimpering. His shoulder blades were wings. His toes were curled. Slants of dusty sunlight reached through the peeling bleachers. One beam of this fell across Pinky's head, making his hair look as soft as the fluff of a newborn chick.

Bernard was amazed. His instinct was to back away as quietly as possible but something stopped him. He stood conflicted for a moment, watching them. Then, loudly, he cleared his throat.

Their eyes shot open. In one swift motion, Ned pulled out, covered himself, scrambled to his feet and yanked up his pants. Pinky made no effort to hide his nakedness. He just sat on his jacket Indian-style, pouting. His skin was so white it was almost blue.

"You're not going to tell, are you?" Ned scoffed.

Pinky scratched at a mosquito bite on his shoulder and watched Bernard with the sort of expectation an infant watches the mobile above his crib. Both of them waited to hear what he was going to say.

"You're both going to have to give me something."

"What do you mean?" said Ned. "We don't have to."

"Yes you do," said Bernard.

"Put on your clothes, idiot," Ned told Pinky.

"Or else I'm going to have to tell a few people about this here."

Pinky stuck his arms in the sleeves of his shirt. He put the second button in the first hole and progressed downward.

"Cigarettes," Ned offered. "How many do you want?"

"I don't smoke."

"All right, Saint Bernard," seethed Ned, "what do you want?"

"I want your bed," Bernard said, "and I want his solo."

It was that simple.

❦

On the day before the boys choir of St. Ignatius left for Rome, Monsignor Malcon wanted to see Bernard in his office. By this point he'd shrunk so much he wasn't much taller than the boy. His shirt was loose as a choir robe.

"Now that you worked off the flight and are going abroad, we won't see each other so much anymore," he said. "I want to give you a parting gift."

The frame containing his foreign coin collection was face down on his desk without its backing. He was carefully removing the coins from the circles cut in the felt mounting and dropping them in a nicked wooden box with a hinged door and a dark glass eye. He must have been at it for a while. He was on the last row. These were coins from China, with squares cut out of their centers. The box was almost full to its brim. Cannonhead patted it on the side, where a little brass maker's plaque was screwed. "The Blair Camera Co.," it said.

"Do you know why I collect foreign coins?" he wheezed.

"I can't take those," said Bernard.

"For the same reason anybody collects anything. To fill a hole." He dropped the last coin in the camera and pushed it toward Bernard. "There you go. That's for you, *defan* Shine."

"I'm Bernard," he said, but he picked up the box anyway.

◈

Word came to them in Rome that Monsignor Malcon was dead. Principal Father Pierce lined them up in front of the Trevi Fountain like a row of ducks. He held the telegram in his shaking arthritic fingers and read it aloud over the roar of the water. His posture was somber, his face grievous, but when he got to the end, a pigeon shat on his toupee. The boys contained themselves by looking at their loafers, except for Ned Drake, who brayed like a donkey.

"Really, Ned!" said Mr. Wainright. A flat-footed gypsy snatched his sleeve and pointed at the dirty baby in her arms. He recoiled. "I don't have any money."

It was November, the boys were cold, their fingers were raw, they had an epidemic foot fungus and they were tired from endless sightseeing. In a flurry, they'd visited the Vatican, the Sistine Chapel, and the Coliseum. They'd sung the requiem at St. Paul's Basilica, and not butchered it, and been rewarded on the Spanish Steps with paper cups of pistachio gelato.

Bernard had bought a postcard and sent it home. It read:

Dear Nan & Uncle Luscious,
This is the Pantheon. It's a building that looks like a rectangle from the outside but inside it's perfectly round. There's a hole in the top of the dome so you can see the sky but when it rains the water comes right in. I miss you.

Love, B.J.

He didn't write how the oculus had filled him with wonder, how gazing up at it he'd felt the privilege of looking through a new eye onto something he couldn't name. It had made him dizzy, that feeling, because simultaneously he'd felt he was being looked at and seen. He didn't write how his voice moved like water when he sang his solo, nor how Pietro Cardinal Ciriaci had wept. There were no words to describe the source of those things, and even if there were, there wasn't enough space to write them down on the back of a picture postcard.

"Let us bow our heads in memory of the Monsignor, and pray," Principal Father Pierce intoned. The boys tucked their chins. The gypsy woman tugged insistently at Mr. Wainright. Insistently, Mr. Wainright ignored her.

Bernard reached into his pocket and fished out a Chinese coin. He tossed it backward over his shoulder into the fountain and made a wish.

# RESPIRATION

Click click boom. Breathe in. Click click boom. Breathe out. Click click boom. Breathe in. Click click boom. Breathe out. Click click-boom. Breathe in. Click click boom. Breathe out. Click click boom. Breathe in. Click click boom. Breathe out. Click click boom. Breathe in. Click click boom. Breathe out. Click click boom. Breathe in. Click click boom. Breathe out. Click click boom. Breathe in. Click click boom. Breathe out. Click click boom. Breathe in. Click click boom. Breathe out. Click click boom. Breathe in. Click click boom. Breathe out. Click click boom. Breathe in. Click click boom. Breathe out. Click click boom. Breathe in. Click click boom. Breathe out. Click click boom. Breathe in. Click click boom. Breathe out. Click click boom. Breathe in. Click click boom. Breathe out. Click click boom. Breathe in. Click click boom. Breathe out. Click click boom. Breathe in. Click click boom. Breathe out. Click click boom. Breathe in. Click click boom. Breathe out. Click click boom. Breathe in. Click click boom. Breathe out. Click click boom. Breathe in. Click click boom. Breathe out. Click click boom. Breathe in. Click click boom. Breathe out. Click click boom. Breathe in.

Click click boom. Breathe out. Click click boom. Breathe in. Click click boom. Breathe out. Click click boom. Breathe in. Click click boom. Breathe out. Click click boom. Breathe in. Click click boom.

I see a song. It looks like:

Click click boom. Breathe in. Click click boom. Breathe out.

That clicking. It looks like train tracks leading into a tunnel. Click clack train track. The rails are rusting. The tracks are splintering. They are old and gray. In between the tracks are weeds and broken bottles. Off to the sides is tall grass coming up from red dirt. Dry grass as far as I can see, fields of it bowing down and standing up again in the wind. The tracks part the grass like hair. They run into the tunnel. The tunnel is a black hole in the side of a mountain. The mountain has knuckles made of rocks. I cannot see over it. Before me, behind me, the train tracks stitch the red ground together.

I think I have been here a long time. It's hot in this place. I wait for the train to come.

Click click boom. Breathe in. Click click boom. Breathe out.

That breathing. It looks like the dry grass bending down and standing up and bending down again. It looks like the cloud mass over the mountain, shrugging and changing shape. Hushing across the sky. The sky is gray. The clouds are white. The clouds roll in and out. They look like waves at the ocean shore. The breath moves the clouds and the grass. The grass stands tall. The grass bows down. Who is breathing?

Click click boom. Breathe in. Click click boom. Breathe out.

I see a new sound. Metal sliding on metal. I see a broken playground swing to my left. Two chains drop from a bar held up by other bars. The bars are painted blue. A link in one chain has snapped. The swing dangles in the grass. It is made of dirty canvas.

The canvas is coming unstitched. When the grass bows, the swing spins from its chain. This swing wasn't here before.

*"Bernie?"*

I see a voice. It looks like a bird landing on the bar above the broken swing. It is a little brown bird with a white breast. It cocks its head to the side and looks down at me.

Click click boom. Breathe in. Click click boom. Breathe out.

Whose song is this?

*"You look like shit."*

I see the bird transform into crow. Its feathers turn black and oily and its beak and legs grow longer. Its eyes are black beads. One eye points at me.

*"Can you hear me?"*

I see the crow raise its wings.

It looks like an umbrella opening. With its wings open, the crow has tripled its size. The wings flap.

*"Blink your eyes if you can hear me."*

I remember this swing. I used to play on it. I used to pump my legs and fly up and down and back. My stomach would flip and I would close my eyes and pump higher and higher. When I couldn't get any higher I would launch myself from the swing like an arrow. I touch the broken chain. I have nothing to fix it with. My pockets are empty. I touch the seat.

Click click boom. Breathe in. Click click boom. Breathe out.

The dry grass bows down. The clouds roll in. The dry grass stands up. The clouds roll out. The train tracks stack like stitches into the tunnel. The mountain knuckles its rocks. The broken chain swings back and forth. It is rusty and it sounds like it's crying.

*Bernie.*

What is that voice?

*I wrote you a haiku.*
I remember. It is a girl's voice.

*I won't mind, brother,*
*if you leave your brokenness*
*in the bed and go.*

I know her. She looks like me. She has eyebrows like a blackbird. I used to push her on a swing.

Her voice looks like a crow. It flaps its wings and lifts off. The swing set falls apart at its joints, the bars and the chains come down, metal scraping on metal. The crow is flying to the mountain. I see it dart into the tunnel's mouth.

I follow it. I walk along the train tracks. The tracks are uneven. I'm walking on a broken spine over the dry red dirt and it's hot in this place.

Click click boom. Breathe in. Click click boom. Breathe out.

I see the song changing. Beneath the clicking and breathing is a beat. It is throbbing out of the tunnel. The tunnel looks like a cave opening its mouth wider. I cannot see the other end of it. I step inside. I follow the crooked tracks into the dark. Behind me the opening gets smaller and smaller until it's just a bright little dot. The beat is deeper here. The tunnel is vibrating. I keep walking. I'm in a drum. I'm in a tight throat. When I turn around now, I can't see anything. Inside, it's blacker than the crow's eye. What is this place?

Click click boom.

I can't see my hands in front of my face. I have no face. I have no hands.

Click click boom.

I'm trapped in the beat and the breath of the dark. I'm trapped in a fist pounding

a drum. I'm a vibration. The beat gets fast and frenzied. It turns itself into a train. I hear its wheels behind me click clacking on the tracks. It's singing on the rails now. I hear it behind me, chugging, churning, pushing, coming. I hear:

Click click

Boom.

Emma Boudreaux
Postcolonial African Novel
Professor Kagunda

## THE ORIGINS OF LITTLE WILLA

(A story based on the early life of South African novelist, Bessie Head)

> When you examine at close quarters the colonial context, it is
> evident that what parcels out the world is to begin with the fact
> of belonging to or not belonging to a given race, a given
> species.
>
> —Franz Fanon, *The Wretched of the Earth*

Willa was born with the weight of Africa hunchbacked on her shoulders at the topsy-turvy bottom of the continent, a place of distortions not far from the sea. Within Natal Province, within Pietermaritzburg, within a madhouse, within the womb of a white woman resembling a moth, also named Willa, Willa for Wilhelmina, who spoke Afrikaans with a lisp and smoked cigarettes like a man. Willa One with a crumbling will; Willa who hadn't had her wits about her since watching her goldenboy toddle under the wheels of a taxi speeding four well-fed cigar-puffing businessmen to an East Rand race meeting. Crushed like a beetle, or rather, a piece of fruit. A cantaloupe with bird-bones and teeth like freshwater pearls.

Jan Janssen had been away that day, that week, that month, working the South African Railways, spreading it over the Cape hills like a scar, his red face blackened with earth and steam engine soot (almost as black as the faces of the pile-drivers). Although he bellowed like a locomotive when he returned, although he cursed the land into which the mangled body of his boy was dropped, Jan was away that day. He hadn't been there to comfort his wife. In fact, it was the stable boy who lifted the child from the street and built the teeny tiny coffin from planks of imported pine. So it was. And after that day, you could say, things were not the same.

❦

It wouldn't have mattered if her birth had transpired outside the white walls of the madhouse; Willa Two was crowning into a mad world, marked for misfortune, the umbilical cord wrapped round her neck like a hangman's noose. "Gracious, what an odd-looking baby," Nurse Matron thought but did not say, so as not to upset the mother. She wiped the blood and gook from the little limbs and passed her off to Willa's breast, a breast that had slipped from the white nightgown and resembled one-half of a sandless hourglass.

"What will you name her?" asked Nurse Matron.

Willa didn't answer. She just gazed at the grasping child with eyes flat as coins.

"No ideas, eh? We'll give her your name then," reasoned Nurse Matron, flourishing a fountain pen. "How does that sound? Little Wilhelmina." In her hurry, she spilled a large drop of ink on the birth certificate. It bloomed like a spider under the text "Father: *Unknown.*"

"*Gelukkige verjaarsdag, dogter,*" said Willa, deadpan, deep-voiced. Happy birthday, daughter.

These were the last words she spoke, more like a denunciation than a greeting. Perhaps the labor exhausted her wits completely. Perhaps she was resisting something, who knows what. Perhaps she simply preferred silence from then on. She paid no attention to her child. Her breasts had no milk.

Nobody, not even Old Saartje with her crackpot antics could wake Willa from her daze. Willa didn't blink an eye the day Old Saartje mistook the baby for a sack of diamonds, snatched her out of the crib by the nappies and worked herself into a frenzied escapade to swim home to Holland over the red linoleum tiles. The baby being used for an unwilling flotation device. The baby being used to mop the floor. All Willa did was drag on cigarette after cigarette, watching her hands.

It was decided the asylum was no place for a child.

As for Old Saartje, she was stitched corset-tight in a straitjacket. "What have you done with my diamond dowry? I'll be late for my wedding," she whined, even though her husband had been skewered on an Englishman's bayonet in the Boer War four decades before. "I need to get home to Holland," she mewed until Nurse Matron held a hand mirror before the old woman's prune of a face. Old Saartje was silenced by the sight of her own slack bloodhound jowls, the skin of her nose pitted like the peel of an orange. "I forgot," she whispered, turning her shaved skull to the bars at the windows. "I forgot this place was home."

Home. Here the walls were smeared with human excrement, the linoleum tiles wet with diluted bleach. Combined, the two smells reeked of death. When it was time for Arts and Crafts, the madmen chewed on their paintbrushes and wiped the watercolors on the pants of their pajamas. When it was time for Recreation, they were sedated and wheeled about the grounds with strings of drool hanging from their chins, their fingers and toes curled into fists that dangled like weights from their atrophied limbs.

On the day Willa Two was powdered and doll-dressed in a white lace bonnet and embroidered booties and lifted away from the madhouse, Willa One reclined dead-faced on a deckchair while Old Saartje, still stitched in the straitjacket, rocked herself babbling, *"Vandag, gister, more,"* over and over into oblivion. *Today, yesterday, tomorrow . . .* In packs of two and three, the madmen bayed like wolves.

The child was delivered to Kees Peterson, a rich Durban dairy farmer, and his barren wife, in a basket meant for kindling. *"Goed?"* asked Kees. "Has it all its fingers and toes?" "By God, yes!" his wife exclaimed, inspecting little Willa. "She's a perfect specimen!" Over the years they'd been sent a half-dozen defective babies to foster—club-footed, hair-lipped, cross-eyed, colicky changelings. They'd returned every one.

"Except for her complexion. The poor dumpling must be frozen, she's nearly purple." Mrs. Peterson brought her to the fireplace under the cuckoo clock and warmed her at the hearth. She rubbed the baby furiously between her palms to make her color normal. The clock struck the hour, but its face had no hands. The cuckoo bounced crazily on its spring, a tuft of real feathers glued to its wooden head. Weeks passed. Willa might have passed too had her fine silky hair not begun to nap, had her "strangeness" not made itself apparent. Kees was startled awake by a clatter in the larder early one morning. His wife was shrieking and waving a wooden spoon over her head when he rushed in from the bedroom in his longjohns. Her face was screwed up like a juiced lemon, her hair wisping wild from her pretzel bun. "Look at it! Look at it!" she spat, pointing a bony finger in the face of the wailing child.

"What is it?" asked Kees. *"Ek verstaan nie.* This one is an angel."

*"Nee, Man!* A filthy monkey! Look carefully. Look at the hair. Look at the skin. We were blind!"

"Do you mean—?"

*"Ja!* We were fooled!"

Mr. Peterson's wife returned Willa dangling upside down to the madhouse, one gloved fist wrapped around the baby's ankle as if holding a plucked chicken.

"What's the matter?" asked Nurse Matron.

"It's a *coloured*," snapped Mrs. Peterson, flinging the child through the doorway. She straightened her hat, wheeled around on her high heels and clipped off down the crooked pathway, trip-trap, trip-trap.

Nurse Matron pleaded with Mrs. Peterson's retreating back. "But we can't keep her here! Her mother's not well," and a last ditch attempt, "This is no place for a child!"

"Not my problem!" came the reply.

The madhouse was understaffed and overflowing. There were not enough bedpans and the stairwells were puddled with urine. You could shave a madman's head but the lice would only migrate down to his eyebrows and farther south. Nurse Matron was fatigued. She stood in the doorway wondering what to do with the blacky-white changeling in her arms. It occurred to her to toss the thing in the rubbish bin. Her feet hurt. Her heart was a coal hard lump.

Black Sally, the madhouse laundress, came up with a solution. Her Jo'burg half sister was a kind woman, childless *and* coloured, the result of a rape by an Englishman. So, for the second time, Willa was lifted away from the madhouse—this time in a basket meant for carting laundry.

As for the first Willa, nobody was surprised a few months later when she slipped quietly out of her body. She'd been dead to the world for so long it was the rigor mortis alone that indicated she was a corpse and no longer a living human being. Jan Janssen, sunburned and long estranged, was notified of his wife's death by telegram somewhere along the Botswana border where the railway slices through the tall, tall grass. He had done with tears. He was a businessman, after all, with an important role to play in an industry that clawed from the highveld to the Transvaal savanna. He let the paper loose into the wind where it drifted for nearly a minute, fluttering like a moth before lighting next to the tracks. He knew nothing about the baby.

Back in Natal Province, however, word of the darkling child spread from the mouth of the madhouse like wildfire. This word was a hungry thing. A small black man who sufficiently resembled the stable boy on account of his spectacles was hunted down. His body was found months later, wedged between two rocks at the bottom of Albert Falls, minus its head, hands, and feet. The true stable boy who'd been there that day, the day, the week, the month Jan was away, the one who'd tenderly lifted Willa's boy from the street and built him a teeny tiny coffin of imported pine, lived on for many years in an eroded Bantustan on a plot of land the size of a postage stamp of the queen's face. He was shot in an unrelated incident on a bright afternoon in Sharpville with his spectacles folded neatly in his breast pocket.

❧

What Black Sally failed to mention in regards to her sister was that she lived outside Johannesburg on the skirt of a mining compound in a two-room shack where she ran a beer house in the front room and a once-in-a-while one-woman bordello in the back. On the other hand, she *was* kind. In fact, she had a tremendous heart, for which she was called Sunshine. So. Years passed. Willa grew under Sunshine, never suspecting this woman wasn't her true-blue mother, or that there was anything strange about falling asleep to the sound of drunken miners gambling at dice, whooping it up, singing marabi or fistfighting in the next room.

Willa was not a pretty child. Her eyes were spaced too far apart, like a rabbit's, and her head was disproportionately large, but Sunshine twisted the little girl's hair into elaborate Bantu knots and tied pastel-colored ribbons around every one. Pink, yellow, green. She sat the child on her lap each night as she penciled in her eyebrows, combed out her red wig, and sang American blues songs. She'd smile and her smile was a crescent moon lying on its back. "How do I look, queenie?"

"Beautiful, Mama." And she was, with her caramel skin and her luscious behind, round as a plum and high enough to set a pint of beer upon.

Professor Kagunda, are you reading this? I suspect you've stopped reading by now. I tried to do the assignment but I couldn't. My brother died eight days ago. Do you know what loneliness is? Check this box if you are reading this:

One day, when Willa was five, Sunshine found her weeping in the yard with her thumb jammed in her mouth.

"What's wrong?"

"I haven't ate since Tuesday!" cried Willa.

"Have some mealie bread."

"We got no mealie bread."

"Let's make some!"

"We got no mealie meal."

"Is that so?" asked Sunshine, knitting her eyebrows. "Well, what would you like to eat?"

"Ice cream."

Sunshine smiled and clapped her hands. "Buckle your shoes, queenie! We're going to town!" The banana split she bought Willa was bigger than a toy boat. Neither of them knew that the waitress had hocked a glob of her phlegm into the whipped cream before spurring them to eat it outside. It took Willa so long to eat it on the bench at the bus stop that it melted to a soup and had to be drunk.

On the way back home she vomited it up over her patent leather shoes.

Sunshine forgot to enroll Willa in school. When she had money she spent it on perfume and nylon stockings. When she didn't, she prostituted for amputees, pitiable men who caressed her with their phantom hands. Once, she took a notion to brew a batch of sour-mash whiskey in the tub. She botched the recipe and poured the useless slop out into the dusty yard. For days afterwards the bathwater reeked of alcohol.

Most nights the beer-house fights got out of hand. Someone would drink himself mad and trash the establishment roaring that he was a man, not a beast. There was sure to be bottle smashing, bloodshed, liquor-loosed anguish. The walls would shake. The men would turn on each other like dogs spat up out of hell, quite literally, for that's what the mines of the Witwatersrand Basin was, the gouged rotten mouth of hell, all veined with gold. The men were made to toil there underfoot in the root canal bowels of the land, to crawl like crabs with pickaxes in the grinding winding dark, to work off their fingernails, to bruise, to lose their legs and lungs, to rip out the gristling treasure from the muscle of the earth and give it away for enough to buy a drink a day. They drank to forget; they fought.

The rough black shadows of the Africans leaped under the door separating the shebeen from the back room where Willa slept. She mistook the shadows for living things. She thought they were reaching for her. One time, a man ambled in, demanded she undo his pants, broke into sobs and passed out on the floor. Another time, a man ambled in and didn't pass out until she met his demands. But that time is too ugly for words. On nights like these, when things were being broken, dishes and promises, bones and order, Willa would creep through the window with her blanket and stretch out under the streetlamp at the corner to catch a few nods in its thin pool of light, dreaming of flying.

There were also times, such as when Sunshine sang in Xhosa hanging the laundry out to dry in the yard, when Willa's heart would swell with joy, just to see the dresses dancing in the wind.

❧

Then came the butcher and disaster right behind him. Mr. Tibbs fell head over heels in love with Sunshine in his shop while wrapping her a greasy cut of meat in thick brown paper. The sight of her melted him like a pat of butter. He noticed the little thumb-sucking girl at Sunshine's side looking for the life of her like a malnourished lollipop and added another two pounds of meat to the bundle at no cost, never mind they were coloured and shouldn't have been in his shop at that hour.

"Thank you." Sunshine smiled her smile as easy as a hammock and he was won. If he'd noticed his reflection in the scale atop the counter at that moment, he'd have seen that behind his walrus mustache his face was apple-cheeked, miraculously stripped of twenty years. He'd have seen that in an instant, he'd stopped feeling confused about his purpose.

Some good resulted from the affair. Walter Tibbs taught Willa to read enough English to learn all about John and Jen and their cat, Kit. He gave Sunshine enough cash to stop running the shebeen out of the front room.

"Are you growing a baby in there?" asked Willa once, laying her ear on his round belly. "I want a brother." He roared with laughter, grabbed her with his sausage fingers and tossed her in the air. He bought her a baby doll with curly yellow hair and blue glass eyes.

The end result, though, was disastrous. How could it be otherwise? In another time, in another place, the distant future on a distant planet perhaps, if he hadn't been married, if she hadn't been coloured, if he hadn't been white, if it hadn't taken place there, atop a mine where the earth trembled and roared and the weight of the continent warped things with its load, if he hadn't been seen giving her forget-me-nots, if this, if that, their love might have gone on without notice. Never mind in Willa's eyes he was Kris Kringle because he always brought a brown bag of licorice ropes. Never mind he made them laugh.

This was a place of distortions. Breasts had no milk. Clocks had no hands. Men had no legs. Love was a thing with no space to stretch itself out. The catastrophe unfolded itself.

The pertinent details are these: Mrs. Tibbs, a frigid little woman who was gifted at needlepoint in spite of being myopic, shot herself in the mouth with a hunting rifle because of the humiliation. Sunshine was clapped in a women's prison for life. Before she was carted off, a mob destroyed her smile with a barrage of gold-drained mine stones which broke her jaw and cracked off half her teeth. Mr. Tibbs was deported and found himself in a London flophouse where he swelled to three hundred pounds and could no longer take the stairs. And Willa?

Willa wound up back in Durban, in a Catholic orphanage mission school for coloured girls called Mother of God, Joy of All Who Sorrow. The school was situated just a hop skip and a jump away from the Petersons whom Willa had unwittingly deceived as a baby. The headmistress was Sister Mary Margaret, a gaunt old woman with arthritis, no patience, and a paddle she was quick to use against "cheekiness." She'd come on a creaky boat from the white cliffs of Dover at eighteen with the dream of bringing light to the savage darkness. The entire voyage she'd been seasick and anxious, and at long last when the vessel docked at Capetown she was dismayed to find the heathen darkies dressed in trousers.

The other nuns at the mission school resembled seagulls and regularly checked the girls' fingernails for dirt. Merit stickers were handed out for hygiene. The girls wore pleated navy wool skirts and crisp white blouses, stiff with starch.

"Here is your uniform. You are to keep it impeccably clean," said Sister Mary Margaret to Willa on her first day at Mother of God, Joy of All Who Sorrow. "We do not tolerate cheekiness here. Do you know the Lord's Prayer?"

"No," whispered Willa.

"Speak up, child. I can't hear you. Lift your head." Willa was crying. "What's this? What's this? Didn't I just tell you we don't tolerate cheekiness? You ought to be grateful—you're here to be saved."

"I—I want my mother," Willa wailed.

"Gracious child, your mother died years ago. Mary is your mother now."

"No, she's not! You're lying. She's not dead!" shouted Willa. The paddle came down across her cheek with a thwack.

"Cheekiness! I'm warning you. I've got a full docket on your case. Your mother was a white lady. She went insane as she was with child from a native. She had to be locked up where she gave birth to you and died. If you're not very careful, you'll go insane just as your mother did. It's in your blood. Do you hear me? Your only chance for salvation is Christ."

Willa felt as if her skin had been torn off by a hyena and she'd been issued a new skin. A filthy uniform. The mantle of insanity. She was eight and being eaten. That winter was slung with perpetual thunderstorms. Willa spent long periods indoors staring at her blank face in the mirror, trying to trace the origins of her features. She started to hate her hair, her eyes, her lips. She saw herself ugly, homeless, strange. She didn't know she was more South African than South Africa. She only knew that she didn't belong. At night

she watched her reflection contorted by raindrops in the windowpane and the gaping stretch of blackness behind it. Through this
window, from time to time, came the long low howl of a train.
Under the train, the wet ground moaned. Bones rotted. Diamonds
gleamed.

# AUNT PATTY ON THE WAGON

While walking the five blocks home from the university one rainy evening in November, Professor Bernard Boudreaux Jr. was filled with the usual sense of dread. The rain was hard and relentless. He was used to heavy storms, having grown up in the arch of Mississippi's foot, but this had none of the warmth of the downpours of his boyhood when the humidity had licked his skin and the sky had come low like a merciful hand stretching the afternoon, giving it drink, turning it into a red endless muddy road. This was a menacing rain, a cold nor'easter, and now he lived on the long avenue of the eating clubs.

There was the gothic Tower, the Canon, the Quadrangle, the florid Ivy and the Cap and Gown. He passed these using his cane, which was a recent acquisition, a gift from his friend Lester, who'd urged him to "turn that limp into a pimp walk." The cane was polished ebony and had a silver handle, but it was not for show. Therefore, rather than making him feel distinguished, the cane made him feel weak. That was part of the dread. It was a constant reminder of his deformity.

He walked with a bent head. The rain was driving on a sideways slant. It tore like artillery against the black hide of his umbrella, which the wind was threatening to yank away and hurl into the road. *Tap,* went his cane, like a blind man's. *Tap tap.* He hated the sound.

They loomed on either side of him: the Cloister Inn, the Charter Club, the Court, the Dial Lodge, the stately Colonial, and the Tiger Inn with its epaulets. It was dinnertime. Each club was lit like a jack-o'-lantern and buzzing with student life, but the street itself was deserted. The rain ricocheted white on the dark pavement. The professor was alone.

His anxiety increased as he crossed into the residential zone. All along the curb, the last leaf piles of the fall were clogging the gutters and giving up their damp despairing smell of rot. It was a neighborhood of outlandish property taxes and implicit understandings. Having a swimming pool was looked upon as tacky but having a gardener was not. The professor had been mistaken for a gardener four times in the four years he'd lived there, twice by the same woman who'd welcomed him and his family with a box of macaroons on the day they moved in. He had worked as a gardener's assistant in his youth, and he wondered if they could smell it on him. That was part of the dread too, though he never talked about it.

He was slogging by the macaroon lady's mansion now. He cut his eyes through the dripping hedges to glance at it. It had been added onto and added onto until it was ready to fold like a house of cards under the weight of its own Tudor sprawl. Its windows were mismatched and, like a funhouse, it had too many doors. When he was past it, he had the uneasy feeling he was being watched from behind.

Measured against the macaroon lady's house, Professor Boudreaux's two-story brick colonial was modest but tasteful, he thought. In fact, it resembled the pointy-roofed dream home he'd drawn as a boy, except in place of the lollipop tree stood a towering blue spruce. He was proud of the house, but it built a nebulous anxiety in him. He imagined coming home from work and finding it in blazes, boarded up, burglarized, or as in *The Twilight Zone,* in the sudden possession of another man. Some nights these thoughts were so real that he stayed in his office on campus rather than face what he might find.

"Who are you?" he feared his wife and children asking him. "This isn't your house."

There were games he'd devised for the walk home to protect against that sort of catastrophe. For example, he might hold his breath for one hundred steps and make eye contact with everyone he passed. This evening, the game was to avoid touching the seams in the wet sidewalk with his new cane, while keeping his umbrella from inverting in the wind. The rain was playing tricks on his eyes by fogging up his glasses. Periodically, he reached up to wipe them clean with his thumb. He flinched at a fire hydrant that looked like a dog.

The road was beginning to flood. He tried to avoid the puddles on the sidewalk without success. Above his galoshes, the cuffs of his pants were now sopping wet and tugging downward. The puddles reflected the mean orange glare of the streetlamps and it became difficult not just to discern where the seams of the sidewalk were, but whether or not he was contacting them with the tip of his cane.

When he reached his block, he heard a car approaching from behind. Quickening his pace, he tripped on an angry root. He dropped his briefcase and cane, crashed on his kneecaps, and found his shins submerged in water.

He inhaled and held his breath until the car passed. Then he erected his cane and pulled himself to his feet. A thousand needles of pain shot from the sole of his bad foot up his calf. He shook himself off and, cautiously, staggered on.

Mrs. Turner's pair of lawn jockeys leered at him from across the street, their faces slick as patent leather in the wet. They followed him home with their popping eyes, as if to say, *Stop pretending. We saw you fall.* The house rose before him intact. Relief. He exhaled, and took the flagstones toward his front door.

Then, horribly, his distress was confirmed. Through the rain-streaked dining room window, he'd spotted his sister-in-law sitting at the table with his wife and two children.

She was in his seat. He wiped his glasses to be sure. There was no mistaking her, even at this distance, even with the rain giving the window the appearance of an impressionist painting. She looked like an actress in stage makeup, a wide-jawed, redheaded replication of his wife.

He stalled in the front yard under the shelter of his wide umbrella to spy on them. Could they see him? No. It was dark and so was he. He felt his heart pound. What were they doing? He drew closer, right up to the holly bushes beneath the window. There was some-thing cabalistic about the manner in which they sat. They appeared to be using the eggcups as finger bowls.

His sister-in-law was giving a speech. He was convinced she would change the subject when he entered, but he couldn't make out her words through the rain. He watched her mouth in an attempt to read her lips, and was dismayed to find that his daughter resembled her. His son, he observed with some satisfaction, did not. Still, the four of them looked alike in a way that did not include him.

They were laughing now. He could just make out the low stac-cato bark of his sister-in-law's laughter through the windowpane. Suddenly, a gust of wind sucked the professor's umbrella inside out, tore it from his hand and flung it up into the middle branches of the blue spruce tree. It flapped there like a mangled pterodactyl. Fearing that the neighbors would mistake him for a Peeping Tom, he went inside.

The reek of her Shalimar perfume had extended to the vestibule. With a terrible sense of foreboding, he shook out the rain spit from his overcoat and hung it on the peg.

Then he closed the front door behind him and heard it latch.

"Is that you, Smarty-pants?" she bellowed.

"Dad? Aunt Patty's here," sang his son. They adored her. "She brought us walkie-talkies."

"Is that right?" he called, stabbing his cane into the umbrella stand. He sucked in his stomach, limped into the dining room and forced himself to kiss her on the cheek, which tasted of pancake makeup. Her eyelashes were clumped together with mascara, like the little legs of flies. "Hello, Patricia. You look well."

"I'd better. I've had a face-lift." Her voice was loud as a newscaster's and characterized by the squashed vowels of the Midwest. "You've gained weight."

"Glad you noticed."

"Surprised to see me?" She showed her horse teeth. They were bleached so white they were blue.

"We're all surprised," his wife stressed. She knew he didn't like her sister. "Patty came all the way from Milwaukee to surprise me for my birthday, Bernard." There was a hint of apology in her voice.

"Imagine that."

"Well, let's not be misleading, that's not the only reason I'm here. I'm giving a seminar in Atlantic City, so I thought what the heck— why not combine the trip with my kid sister's birthday."

"You shouldn't have," said Bernard.

"I wouldn't miss it for the world. This is a real milestone. You only turn forty once."

"You only turn *any* age once," his daughter pointed out. She was nine. "Then you die and that's that."

"Don't be morbid, Emma," said Lynn, whose birthday wasn't until November twentieth. Today was only the twelfth.

"I'll be in your hair for a whole week," Aunt Patty boomed.

"Aunt Patty's going to sleep in my room," said Emma, "and I'm going to sleep with Bernie."

"That's fine."

"Put down your briefcase. Take a load off, why don't you," Aunt Patty invited, as if it were her house and not Bernard's. He realized with some embarrassment that he was gripping his briefcase against his chest like a plate of armor and dripping on the Moroccan rug.

"Make yourself comfortable, Smarty-pants."

Nobody called him that. It was her special belittling nickname for him. She'd started it at the rehearsal dinner the night before he married Lynn, and he'd politely asked her not to call him that again.

"Cool down, Smarty-pants. Don't be such a square," she'd teased, drawing a wobbly rectangle in the air with her pointer fingers, before spilling her highball in his lap.

She'd been the only member of Lynn's family in attendance. Everyone else had disapproved. Knowing how grateful Lynn was to have her sister as her maid of honor, Bernard had held his temper and excused himself from the table in the back room of the musty lodge where they were celebrating. In the dim hallway leading to the men's room, he crossed under the enormous mounted head and neck of a moose with moth-eaten fur. Patty had tracked him down, locked the men's room door behind her, and reached for his crotch, which he was dabbing at with a towel.

"No, no. Let me do it," she'd insisted. "It's my fault."

"I'm fine," he told her, but she'd laughed and snatched at his fly.

"Let's see what you got hiding in there."

"Stop it," he said, backing against the sink.

"I never did it with a black guy. Is it true what they say?" she panted.

"Get off me!" he cried, pushing her away.

Her face turned evil then; her freckles darkened. "If you don't show me your big black dong right now, you cripple, I'll scream."

Much later, as one of her twelve steps to recovery, she'd apologized to him and Lynn for that night. They were on a list of people she'd harmed under the influence and become willing to make amends to. The details of her apology were amazingly accurate. She remembered the moose, the pink odorizor cakes in the urinals, and even having used the word *dong*. Lynn had burst into tears and embraced her. She'd been pregnant with Emma then, and her arms barely reached around her sister's back. "Of course, we forgive you, Patty," she cried. "We're so proud of you."

But it was never his sister-in-law's drunkenness he objected to.

"Aunt Patty's giving us all manicures," said Bernie, "even though I'm a boy."

"It's perfectly acceptable for a man to have a manicure, not in a pink or red, of course, but a clear polish is just fine," Aunt Patty rationalized. "Commendable even. A man with manicured hands says to the world, 'Hey world, I'm impeccably clean. I care about my appearance. I pay attention to the details.'"

Aunt Patty was now a motivational speaker.

"On the other hand, a man with dirt under his fingernails, or who bites them, who's going to want to do business with a man like that?"

"Not I," said Emma.

"Exactly. It sends a message. Let's stop soaking." Aunt Patty lifted her fingertips from the mysterious solution in the eggcup. "Time to push back our cuticles."

She did phenomenally well for herself. At her sold-out seminars she wore Republican red suits with linebacker shoulder pads and used a laser pointer to highlight her transparencies. Her theme was "Accept Your Wisdom." She carried ballpoint pens stamped with this phrase and handed them out whenever meeting someone new. "Accept Your Wisdom" was also the title of her self-published book, which had come into print the same year as Bernard's book on burial rites in the Black Diaspora, and sold more copies by a landslide.

"Sit," Aunt Patty instructed Bernard, but there were only four high-backed chairs in the dining room, and she had usurped his.

His foot prickled.

"Don't you want a manicure?" she badgered.

"I have to change," he said, escaping.

⁂

Over lasagna, after everyone's fingernails had dried, she asked the children what their dreams were for the future.

"When you close your eyes and envision your possibilities, what do you see? Be specific."

"I want to be a motivational speaker," said Emma, "or a hermit poetess."

"Excellent choices. What about you, Bernie?"

"His grades will have to improve first," said Bernard. Lynn shot him a look. Their son was ten and read at a second-grade level, at best. Down in the Delta, he was the kind they would have called "touched." He claimed that every letter of the alphabet had its own color, as did every number. *C,* for example, was aquamarine, *S* was hot pink, and *2* was brown. Words on a page presented pictures to him that did not generally correlate to their meaning. Synesthesia, the tutor called it, but it seemed more to Bernard like his son was hallucinating. Either that, or lying.

"Once his grades improve he can be anything he wants," Bernard added. This was his genuine wish: that his children achieve unfettered success without undue hardship, but somehow nobody understood that. He couldn't express it. He heard himself now sounding like the bad cop to Aunt Patty's good one.

"She's not a good cop," he reassured himself, "she's a sad clown."

"Go on, kiddo," Aunt Patty pressed. "Look into your crystal ball. What does your future have in store?"

Bernie wiped away his milk mustache with the back of his hand. "I'm going to fly," he said, without hesitation.

"I didn't know you wanted to be a pilot, honey," said Lynn. "Your grandfather wanted to be a pilot too, you know, in the Second World War. A fighter pilot."

Bernie's face lit up. "Bernard the First?"

Bernard bristled.

"No, no. Elbows off the table, please. *My* father. Aunt Patty's and mine," Lynn clarified. "Your Pops."

"The old coot," said Aunt Patty.

Emma giggled.

"Oh." Bernie removed his elbows from the table. "I thought you meant Dad's dad." He looked at his father. "What did your dad—"

"But Ed's feet were too big," the professor interrupted his son. "Isn't that right, Lynn? Tell him the story."

"The air force wouldn't let your Pops enlist because they didn't have big enough boots," Lynn finished.

"No boots for the coot," Aunt Patty joked.

"Yeah, well, I don't want to fly an airplane. *I* want to fly," Bernie explained.

This wasn't terribly surprising. The boy had always had a predilection for height. As an infant, he'd loved being tossed in the air; as a toddler, his favorite toy had been an aluminum ladder; at the age of five, he'd learned to scale the refrigerator. *Higher,* he used to shout, when they pushed him on the park swings. *High as the sky!* They were charmed by it. However, it was a little upsetting to hear a ten-year-old, in all seriousness, indulge the fantasy of flight.

Bernard put down his fork. "I think your aunt is asking you what you'd like to be when you grow up, son," he suggested.

"Actually, no. What I asked you, Bernie, was to visualize your possibilities, which you did perfectly well. What's more, you can actualize your dream to fly just as long as you accept your own wisdom. Don't let anybody tell you otherwise. Flying is a beautiful dream."

Bernard couldn't tell whether or not his sister-in-law was speaking metaphorically. This irritated him.

She raised her lipstick-stained glass of seltzer and toasted her nephew. "To flying!"

"Thanks, Aunt Patty. Watch this." Bernie blew a spit bubble the size of an avocado pit. "Did you know that I'm named after—"

"Not at the table," Bernard ordered. "Finish your spinach."

"Can you see me?" said Emma. She'd covered her face with her hair. "Am I here? Can anybody see me?"

"I see you, sweetie. Watch this," said Aunt Patty, rolling her tongue into a taco. It was more than a little obscene.

❧

"What have you got against my sister?" Lynn asked him later, in bed. The rain was still drumming on the roof.

He closed his book and chose his words carefully. "She's a phony," he said.

"A *phony?*" She spoke in a stage whisper, in case Patty was eavesdropping through the adjoining wall. "I'll be the first to admit she's not perfect, but I would never call her a phony."

"No?"

"Never. How can you call her that, with all she's overcome? I mean, I really admire her." Lynn's face flushed. "I do. You have to acknowledge how honest she's been with herself, and how brave. Don't you think?"

"Are you referring to her recovering alcoholism?"

"I'm referring to the choices she's made to improve her life and to help others improve theirs."

He snorted.

"You could learn a thing or two from her if you kept an open mind. You two are more alike than you think, Mr. Smarty-pants."

Bernard felt the blood rush to his temples. "Don't you ever call me that again."

Lynn rolled her eyes. "Just promise me you'll make an effort, Bernard. Don't be so judgmental."

She'd told him stories about how fiercely protective of her Patty had been as a teenager, how Patty had shouldered the entire burden of Ed's abuse. He tried to focus on that Patty, the saintly one whom he'd never met.

"Fine." He reopened his book and pretended to read.

"Thank you." She reached into the drawer of her bedside table, fished out a bottle of lotion, and slowly, deliberately, moisturized her hands.

"I only wish my dad could have been as strong as Patty," she added, tearing up. Ed had died that summer from acute liver failure. Lynn's mother had discouraged her from bringing Bernard to the wake on the grounds that he would be the focus of attention due the corpse.

"Penny for your thoughts," said Lynn. It was her favorite phrase. But even for a thousand pennies, even for ten million, he couldn't explain his thoughts to his wife. He ignored her instead.

She squirted some more hand lotion into her palm and held it out to him like a peace offering. The scent was called ylang-ylang myrrh, and it stunk.

"Why don't you let me do your foot," she said.

"No thank you." He didn't like her to touch it.

"Remember what Dr. Rudolph said," she warned, as if he could forget.

During a panic attack at the start of the semester, the foot had fallen asleep and refused to wake up. At rest, it was completely numb. When pressure was applied, it bristled with phantom pins and needles. Lynn had forced him to go back to the orthopedist who fitted him for corrective shoes. "Maybe your foot grew," she'd speculated. "That can happen when you gain weight, you know. It happened to me when I was pregnant with Bernie, remember how my feet spread? Maybe your shoe is too tight."

He hated going to the doctor, unpeeling his sock and setting his clubfoot on the cold examination table for the doctor to prod. The joints were misaligned, the toes were twisted in, the heel was twisted out, the arch was askew, and the nails were thick as mollusks. The entire appendage was a loathsome reminder of the place where he was shamed.

Dr. Rudolph had a comb-over and an Adam's apple as pointy as a crayon. A model skeleton dangled by the crown of its skull, next to the file cabinet in the corner of the examination room. It put Bernard in mind of the song his Nan used to hum while hanging the wet wash to dry in the yard:

> *Dem bones, dem bones, dem dry bones*
> *Dem bones, dem bones, dem dry bones*
> *Dem bones, dem bones, dem dry bones*
> *Don't you hear the word of the Lord?*

The doctor measured Bernard's foot to the millimeter with a pinching slide-rule contraption, which looked like a phrenological tool imported from the nineteenth century, as the skeleton watched on with a maniacal grin.

> *Toe bone connected to the foot bone*
> *Foot bone connected to the leg bone*
> *Leg bone connected to the knee bone*
> *Don't you hear the word of the Lord?*

"Hmm," Dr. Rudolph said. "Interesting." He whacked the sole with his miniature rubber hammer once, twice, three times.

"What?" asked Bernard, "what is it?"

"The foot hasn't grown but there seems to be some nerve damage. You can't feel that?" He traced an infinity sign on the ball of the foot with a cotton swab.

"No."

The bone doctor slapped the foot with his rubber glove, as if he was challenging it to a duel. "And that?"

"It tingles a little."

Dr. Rudolph studied Bernard's chart. "Let me ask you this. Do you ever experience abnormal hunger or thirst, a trembling in the hands, an elevated pulse, confusion or distress about your place in the world, blurred vision, irritability? Do you often feel threatened? Would your loved ones describe you as paranoid? Are you suspicious, for example, that you are being watched? Are you stubborn, do you sometimes suddenly awaken from sleep, lack physical coordination or pound your hands on tables or walls? Are you African-American? Do you suffer from unbearable nightmares? Do you find your breathing becomes rapid and shallow? Lastly, are you sometimes nervous, angry, or upset for a reason you can't articulate for fear of being misunderstood?"

Bernard was alarmed. "Yes," he admitted. "Why do you ask?"

Dr. Rudolph clicked his pen. "Some, none, or all of the above?"

"Why?"

"Those are the telltale symptoms of diabetes. So is your sleeping foot. We'll have to test your blood sugar."

After two agonizing weeks, the results came back negative. Dr. Rudolph told him, "The good news is, you're not diabetic. The bad news is, if your foot doesn't wake up, it might have to be amputated anyway.

"Now, it's not as bad as it sounds," Dr. Rudolph reasoned. "Today's prosthetics are extremely lifelike, and they come in all flesh tones. Think of it this way: I could give you a brand-new right foot, size ten and a half, the mirror image of your left foot. It would be fake, but it would be normal."

Bernard had a vision of his severed foot on display as a good luck charm in the front window of a dusty curiosity shop.

"No, I don't want to lose my foot. What can I do?" he implored.

Dr. Rudolph knitted his eyebrows. "Try massaging it. It's a crapshoot, but it may help with the circulation."

"You're sure you don't want me to massage it? How's it feeling?" asked Lynn.

"Better," he lied.

"That's good." She saturated her hands with the lotion he refused. "What do you think?"

"About what?"

"My manicure." She wiggled her greasy fingers. The nails were painted coral pink. The color made her hands look old.

⚜

In the middle of the night, a great clap of thunder woke Bernard from a nightmare in which his foot was being set on fire by an angry mob.

The dream foot had caught fire like a dry thing of tinder. The flames licked up his ankle, but he was paralyzed. The paralysis continued for several seconds after he'd woken up. He lay there with a terrible thirst until the dream ebbed away and he was able to wiggle the toes of the bad foot. Lynn slept peacefully beside him on her stomach. She was a talented sleeper. He rested his hand on her back, felt the slow rise and fall of her breath and tried to match it with his own. After a while he gave up, put on his glasses, slippers, and robe, and made his way downstairs, with the aid of the banister, to fix himself a snack.

He didn't notice the kitchen light was on until it was already too late.

"What are you doing up, Smarty-pants?" she asked. She was down on the floor with a bucket and sponge, in a plaid flannel nightgown and rubber gloves. The sleeves of her nightgown were rolled up. Her arms were a chaos of freckles. Her hair looked suspiciously like a wig, and without her makeup her face was freakishly washed out. The room smelled of cleaning spray. The dishwasher was running. The countertops and floor were gleaming. The magnets on the refrigerator had been straightened. He was immediately on edge.

"I was hungry," he replied. "Did you move the kitchen table?"

"Yes. I thought it made more sense there. Feng-shui. It opens up the room and frees mental clutter. Did you know that your environment is an outer manifestation of your inner state?"

He didn't answer.

"It's true. This is the landscape of your mind."

She scrubbed at a persistent rust-colored stain on the tile. "Elbow grease, elbow grease," she said, dumping out an anthill of Ajax.

"That won't come out," he warned her. "It was there when we moved in."

"Says you." She dunked the sponge in the bucket, wrung it out and continued scouring. "You have to want it badly enough. You start with visualization. I want this stain gone. I'm visualizing it gone. I'm a true believer in human grit and I'm capable. That's my attitude." She swiped at the floor, grunting like a tennis pro.

"There."

The stain was gone.

"It's not magic," she told him. "It's pluck."

Her knees cracked when she stood up to empty the bucket in the sink. Her feet were bare and he felt a flicker of sympathy when he noticed that her ankles had grown fat.

"I hope you don't mind, I also reorganized the cabinets, alphabetized the spice rack, and cleaned the insides of the oven and fridge. I'm an insomniac," she explained. "It helps to have a project. What would you like to eat?"

There was something wrong with her. All he wanted was to leave.

"How about some cinnamon toast and hot cocoa?" she offered. "Have a seat."

A yellow legal pad lay on the table. The top page was scribbled with notes. "That's my list," she said, popping two pieces of wheat bread into the toaster. "Those are the things I'd like to accomplish this week, in no particular order. Take a look."

While Aunt Patty warmed a pot of skim milk on the stove, Bernard read her list and his sympathy vanished.

1. Clean house spic and span! Redecorate/Rearrange.
2. Coach Bernie in flight.
3. Cut Emma's hair. Bangs?
4. Help Bernard tap into his serenity.
5. Girl's night with Lynn in Atlantic City.

"No," said Bernard, not knowing which item to take issue with first. "Absolutely not."

"Look. The house is a mess. Lynn's tired. She's frazzled. She's in over her head. A getaway is just what she needs and it wouldn't hurt for you to spend some quality time with the kids. Bernie's crying out for your attention and Emma doesn't even think you notice her. She's biting her fingernails and chewing her hair. I found this under her pillow." She handed him a piece of paper folded as small as a tooth. "Something's got to give and it's you."

Bernard unfolded the paper. It was a sheet of his own dove-gray stationary, embossed with the Princeton seal. In spidery letters almost too small to read, Emma had penciled a haiku:

> *In my nowhere room*
> *That nobody will visit*
> *Invisible ink*

❧

Aunt Patty set down the plate of cinnamon toast and the #1 DAD mug full of hot cocoa before him. "Eat it while it's hot," she said. Her breath was antiseptic with mouthwash. Another roll of thunder sounded.

"By the way, do you store emergency candles? You could lose your power any minute." She snapped her fingers. "Just like that. Are you prepared?"

His hands shook as he took a bite of the toast, chewed and spat it out. It tasted awful.

"I used Sweet'N Low. You'll get used to it," she said. "You need to shed some pounds. It's too much baggage, Bernard."

He stood up. Who was she to cast stones? He would have liked to rip her list in half, banish her from his house and throw her out in the rain. But she was his wife's sister and his children adored her. They would take her side, so he held his tongue.

"Where are you going?" she asked.

"I lost my appetite," he lied. "Goodnight."

"Wait a minute. I'm not finished with you, buster. We need to talk."

Bernard fled as fast as his sleeping foot would allow and took refuge in his son's room at the top of the stairs. It was his habit to check on his children after they were asleep but tonight he locked the door behind him. The room was illuminated an eerie green by the light of the fish tank.

The children were snuggled under the triangle comforter in Bernie's twin bed. Bernie had one arm thrown over his sister, as if to protect her. Clutched in his manicured hand was a walkie-talkie transmitting a low crackling static.

Bernard stepped over the mess of socks, T-shirts, and comic books on the floor and sank down at the side of the bed. He lay his cheek on the mattress eight inches from his daughter's face, felt the hot breath from her heart-shaped nostrils, and reached out to pull the strand of hair clenched between her teeth. Her hair was long and full of snarls; she howled whenever Lynn took to it with a brush. Underneath her eyelids, her pupils were agitating.

He pushed all of the buttons and flipped the switch on the side of the box. The disturbance wouldn't die. Gently, he tried to work the walkie-talkie from his son's hand in order to dislodge the batteries, but Bernie's grip tightened around the thing and his eyes opened. The boy was suddenly alert.

"Dad?"

"Shhh. Emma's asleep. You left your walkie-talkie on."

"Don't turn it off," Bernie whispered. "I'm listening."

"KKKKKKKKKKKKKKKK," went the walkie-talkie.

"To what?" Bernard asked, frustrated that his son didn't understand how these things worked. "Someone needs to be talking into the other one."

"I know."

"Where is the other one?" he asked, but the boy's eyes were already rolling backwards, his eyelids were drooping and just as suddenly as he'd woken up, he was asleep again.

Bernard studied their faces. He worried for them. He remembered the white schoolboys who had held him down and beat him, spat on him, stolen his shoe to expose his foot, and laughed at it. He remembered being denied a public library card. He remembered going uptown to the movie house with his uncle, having to use the back door and squeeze into the last three rows where the seats were broken and cushionless. He remembered his Nan's hands, spoiled by the acid bluing with which she laundered white folks' clothes to make a wage. He remembered wetting his pants in the drugstore when the soda jerk refused to let him use the toilet. He remembered the hot urine running down his leg and over the clownish shoe, running down his leg like a dog's. He remembered the terror of being seen. He had promised himself it would be different for his children.

Their faces were greenish and alien in the light of the fish tank. They didn't really look like him, and in a way, he was glad. In a way, that was the whole point.

"Will you mind," Lynn had asked him on the night he drove her to the hospital to give birth to Bernie, "will you mind if the baby comes out light-skinned?" Her eyes were wild awake; her face was red as a slap. They'd just been pulled over.

"I'm having a baby," Lynn had shrieked at the cop. Her water was broken all over the seat. Her hands were fisted between her thighs. There was a heavy smell in the Volkswagen Beetle, like graphite and blood.

"License and registration," the cop ordered.

"I'm having it right now!"

"License and registration."

"Here," said Bernard, "take it."

The cop looked from the license to Bernard to Lynn and back to the license.

"This your car?" he asked.

Bernard deadened his voice. "Yes."

"That your wife?"

"YES, I'M HIS WIFE," Lynn yelled. Her face was contorted in pain. "It's coming!"

The cop shook his head. "I wasn't asking you." He smiled and tapped Bernard on the shoulder. "That your wife?"

Bernard gripped the steering wheel at ten and two and stared straight ahead. "Yes."

"In that case, I'm gonna have to write you up a speeding ticket." He proceeded to do this, as slowly as possible, before dropping the ticket in Bernard's lap like a piece of toilet paper. Bernard was terrified he wouldn't be able to stop his dead foot from leveling the gas pedal to the floor, causing the engine to roar like a beast. He held his breath for the time it took the cop to swagger back to his squad car. It was a game to protect against evil.

Lynn grasped his arm, awake to the distance between them. "You won't mind if it comes out white? You'll love it anyway?"

"It's mine isn't it?" he'd snapped, unable to look her in the face.

They were his children. And in a way, they weren't.

Bernard turned his head to the aquarium. A lone Siamese fighting fish wove between the plastic seaweed columns, through the snowy flotsam of its own waste, over the fake treasure chest and the fluorescent yellow pebbles. It was the last remaining fish, having eaten the others. Bernard watched the fish for a long time, and listened to

Aunt Patty pacing the rooms downstairs. The numb sensation in his foot began a slow rise up his right leg.

In a panic, he stood, supporting himself at the windowsill where Bernie had lined up his soccer trophies. Dark rivulets of rainwater trailed the windowpane. Not ten feet away, in the grasp of the spruce, the spokes of his vanquished umbrella glinted like knives. He wiped his breath from the glass. Farther off, down on the opposite side of the street, the midget lawn jockeys were just visible under Mrs. Turner's dim porch light. From this angle, they appeared to be crouching. Bernard quickly removed his glasses and put everything out of focus. The rasp of the walkie-talkie grew suddenly louder then, like a great vacuum in the void of outer space.

❧

The next morning Bernard overslept. By the time he woke up, the storm was finished and his family was gone. He searched the rooms for signs of them in a dull anguish, not trusting them to return. The living room had been rearranged in such a way he barely recognized it. All of the furniture was now raked on a diagonal slant. Affronted, he kicked his foot against the wall and heard his daughter scream. He followed her voice to the backyard.

The four of them were out there, but it wasn't normal. The ground was covered with earthworms, millions of them, as far as the eye could see. He stepped onto the back porch in a state of disbelief. The worms wriggled over each other like boneless blind fingers of the apocalypse. The air was unseasonably warm. The sky was clear and blue.

"Look, Dad," Bernie shouted. He was trying to force a handful of worms down the back of his sister's jacket, as if it were a snowball.

"No," Emma squealed in delight, "they'll eat me alive. Dad! Watch me." She did a pirouette. The worms crawled over the toes of her boots. "This is the ballet of the worms."

Lynn and Patricia were filling an empty Maxwell House can with the squirming creatures.

"Aunt Patty's taking us fishing!" Bernie gushed.

"She's soooooo fun," Emma added.

"We've got to take advantage," Aunt Patty explained loudly, picking out the dead ones with her long red fingernails and flinging them over her shoulder. "It's a perfect day for fishing." She was teetering in high heels. If he didn't know better, he'd have thought she was drunk. "Most people would look at this as a problem. Not me. I look at this as a lesson. When the world gives you lemons, make lemonade."

"We might have fresh trout for dinner," said Lynn. "Wouldn't that be nice?"

Bernard couldn't tell if he was awake or dreaming. "I don't understand," he said, pushing his glasses up the bridge of his nose. "Where did they come from?"

"They were hibernating in their tunnels," Bernie guessed. "But they didn't want to drown."

"Look, Dad, look," said Emma, holding up a worm at least twelve inches long. "This one is the king. He's in a bad mood. Accept your wisdom," she admonished the worm.

"You're talking to his butt," Bernie told her. "His face is at the other end."

Aunt Patty glanced at her watch. "We better get the show on the road. Morning's the best time to bait and hook. Get dressed, Smarty-pants. The early bird catches the worm. Ha! No pun intended."

"I'm not going."

"What?" said Lynn, giving him a look.

"Why not?" asked Emma.

"Be quiet, guys," Bernie said, yanking his walkie-talkie from his back pocket.

"I've got to work," Bernard explained.

"It's Saturday," countered Aunt Patty. "Besides which, I thought you were on sabbatical."

"I am," he said. "In order to work."

"He's editing a new book," Lynn told her sister with a combination of disappointment and pride.

"Be quiet!" Bernie shouted. "I heard something." He clutched the toy desperately to his ear. "Roger, Roger!" he called into the mouthpiece. "Hello?"

❧

Bernard was editing a collection of slave narratives to be called *Strangers in a Strange Land*. He spent that entire Saturday holed up at his office in the History Department while his family was at the lake, reading and listening to the accounts of ex-slaves recorded for the WPA. They spoke of omens, of unspeakable evil and of bottomless faith. How could they do it, he wondered. How could they testify with such music and ease? Each story was a nightmare and a lullaby all in one. They had a power over him.

He spent several hours contemplating a story told by Sarah Gudger, at the impossible age of one hundred twenty-one. It caused his foot to shiver.

> I 'membahs de time when mah mammy wah alive, I wah a small chile, afoah dey tuck huh t' Rims Crick. All us chillens wah playin' in de ya'd one night. Jes' arunnin' an' aplayin' lak chillun will. All a sudden mammy cum to de do' all a'sited. "Cum in heah dis minnit," she say. "Jes look up at what is ahappenin'," and bless yo' life, honey, da sta's wah fallin' jes' lak rain. Mammy wah tebble skeered, but we chillen wa'nt afeard, no, we wa'nt afeard. But mammy she say evah time a sta' fall, somebuddy gonna die. Look lak lotta folks gonna die f'om de looks ob dem sta's. Ebbathin' wah jes' as bright as day. Yo'

cudda pick a pin up. Yo' know de sta's don' shine as bright as dey did back den. I wondah why dey don'. Dey jes' don' shine as bright. Wa'nt long afoah dey took mah mammy away, and I wah lef' alone.*

How was he to interpret that? Had Sarah Gudger witnessed a meteor shower or was she describing the dreamscape of her suffering mind? And what of her age? It was doubtful that a human life could span a hundred twenty years. And even if it could, wouldn't the passage of so much time serve to distort a childhood memory? Yet, he believed her. He knew firsthand the lucidity with which an orphan remembers a parent being stolen away. He believed her in his bones.

He drifted with his thoughts for hours until he found himself doodling stars with streaming tales on his desk blotter. He hadn't accomplished any real work. By the time he left for home, it was dark outside and the worms had burrowed back into the earth. The ground was marked with a million tiny holes, like a freshly aerated football field. Here and there on the pavement remained the flat carcasses of worms that had been squashed. Tonight, the professor's game was to count the flattened worms with his cane. There were ninety-six of them leading to his front door.

Inside he was confronted by the nauseating smell of fish. He hung his coat on the peg and listened. The house was quiet. When he tried to put his cane in the umbrella stand, something obstructed it. He reached his hand in and pulled it out. It was his broken umbrella. The handle was missing but someone had folded it properly inward like a sleeping bat.

The rescued umbrella gave sentience to his dread. He carried it into the empty kitchen where the sink was full of soaking pans and

---

*Born in Slavery: Slave Narratives from the Federal Writers' Project, 1936–1938, Manuscript and Prints and Photographs Divisions of the Library of Congress, http://memory.loc.gov/ammem/snhtml/snvoices03.html.

the counters were messy with little bones. Silver scales twinkled on the floor like magic dust. His family had been stolen away. In a bout of rage, he slammed his fist against the freezer door.

"Is that you, Smarty-pants?" Aunt Patty whooped from below.

They were down in the den playing Uno at the card table. Again, there was something exclusive about the way they sat. He surveyed them from the middle of the staircase without descending any farther. His foot was completely numb and he was afraid he would fall.

"Dad!" said Bernie. "I caught a trout this big and we fried him. Em caught one too but she threw him back."

"I'm considering becoming a vegetarian," Emma said, examining her cards.

"Excellent idea," said Aunt Patty. "A meat-free diet is good for the complexion."

"Aunt Patty caught five trout, Dad. Can you believe it?" Bernie went on.

"I learned it from the old coot when your mother was a baby," Aunt Patty told the children. Her face was slightly sunburned. "He used to make me a bologna sandwich and take me out to Lake Michigan in the freezing cold before the sun came up. Me and his pole and his hip flask. Fishing is the only thing he ever taught me how to do, aside from drinking. Not that I bear him a grudge. Fishing is a fine lesson. Give a person a fish and they won't be hungry for a day. Teach a person to fish and they won't be hungry for a lifetime. Isn't that right, Smarty-pants?"

"Don't call me that," he seethed.

There was an awkward silence.

Bernard cleared his throat and held up his umbrella like a piece of evidence. "I'd like to know how this got down from the tree."

"I found it," Bernie said.

"What were you doing up there?"

"I tried to fix it for you, but this part fell off." Bernie showed him the long curved handle of the umbrella. "Can I keep it?"

"I asked you what you were doing up in that tree."

Bernie shrugged.

"Answer me."

Bernie and Aunt Patty exchanged a look.

"Uno," said Emma.

"Why were you up in the tree, boy?"

"I was giving him a flying lesson," Aunt Patty said.

"Are you *insane*?" he shouted.

"Uno," said Emma.

"Calm down, honey. He's fine," Lynn said. "We saved you some fish. It's warming in the oven."

"Uno," said Emma. Her voice was shrill. "Doesn't anyone want to stop me from winning?"

"You'll have to help yourself," Lynn told Bernard, returning her attention to the cards. "We waited for you until we couldn't wait anymore."

"That's right," Aunt Patty added. "It was your choice to be absent."

He ate by himself that night, at the relocated kitchen table, with a paper towel for a napkin and the sinking feeling he was being judged. Their laughter came up through the floorboards and he sensed they were laughing at him. The fish wasn't enough to fill the emptiness in his stomach. Later on, he woke up from the usual nightmare with a desperate hunger pang.

He avoided going to the kitchen. She was down there again. He could hear her, closing and opening drawers. He limped across the hallway to check on his children with the nagging suspicion that they'd be gone. But they were there, the same as they had been the night before, tucked in with the hissing walkie-talkie, washed in the green glow of the tank. He locked himself in his study, sat down at his desk overlooking the backyard and tried to get some work done. He massaged his anesthetized foot, but it was no use. He dropped his Bible on it. It was the heaviest book in the room. Nothing. Until he thought he heard his son's voice muffled through the wall.

"Roger, Roger."

He rested his cheek against the wall and listened.

"Roger," Bernie was repeating. "I'm here. Over and out . . . Roger. Can you hear me, Bernard One? This is your grandson speaking from the planet Earth. This is Bernard Boudreaux the Third. What did you say? Over and out."

Bernard felt dizzy suddenly. The room grew close. He sank to the floor. The walls were breathing.

✿

"I want her to leave," Bernard told Lynn in bed on Monday night. He'd come home at 11:30 PM to find Aunt Patty chopping off Emma's hair. It was short as her ears and two hours past her bedtime. He'd picked a lock off her little shoulder and wound it around the tip of his finger until it turned purple.

"Doesn't she just look cute as a bug?" Aunt Patty asked, taking one last snip and styling it with her fingers.

He stared at his daughter. She was sitting on a phone book. Her feet didn't touch the floor. She looked decidedly middle-aged.

"You don't like it, Dad?"

"No, Emma," he said, "I can't say that I do."

It was the last straw. Aunt Patty was presumptuous. She was

reckless. She was a bad influence. He wanted her out of his house. "By tomorrow," he told his wife.

Lynn stopped writing in her sunflower journal. "You're being irrational."

"I don't trust her. She has no respect for me or my rules."

There was a knock at the door.

"Come in!" Lynn called.

Aunt Patty opened the door. "Hey, kids. Am I interrupting?"

Before he could answer, she came in and sat at the end of their four-poster bed. "We need to talk," she said. "I've agreed to facilitate."

Lynn quietly began to cry.

"Go ahead, sweetie," Aunt Patty told her, "Get it all out. I'm here."

"What is this?" he demanded.

"This is an intervention, Bernard. Go on, Lynn. Say what you have to say."

"I don't know if this is such a good idea," Lynn said.

"Of course you don't. You're scared, and when we're scared, we feel confused. All you have to do is take a deep breath and speak from your heart. It's time to infuse some honesty into this marriage, before it's too late."

The dread rolled up like a wave. The bed was a boat going under. He threw back the covers and leapt out, only to collapse.

Lynn gasped. "Are you okay?"

"He's fine," Aunt Patty answered. "But he's avoiding the issue."

His temples were pounding as he rose to his feet.

"If you don't tell him, I will," Aunt Patty said. "Your wife thinks you're having an affair."

"It's just that you're never home," Lynn called after him as he made his way out the door.

❧

In a blind rage, he drove to Professor Lester's house, where he was handed a black silk robe and a short thin Cuban cigar.

"Now, Brother Bernard," his friend grinned, easing into his leather recliner and crossing his legs, "what brings you to my bachelor pad?"

"My sister-in-law," Bernard began, but when he tried to put into words the dread she had made manifest, he realized how foolish he sounded. What had Aunt Patty done to him that was so terrible? Taken his kids fishing? Given his daughter a haircut? Cleaned his house? Talked to his lonely wife? How could he articulate the doom that had driven him from his own house without it sounding like self-sabotage?

He simplified his tactic. "I'm not well," he admitted. "My foot . . ." He stopped.

Lester drummed his fingers on the humidor. Bernard noticed that his fingernails were polished.

"When you were small," he was surprised to hear himself asking, "what did you envision for your future?"

Lester held the sweet blue smoke of his cigar in his mouth and let it roll off his tongue. "You mean what did I want to be when I grew up?"

"I guess that's what I'm asking."

"Marvin Gaye." Lester smiled. His gold tooth twinkled.

"Seriously."

"I'm dead serious. I wanted to be Marvin Gaye."

"What went wrong?"

"I can't sing for shit compared to Marvin. Just listen to this." He got up to leaf through his enormous record collection, pulled out *What's Goin' On* and put it on the turntable.

"That's what I'm talking about right there. Makes a grown man want to cry."

Bernard stubbed out his cigar. It was making him sick.

"And a grown woman want to open her legs." Lester sighed, slow-dancing with an invisible woman before resettling in his recliner. "How about you? What did you want to be?"

"I don't know."

"Sure you do."

"I had the book smarts. As far back as I can remember, people always said I'd make a fine professor."

Lester pointed his cigar at him. "You done good, then."

"Right."

"But what did *you* want to be, man?"

Bernard thought about it. "I guess I always just wanted what white people told me I couldn't have."

Lester pulled on his goatee. "You done good, then."

"Right."

"So, what's the problem?"

"I keep feeling like something's not right. Like it's all going to disappear. Like someone's going to take it away from me."

The record started skipping. *What's going on? What's going on? What's going on? What's going on? What's going on?* Lester made no move to correct the needle.

"You want to know what I think, brother?"

Bernard waited. Lester wasn't a historian, but a cultural critic. His perspective was different.

"One of two things is going on. Either you're participating in the notion that you're undeserving, or this"—he made a wide gesture with his cigar—"isn't actually what you want."

*What's going on? What's going on? What's going on?*

"Are you going to fix that?" Bernard asked.

"You never answered the question."

"What question?"

"What did you want to be?"

Bernard could no longer feel his foot. "I honestly don't know."

❊

He slept at Lester's that night, and in his office at the university the next. On Wednesday he slunk home after midnight to find Aunt Patty sitting alone at the dining room table in the dark, with a near-empty bottle of Jim Beam and a shot glass. He could smell the sourness sweating through her pores.

"Patricia?"

"The prodigal son returns," she slurred.

He turned on the light and she shrank from it. Two black streaks of mascara ran from her bloodshot eyes to her chin. "Turn it off," she said. "Please. Turn that off."

He did.

"Thank you."

"You're drinking," he stated.

"Yes. And also, I'm drunk."

The room was charged with an electric quiet.

"Why?" he asked.

"Something bad happened," she said. Her voice was as dry as straw. "Something very very bad."

"What?" he asked, gritting his teeth.

She started to pour herself another shot. There was the clink of the bottle neck against the glass, but she couldn't work her hand. Her fingers were too loose. The liquor spilled and she lost hold of the bottle, which rolled slowly off the oval table and landed on the rug with a mute thud.

"Tell me what happened."

"He's gone," she said.

Bernard felt his hackles raise. He left her there, propelled by the dread. The stairs creaked as he climbed them, and he knew. The door was ajar, and from its base, a line of green light ran across the floor like an arrow with no point. He knew even before he pushed the door open, widening the line into a green band that encompassed his insensate foot. His son was not in the bed.

Emma was asleep diagonally on the mattress. Her arms looked broken. Her cropped hair stood at odd angles. The crackling walkie-talkie rested on the pillow where Bernie's head should have been. He shook her awake.

"Where's your brother?"

"Huh?"

"Where's Bernie?"

"Let go, Dad," she whimpered. "You're hurting me."

Horrified, he released his grip on her shoulders, hobbled back down to the dining room and turned on the light.

"Turn it off," Aunt Patty winced.

"What have you done with him?" Bernard demanded.

She squinted. "Turn off the light, Smarty-pants."

He stalked toward her, balancing himself with the backs of the dining room chairs. "Where is he?"

"Who?"

He lifted her from his chair and slammed his fist into the center of her face. He felt the sweet crunch of bone against his wedding ring and, as in slow motion, watched his sister-in-law crumple to the floor like a rag doll, her nose spurting more blood than seemed possible. His ears filled with a roaring. Before he unclenched his hand and began to feel the sting of remorse, he had the time to think: how right it feels that it would come to this final degradation, a black man striking a white woman. How easy to be the animal they feared.

"My son," he growled, standing above her, "you said he was gone. Where is he?"

"I don't know." She spoke through her hands, suddenly sober.

"You said something terrible happened. You said he was gone."

"No." She shook her head. "I wasn't talking about him." She wiped her hands on the front of her nightgown. She looked up at him. Her teeth were red with blood. "I was talking about my father. Ed." She grabbed the edge of the table and pulled herself to her feet. Her eyes focused on something behind him.

He turned his head. Emma was standing in the vestibule in her pajamas, hugging the walkie-talkie like a teddy bear.

"Dad?" she said, softly. The word broke his heart.

"What are you doing up?" he asked.

"It's Bernie," she said holding out the walkie-talkie. Her eyes were wide. "He said he's just about to land on the roof." The walkie-talkie hissed like a cat. That and his heavy breathing were the only sounds in the room.

"What happened to Aunt Patty, Dad?"

"It's okay, honey," Aunt Patty said. "I just got a little nosebleed is all. It happens to all of us sometimes, but it's nothing to be afraid of."

Emma rubbed her eyes. "Are we in a dream? Is this a dream?"

"Yes, sweetie," Aunt Patty lied. "This is just a dream."

"Oh." The static from the walkie-talkie grew louder. "Whose dream is it?"

"Yours, of course," Aunt Patty said, weaving toward the kitchen. "I'm just going to ice my nose. A little ice would be nice."

"Bernie's on the roof?" Bernard asked.

Emma nodded her head. "I asked him if he would come down the chimney but he said he doesn't want to get dirty so he's coming in the attic window. C'mon," she urged.

"Is this a joke?"

"No. C'mon, Dad. He's okay. Come see."

She led him back upstairs by the hand. "Be quiet," she said on the second floor, "Mom's sleeping." Lynn's snore seesawed from the master bedroom. Bernard opened the attic door and was consoled at the sight of his son tapping down the staircase with the handle of the broken umbrella as a makeshift cane. He was smiling, and he carried the cold chill of the outdoors.

"How far did you get?" Emma whispered. "Did you see him?"

"Not this time."

"This is not a funny joke," Bernard said.

"It's not a joke," Bernie argued.

Bernard looked at his watch. "It's one o'clock in the morning on a school night. Go to bed. Both of you are grounded. Wait," he said, stopping Emma. "Give me that." He confiscated the walkie-talkie. "Where's the other one?" he asked.

"We don't have it," Bernie said.

"Where is it?"

Bernie solemnly lifted his finger and pointed upward.

❄

Under the glares of the fluorescent light and the uni-browed admitting nurse in the emergency room, Aunt Patty and Bernard reached an agreement. "I won't tell Lynn you attacked me if you don't tell her I was drinking," she said. "Either thing would ruin her birthday."

"Fine," he agreed. He was extremely contrite.

"And I need you to do one other little thing for me."

"What?" He was willing to do anything.

"You have to take me to an AA meeting in the morning." She held out her hand. The red polish at the tips of her fingernails was chipped. "Is it a deal?"

"It's a deal," he said shaking her hand. "I'm sorry I broke your nose."

"Don't worry about it," she said. "I know how to take a punch. You didn't do anything to me that hasn't been done before. Besides, it's a good excuse to finally get a nose job."

He studied her nose. It was swollen as a pear. "How are you going to explain this to Lynn?" he asked

"I'll just tell her I walked into a door while I was vacuuming."

While she was having her nose set, Bernard nodded off and dreamt of a sunless poisoned sky with inky shredded clouds snagged in the branches of burning trees. Against this backdrop was a black silhouette, a flying man with a stick. Bernard watched the man growing closer through the smoke-choked air. He felt he was watching himself. Slowly, he began to lift.

"Accept your wisdom," he heard Aunt Patty say a long way off, and he was yanked back down into his body. His eyes jerked open and saw her officiously handing the admitting nurse one of her ballpoint pens. The new bandage on her nose made her voice sound nasal. "I can tell by your choice of profession that you're a caring person, but I'm willing to wager you're not as caring to yourself as you should be. Am I right?"

"Yes," said the nurse. "How did you know?"

❧

At the Thursday morning meeting, there were eight white people sitting in a ring of metal folding chairs in the basement of St. Paul's Church; three women, five men. Bernard was relieved not to recognize any of them. One of the women was knitting what looked like an endless purple scarf. The others held Styrofoam cups of coffee and looked exhausted.

"We have two newcomers today," smiled the knitting lady. She wore a sweater with a row of ducks across the front. "Let's welcome them."

"Welcome," said the others in unison. They sounded like drones.

The last time he'd been down here was for cookies and eggnog after a Christmas pageant in which Bernie had been a Wise Man and Emma had been a lamb. That was almost a year ago. He'd felt out of place then, and he felt out of place now. He looked at the scuff marks on the blue and red tiles of the floor and fiddled with the knob of his cane.

The knitting lady gestured at a poster on the wall. "Let's begin by going over the twelve steps." Each of them had to read one. Bernard's was number two: "We came to believe that a Power greater than ourselves could restore us to sanity."

The group began their testimonies under the tick of a five-minute egg timer. Phillip had lost his job at Johnson & Johnson and had not yet told his wife; Janice had woken up in the bed of a strange man who collected dolls, without remembering how she got there; Karen, the knitting lady, just wanted to give thanks for her brand-new baby granddaughter.

Then, it was his turn. They looked at him expectantly, except for Janice, who was quietly weeping. "Oh," he said. "No, I'm not—"

"Start with your name," the knitting lady encouraged, in the sugary voice of a kindergarten teacher.

"Bernard," he said.

"Hi Bernard," the circle sang in unison.

"But I'm not an alcoholic. I'm just here to support my friend."

The knitting lady's mouth turned into a thin line. The egg timer ticked.

"My name is Patricia," Aunt Patty jumped in, "and I'm an alcoholic."

"Hi Patricia," they said.

She began talking, not in the vocabulary of psychobabble he was accustomed to, but with an honesty he didn't think she possessed. She talked about how her daughter Darlene had just gotten her tonsils out but refused to let her visit her in the hospital and had scribbled "Return to Sender" in magic marker on the get-well card she'd sent. How her kids hated her and how she couldn't really blame them because she used to feed them flour for dinner and lock them out in the cold when she wanted to be alone and other things she was too ashamed to admit. How when she was Darlene's age her father had broken her collarbone with a hammer and she had made a vow to kill him someday but he had gone and died first, in August, without ever saying he was proud of her. How since his death, she couldn't sleep and had fallen off the wagon. How she felt trapped in his shadow and filled with hatred. How she was filthy rich and it didn't mean anything because she was a lousy parent. How she coveted her sister's life.

In a final moment of despair, she sang, "*If you've got weeds then Mead's your man, Mead's the brand to kill your weeds.*' You've probably all heard that jingle on the radio," she said. "My ex-husband Karl wrote it. Every time I hear it I want to put a bullet in my brain."

The egg-timer dinged and Aunt Patty slumped down in her seat like a marionette without a puppeteer.

Bernard was astonished.

❧

On Friday afternoon, Aunt Patty and Lynn left for Atlantic City. Lynn was reluctant to leave. "There's casserole in the freezer," she reminded Bernard. "The left side has turkey, the right side doesn't. Emma won't eat meat. They can have popsicles for desert, but only one each."

"Right," he said.

"The number for our room at Caesar's is on the fridge."

"Right."

"Bernie's supposed to mow Mrs. Turner's lawn on Saturday and then you'll need to help him with his homework. He has a math test on Monday. And, oh, if Emma gets her rash—"

Aunt Patty honked the horn in the driveway, unnecessarily long.

"—the calamine lotion is under the bathroom sink, but you might have to buy more. I know I'm forgetting something. Are you sure you'll be all right?"

"We'll be fine. Just go."

"Don't forget to massage your foot. What else?"

"Have fun." He planted a kiss on her forehead and pushed her out the door. It was the first time she'd ever left them alone.

∗

Later that evening, Bernard sat at the kitchen table eating cream of wheat with his children. He'd burnt the casserole to a crisp, setting off the fire alarm, which he'd had to disable with his cane.

"So," he said, attempting conversation, "how was school today?"

"Fine," they said.

Lynn was the glue that held them together. Without her, it was painfully awkward.

"What did you learn about, son?"

"The solar system."

"How about you, Emma? What do your classmates think of your new haircut?"

She was dumping raisins into her bowl. "They say they like it to my face, but behind my back they say it's dumb."

"Oh, well. Children can be very cruel," he said, meaning to

soothe her. It didn't seem the right thing to say. He changed the subject. "Have you written any poems lately?"

"Yeah."

"I'd like to hear one."

"It's dumb," she said.

"I'll be the judge of that."

Emma swallowed a little spoonful of her mush. "Poisonous mushrooms / Taste good to the girl without / Anything to lose," she recited. "But don't worry, I didn't really eat any mushrooms."

"I see," he said. "Very nice."

"What are we going to get Mom for her birthday?" Bernie asked.

He'd peeked in his wife's sunflower journal and read what she really wanted. Another baby. Lynn was happiest when pregnant and immediately afterward, when she had someone to care for, someone who needed her completely. But there was no way he could give her this gift. He recognized his failure as a father. What could he give her? It would have to be something big.

"A grand piano," he said.

"But we already have a piano," Emma pointed out.

"This one is better." The more he thought about it, the more he liked the idea. There was nothing classier. The children could take lessons.

They purchased it on Saturday morning and had it delivered that afternoon. It was shiny as a limousine. Bernie propped up the lid and stuck his head inside with his ear to the strings while Emma sat with her legs dangling from the bench, playing the keys, one by one from bottom to top. Bernie called out a color for every note she struck.

"Blue," he said, every time she hit a black key.

"You said blue already," Emma complained.

"That one was blue like Mom's eyes. This one is blue like a blackboard."

"Blackboards aren't blue," said Emma.

"They are when they're covered in chalk."

"How 'bout this one?"

"Blue," he said.

"Blue like what?"

"Like the tree out front."

"Time to do your homework," Bernard interrupted. He feared the Steinway's lid would close like a coffin on his son's neck.

⚜

That night turned wild with wind. It howled around the house, bending the blue spruce, this way and that, rattling the windowpanes. Lynn called at ten to check on the kids.

"They're fine," he reassured her. "Emma's back in her bed. They're both asleep."

"What's that noise?" she asked.

"It's the wind. Are you having fun?" he asked.

"Not really," she admitted. "I won twelve dollars on the slot machine."

He wondered if Aunt Patty was drinking.

"Penny for your thoughts," Lynn offered.

"Nothing," he said, but after he hung up the phone he was surprised by how much he missed her. He uncapped her ylang-ylang myrrh lotion and rubbed some of it into his foot, but the foot was cold. He put the lotion back in the drawer of the bedside table and pulled out the walkie-talkie he'd hidden there. He held it to his ear and listened. It seemed to be transmitting the sound of the wind. Again, he tried to shut the thing off, to no avail. He couldn't understand it, unless the other walkie-talkie was on as well. It would have to be in close range to be conducting sound.

He carried the walkie-talkie through the dark rooms like a divining rod, bumping into the furniture Aunt Patty had shifted. The strings of the new piano were vibrating, just barely, unloosing strange chords. The house shuddered around him. It was swaying, creaking like a ship on a turbulent sea. He found himself being drawn upward, to the drafty attic, where his son had pointed. The floorboards there were bare and cold. The wind was in the walls. He searched every corner and inside the dusty cartons of his children's old baby clothes. The lost walkie-talkie was nowhere to be found. He sat in the broken high chair, thinking of Lynn and what he couldn't give her. He thought of what he would say, if a penny were enough to untie his tongue. He thought of Aunt Patty's testimony, and of Sarah Gudger's. What would be his testimony?

He brought the walkie-talkie to his ear and closed his eyes. The sound was sub-nautical. The sound of wind in a seashell. The sound of a womb. He remembered that. He remembered before he was born. The close warm heat of his mother's heart. How the beat of it slowed when she chopped down his father's lynching tree, how the beat of it slowed to match the beat of the ax. It was a moment of perfect clarity, transmitted from mother to son. He could see the widening gash in the black trunk of the tree through her eyes. In that moment, he had made his leg an ax and kicked hard enough to unhinge the tree (which had moaned like a man as it went over), hard enough to unhinge his foot. He remembered the twisting sinews. Was it a dream? Whose dream was it?

He listened. It was the sound of absence.

What would he say?

*This is Bernard Boudreaux Jr. All I have is your name. Help me, Father, can you hear me? I'm drowning. I married a white woman so my children wouldn't inherit our misery. My marriage is loveless. My children are strangers. My foot is hibernating and will not wake up. I cannot walk. Help me, father. Everything I see is you hanging from a tree. They made you a stranger and I am a stranger among them. Restore me to sanity. They're watching me. They want to take my foot. Help me, father. Save me from my torment. Show me your face. Bless my foot, Father; that I may step free, over and out of the reach of their watching. Show me to walk. Wash me in the fire of your blood.*

A sound came through the walkie-talkie. It was disguised by static, but distinctly human. The connection was too poor to make out the words. For a moment, he wasn't sure if he was listening to the voice of his father or the voice of his son.

# THE DEATH OF DEB LEVINE

Deb Levine died at the end of the summer I graduated from college. For a few years she had been an acquaintance of my mother's through their book club. She was also the mother of Simon Levine, a kid I went to high school with, and the wife of Adam Levine, a colleague of my father's at the University, and the sister of Dr. Kahn, my first gynecologist.

Simon and his father were both remarkable for their red hair. It was the exact shade of spanking new pennies. In high school, Simon couldn't participate in gym because of asthma and allergies. He also suffered from such severe scoliosis he had to wear a metal back brace. The brace must have adhered with screws because there were tiny holes punctured in the back of every one of his T-shirts. I remember this clearly because I sat behind him in Advanced Placement Biology and was often distracted by counting the freckles on the back of his neck and the constellation of holes on the back of his shirts. I remember him braying like a donkey in class one day while clutching at his ear and how I laughed at him with the other kids only to feel wracked with guilt about it later on when it turned out that his eardrum had burst.

I remember Mr. Levine because his office sat directly opposite my father's in the History Department. Whenever I went to visit my father he'd invite me in if his door was open, ask me if I knew his son, Simon, and offer me a piece of stale matzoh bread from a tin on his desk. I also remember the hair sprouting from Mr. Levine's knuckles and across the backs of his hands. It was thick, red, and curly and underneath it the skin was a moist raw pink. This struck me as grotesque as did his mangled row of bottom teeth.

I remember Dr. Kahn because among other things, he was the first man to put his fingers in my vagina. My mother brought me to see him when I was sixteen because I hadn't yet started my period.

"Your ovaries are very well formed," he'd told me as he rolled his thumbs over my abdomen. "Would you like to feel them?"

"No thanks," I answered. I remember watching a spider creep in a corner near the ceiling as this was going on.

"Suit yourself. They really do have a lovely shape though. Like cocktail olives."

I thought this an odd thing for him to say, but I figured he should know. That day he told my mother I was twenty pounds underweight and ought to have daily milk shakes to advance puberty. He also gave me a pack of birth control pills to kick-start menstruation, but I flushed them down the toilet one by one when we got home because I didn't believe in mind or hormone control. My mother had started on Prozac after my dad left us that year for one of his graduate students. I thought it was an act of weakness and I did not want to be like her.

It seems strange given our close degrees of separation (the son, the husband, the brother) that I never met Deb Levine. My mom joined Deb Levine's book club in a conscious effort to be more social and to avoid her empty-nest syndrome after I left for college and my brother Bernie died. Deb was considered the resident expert on literature because she was the published author of two mystery novels. Her first book is called *Lot's Wife*. The second is called *The Proof of Anger*. Both are no longer in print.

When my mom called me in New Haven, she spoke about Deb Levine with admiration approaching awe. Deb Levine had been in the Peace Corps, lived in Israel and France before getting married, spoke four languages fluently, and (according to my mother) appeared no older than twenty-eight because of yoga. As if that wasn't enough, she was also a foster mom to a never-ending cycle of AIDS babies *and* had a pottery wheel in her garage. Like me, she was a Yalie, and had been in the first class to admit women.

"That's the kind of life I want for you, Emma," my mother urged. "You should go to France after you graduate. Or Morocco. Can you take Arabic there?"

"Yeah."

"Of course you can. What am I talking about? You could take Sanskrit there if you wanted, right? Tell me all about your classes this semester. What've you learned so far?"

"I don't know. Nothing. Alexander Pushkin was black."

"Wait, lemme get a pen. I want to write down all the books you're reading so I can keep up. I bet Deb has some copies I could borrow. You should see the bookshelves in their house. Floor to ceiling, wall to wall. And most of them are hers, not Adam's."

"Why don't *you* go to Morocco?"

"Me?"

"Yeah, you. There's nothing keeping you in Princeton anymore. You could move to Casablanca if you wanted to. You could ride a camel into the Sahara and become a nomad. You're not that old."

"I don't know, honey. My life is here."

What life? I wanted to ask her. She worked part-time in the children's book section at the Princeton Public Library and sang atonally in the atonal choir at St. Paul's Church. Since she and my dad separated her social life had depleted almost completely. She had no friends that I knew of, not real ones, except for her sister Patty back in Milwaukee. She had the house. My dad was good enough to leave her that, but he'd taken all the things that had made it interesting, the Jacob Lawrence prints and the kente cloth wall hangings and the African masks and the stone fertility statue that used to sit roundly by the fireplace. They were his things, things he'd collected on his travels, so I didn't blame him, but the fact was that the house was decidedly unspecial without them, furnished with yard sale bric-a-brac. In addition to the house, she had the Catholic Church, the book club, her therapist, Prozac, the memory of Bernie and this new fixation on Deborah Levine. I found it pathetic, especially in contrast to the life of my father, which had visibly flourished since their separation, in spite of my brother's death.

At one point during my sophomore year, my mother sent me a signed copy of *Lot's Wife*. The cover featured a sexy white figure blurred onto a lavender background and a curly tilting font. The figure put me in mind of the *Venus de Milo* but was meant, I am sure, to represent a pillar of salt. It was impossible for me to muster any enthusiasm about Deb Levine. I knew her husband and son, after all, and both reflected poorly on her. I couldn't imagine a woman who'd married a man with a mangled row of yellow teeth, raised a weakling boy with scoliosis, and wrote mystery novels to be remarkable, even if she had done Yale and the Peace Corps. Besides that, I resented her for reminding me that my mother hadn't achieved anything noteworthy in her lifetime.

Her book sat unread and forgotten on my shelf until the middle of my junior year when Poresh noticed it one day after we'd just made love.

"What's this garbage you're reading?" He was stark naked standing in the middle of my dorm room. His body was brown and long and perfect from squash and in his hand the lavender book looked ridiculous. We didn't spend much time in my room and it occurred to me that with him in it, the entire place looked slightly ridiculous. As if a Siamese cat had chosen to inhabit a room in a dollhouse.

"Oh, that's not mine," I told him. I wanted to grab the book and put it back on the shelf so he'd just forget about it, but I didn't want to get out of bed because I was also naked. We'd just recently begun having sex and I was still afraid of revealing my body in its entirety. I'd finally gotten my period at the age of nineteen. My hips were unfolding but not yet at their full width. I felt my knees were too big and my breasts not big enough.

"What are these?" Poresh asked me, the first time we did it, clutching my jutting pelvic bones and pushing me into the mattress. I'd been mortified and told him I didn't know. "From now on they are the handles on my sugar bowl," he purred, biting my ear almost hard enough to draw blood. I thought that was a pretty poetic thing to say.

He stood there brandishing the book. "It isn't yours? But it says your name in it right here," he said, pointing to Deb Levine's inscription. "For Emma, a poet and a poem in the making." His eyes were dark suddenly, like oversteeped tea. A muscle jumped in his jaw.

"Oh. Yeah, see, my mom knows the author, so she—"

"You lied to me."

"No! I wasn't."

Poresh shook his head. "You tell me this trash isn't your book. I open the cover and I see your name." He came and banded me in his arms.

"We can't have lies between us. Ever." He smelled powerfully of the olive oil with which he dressed his hair. It clogged my nostrils. "I love you," he said, for the first time. "Do you understand? You can never lie to me again."

"I'm sorry," I tried to say, but the breath wouldn't come. He was clenching me too tightly. "I love you too," I mouthed but he was choking the sound from my words.

⚘

Poresh was the T.A. in my Egyptology section. He'd recognized my last name because he'd been an undergrad at Princeton where my father was one of his favorite professors. Poresh wasn't as beautiful as Bernie had been—nobody was—but he was a close second. He came from Bombay, by way of London. Because of his melodic multi-continent accent and his eyes, which were the precise color of maple syrup drenched in sunlight and dressed with lashes thick as pine needles, we all had a crush on him in that section—the boys as well as the girls. He had a way of stopping dramatically in the middle of every fourth sentence or so to penetrate each of us with those eyes. The effect was that we dangled on his words just like charms on a charm bracelet.

He gave me a C– on my first paper. For me, that wasn't a bad grade. I'd turned into an abominable student after Bernie's accident. My powers of concentration were simply no longer there. But Poresh had written on the last page of my paper, "Admittedly, I expected more of you because you have a wise face. See me during office hours."

I was sweating when I met him. I crossed my arms over my chest to hide the half-moons at my armpits. "Excuse me for a moment," he said, not looking up from the book he was reading. "Please sit down." He read to the end of the page, marked his place with a leather bookmark that had a cryptic design on it, then looked at me for a long time.

"Do you have something you want to tell me?" he asked.

"What? Oh. Um, no."

He was silent. I searched for something to say. I briefly considered telling him about Bernie, then decided against it. I didn't want to use my brother as an excuse. After an awkward pause, I announced, "I like your bookmark."

"This?" he pulled it from the pages and traced the design with his pinky finger. "This is the Eye of Horus. It has a very specific meaning. Do you know it?"

"No."

"The eye is represented as a figure with six parts corresponding to the six senses. See? Touch, Taste, Hearing, Thought, Sight, Smell. The eye is a receptor and it has these six doors, to receive data like a suckling mouth receives milk," he paused. "Am I boring you?"

"No! It's beautiful."

"Here then." he said, handing me the bookmark. "I'm making it a gift to you."

Something bloomed in the vicinity of my stomach. "Thank you, but you don't need to do that."

"I am giving it to you as a reminder to keep developing your senses. You have an astonishing depth about you, Emma." I felt he was right even though I wasn't sure how he knew this. "But it needs to be channeled. Do you like wine?"

"Yeah. I mean, I guess so."

"I would like to bring you to a wine tasting where we can discuss this further."

That was how things began between us. He brought me to graduate functions and art exhibits and cooked exotic curried things for me in his apartment to expand my palette.

All the way from New Jersey, my mother sensed that something was changing. She called me at three one morning in near-hysterics.

"Tell me, are you having sex?"

"No! Jesus!"

"You can tell me, Emma. I want to know."

"That's not really your business. Even if I was, which I'm *not*."

"I was sleeping and I had a feeling. More just like a feeling than a dream—that you were having sex."

"Oh my *God*."

"Bad sex. And it occurred to me, you know, that I never talked to you about masturbation—probably because your grandmother always told us it was a carnal sin and cut off Patty's hair when she caught her doing it."

"Do you even know what time it is?"

"Here me out, I know what I'm talking about, I didn't have an orgasm with your father until I was thirty-one and breast-feeding Bernie. I faked them all before that and a whole bunch afterwards too."

"I don't want to hear about that."

"We read this book in our group about talking to your daughter and when we were discussing it the other day, Deb Levine said the most interesting thing. She said, 'We need permission from our mothers to be happy.' So, I want you to know that it's okay, you know. You can—I want you to be happy. It won't hurt my feelings, okay? And I'm telling you, even though I always told you before it was a loaded gun and you should wait till you were married, I know that's unrealistic. And, honey, you should really masturbate before you have sex or you won't get any pleasure."

"I am not a child anymore."

"I know; I'm sorry. I just wanted to be honest with you."

"Well it's not okay. My sex life is none of your business." I chose my words carefully. "You can't keep defining yourself as just being somebody's mother or somebody's ex-wife. You can't call me in the middle of the night like this. It's cloying."

I placed the receiver gently in its cradle before she could respond. I felt I'd handled her in a profoundly articulate manner and because I couldn't sleep I read Kierkegaard and wrote haikus to Bernie until the sun rose.

That spring, my father remarried. I brought Poresh to the wedding, although it felt more like he brought me because we drove down in his car. During the ceremony, he told me several times to stop slouching. I couldn't help it. My father's new wife looked glossy like something out of a magazine. My mother was not just old, I realized, but ugly in comparison. Then I felt ugly for making the comparison.

At the receiving line, Poresh and my father embraced. "Emma, you've got phenomenal taste." My father smiled. "At your age, this brother blew me away with a term paper on the Malankara Orthodox Church. Did that ever end up seeing print?"

"Yes, in fact. In the *Journal of Ecclesiastical History*."

"Amazing, Poresh. I look forward to reading more of your work in the future and I'd enjoy hearing about your dissertation. Best of luck to you both." He winked at me. Really, I thought, he ought to have said something to Poresh about what a treasure I was, and how when I was little we used to slow-dance to Sam Cooke in the kitchen every night before bedtime with me standing on his Florsheim shoes.

Poresh squeezed my hand. "You're sulking," he whispered. "Don't be rude."

"That's a really pretty dress," I told my new stepmother. The bodice was embossed with cowrie shells. They reminded me of little teeth. She pecked me on each cheek like a European. Like a gull.

At the reception, Poresh had a long conversation with Adam Levine about the history of the Aramaic language while I drew intricate patterns into my salmon steak with the swizzle stick from my drink and imagined what Bernie would think about all this. Adam Levine didn't seem to remember who I was. I figured this was because I no longer resembled the former me. My hair was different. I had hips. My brother was dead. I was with Poresh.

I noticed Deb Levine wasn't there.

"I asked her not to go," my mother told me later. "I knew I'd just end up plaguing her with questions about the wedding and I didn't want to do that."

"Well I hope you're not planning on plaguing me with questions about it. It sucked. That's all you need to know."

"What do you mean, 'it sucked'?"

"Why don't you start dating instead of worrying about Dad all the time?" I needled. "There's nothing stopping you from getting re-married. Bernie's gone. I'm in college. I just don't feel like you're moving forward."

I thought of my mother like a child. I imagined her driving in a square, from home to church to the library to the grocery store back home again, in a state of arrested development, weakness, paralysis. Poresh had started me thinking this way, in the divergent terms of childhood and adulthood. In the adult world, people made grave decisions, traveled the world, tried new things such as anal sex and Camembert.

"You know, we have a lot in common, Emma," he said the night I ended up losing my virginity to him. "We are both stuck between two worlds. I belong to two cultures, while you are suspended between childhood and womanhood." He was stroking the inside of my arm with his fingertips. Our skin was the exact same color. I was sure this meant something. "I am charmed by you because you don't even know what a beautiful woman you could be." He moved his hands to my hipbones. Do you want me to make you a woman?"

"Um. Okay," I told him.

It hurt and I imagined myself tiny and watching us from a distance like the spider on the wall in Dr. Kahn's examining room. I knew I thought of this because Dr. Kahn was the last one involved with my vagina. It seemed like an inappropriate association so I closed my eyes and tried to imagine myself instead as the Eye of Horus.

During the spring of my senior year my mother asked me to come down for Easter. I agreed to go because Poresh was in San Diego for a conference and I thought a restful weekend at home would be a good time to draw up an outline for the thesis I'd been avoiding writing all semester. My mother knew I had a serious boyfriend but hadn't met Poresh. I didn't like discussing him with her. I neglected to introduce them because I was afraid he'd be disappointed by her intellect in the same way he was disappointed by my friends. He was impressed by my father, and that was enough for me.

On Good Friday she asked if I had a picture of him. I was surprised by the question. We were eating whitefish fillets and she had been talking about Deb Levine's newest foster baby's T-cell count all evening.

"I don't know. Maybe," I told her. "This fish is really bland. Do you have any Tabasco sauce?"

"In the fridge, honey. I'd love to see his picture if you've got one with you."

I showed her the picture of me and Poresh sitting side by side on a bale of hay. It had been taken that fall at an orchard in Hamden where we'd gone to pick apples. He had his arms wrapped around me and my head was resting on his shoulder like an egg in a nest. The sun was going down and our skin looked deep orange in its afterglow.

"He looks like a movie star with those thick eyebrows," commented my mother. "Very handsome, but stern. Does he make you laugh?"

"Sure," I lied. "We laugh all the time."

"Good. That's one of the most important things."

I scrutinized the photo with my mother. The color was saturated like someone had dunked the picture in an acrylic rainbow. It hurt my heart just looking and longing for him and the way I felt that day. We had been walking through rows of squat apple trees so burdened with the fruit that their branches were reaching for the ground, when Poresh had asked me what I was thinking about.

I'd been thinking about Bernie, but I didn't tell him that. I told him about the day my father left. How it was a complete surprise. How I started hiccupping violently. How for months after that my mother would sit motionless in the driveway hunched behind the wheel of her Toyota staring at the rusted-out basketball hoop at the top of the garage. How I'd have to go fetch her and lead her back inside by the hand and cook spaghetti dinners most nights up until she went on Prozac and was able to cope. I stopped telling Poresh the story before I got to the part about how I used to have a big brother because I was crying. I climbed up into one of the apple trees so he couldn't see the snot running from my nose to my upper lip but he followed me up the tree. We perched up there on a branch like squirrels, invisible behind the waxy leaves.

"You mustn't be sad anymore," he said, pulling me to his chest. "Listen." His limbs were strong as the tree I had just climbed. "I'm going to take care of you. I'm not going to leave you like he did, so you mustn't be frightened." I trembled when he said that. The tree was so bursting with fruit that it trembled too, shaking loose several apples that plunked down to rot on the ripe resting earth below. I'd never felt closer to him than in that moment.

"How's your thesis coming?" asked my mother as she scraped our scraps into the trash.

"Fine," I lied. "I'm writing about Langston Hughes."

"Really! Deb met him once, you know. In New York, when she was a little girl. Maybe you should talk to her about your ideas. She's a wonderful writer."

"No, I'm doing all right on my own." The truth was that I loved to read Langston Hughes, but I was crippled when I tried to write about him.

On Easter Sunday I suffered through mass. The church was packed with lilies and Christmas and Easter Christians. Father Frank was more stooped over than I remembered, and I was surprised to see him attended by altar girls. When I was a girl there were only altar boys. My brother was an altar boy for about a month, but he kept dipping his fingers in the candles and one Sunday his hair lit on fire. Father Frank dismissed Bernie after that, on the grounds that he wasn't mature enough to perform God's service.

My mother stood singing poorly arranged folk hymns in the second row of the choir with an idiotic, transcendent look on her face. *Christ has died, Christ has risen, Christ will come again!* The choir leader strummed a guitar, badly, while his pregnant wife accompanied him on piano. They sounded awful, but they all looked so happy.

After the service I made Poresh's banana walnut crepes with Chantilly cream.

"These are fancy," she said.

"Not really. They're easy to make."

"They're delicious, honey. What did you think of Father Frank's homily?"

"To tell you the truth, I wasn't really listening. I haven't liked that man since I was eight." When I was eight I'd asked him why there weren't any girl apostles and he told me I wasn't supposed to ask him questions like that while making confession.

"I was in love with the priest of my church growing up." My mother sighed. "Father O'Connell. We all were. Even my mother."

"Really? Why?"

"Because of his voice when he sang the mass. It was not of this earth. Mass was so different before Vatican Two. It's one of my biggest regrets you two had to come up in church not having it like I did."

"Why?"

My mother tucked her bob behind her ears and thought for a moment. "The music was beautiful. That's why I loved it. Plus, everything was in Latin. You felt special knowing how to speak a different language. Father O'Connell sang Gregorian chants with this voice that I swear would break your heart in two, and we'd all chant the response. If you could hear it—a whole church full of people." She was twisting her napkin and I was afraid she was going to start crying. "I really believed that God came down when he heard us singing those words. I could feel God there. So when Father O'Connell said it was the body of Christ, I knew I was eating the body of Christ. It's so different now."

"Wow. So why do you keep going?"

"Habit, I guess. I like singing in the choir. It helps me remember. It's also easier for me to pray there than here." She untwisted her napkin and stared at it for a moment before looking at me. "Do you ever pray?"

"Not really."

"Why not?"

"I don't know." I knew she was praying out there in the driveway when she used to sit in the car for hours. I knew she was praying nonstop for Bernie after his accident—that he would come around in some little way, that he would blink. It seemed hypocritical that she believed in prayer and took Prozac. I wondered which she thought was helping her.

"You used to pray all the time when you were little," she told me.

"I don't remember that."

"You did. You used to talk to God. You remember your First Communion dress?"

"Yeah." She'd stayed up all night at the sewing machine trying to finish it in time. It had been saltwater taffy pink with little red strawberries and lace at the collar and cuffs and when I opened my eyes in the morning I saw it hanging like a dream on the doorknob of my bedroom. When I put it on, Bernie had called me "Queen Em" and bowed.

"You told me God asked you to wear pink instead of white. I didn't question it until we got to St. Paul's and you stood out like a sore thumb. All the mothers were staring at you and snickering, and this one little girl, I'll never forget, she told you you looked trashy."

"Theresa Fabrizio. That girl sucked."

"Yes she did. And I was worried you'd be upset, but remember what you did?"

"I slapped her in the face and told her my dress was a present from God."

"Right. And that's when I knew you were going places. That's when I said to myself, '*This* girl is special.' And you are. You really are."

Before she could get the chance to start reminiscing about Bernie I told her I had to get back to school.

∞

Poresh broke up with me in his car two weeks before the close of my last semester. We were driving back from a foreign film with subtitles through which I had struggled to stay awake. He told me he had agreed upon a marriage arranged by his parents and the wedding was to be that summer, at his grandparents' estate in Dhaka. I began to hyperventilate.

"Do you even know her, Poresh?" I demanded. My voice raised in pitch like the whistle of a teakettle. "Why are you doing this?"

"You're making a scene," he said. "Calm down and show some dignity."

"Who is this girl? What's her name?"

"I don't see what that has to do with you."

"You love me! You don't love her."

We arrived at the gates of my college. "I'm sorry you're so upset, Emma, but really I'm quite surprised. You can't have thought we were going to last forever."

I slapped him then, just like I slapped Theresa Fabrizio. "Shut up!" I shrieked, opening the door, "just shut up!"

I vomited on the stairs leading to my room. The nausea didn't quit. I couldn't stop crying, throwing up, and passing diarrhea for several days. I felt myself pouring from every orifice until I was desiccated as a piece of toast. Fran found me passed out in our common room and at her behest I wound up in the Department of University Health, dangerously dehydrated, dry-heaving, and incoherent.

"Forget about that asshole and get some rest," she told me. I had not yet started writing my thesis and was supposed to graduate in ten days. They hooked me up to an IV drip and put me on a BRAT diet of broth, bananas, and rice. I couldn't keep anything down. I kept retching even after I'd vomited the last drop of bile in my stomach. I resembled a greyhound. I could count every single one of my ribs. When Fran tried to work a brush through my hair, clumps of it pulled right out of my scalp.

A long-legged Nordic-looking woman named Dr. Fangele came to talk to me. Instead of a white lab coat, she wore a black cocktail dress. This made me think she had somewhere important to go afterwards, like the ballet, or the opera. She took notes when I talked. I told her I couldn't eat or write my thesis because my boyfriend had just dumped me and I had no idea what I wanted to do with my life. When I put it simply like that, it sounded pathetic. I sounded like my mother. I didn't like what I had become.

"You're having an anxiety attack," she said, "and we can do something about that. It's called Xanax."

"No. I don't want to."

"Do you want to graduate?"

"Of course."

"Then what's the problem?"

I picked at the tape holding my IV needle in place. "I don't believe in it."

"Why not?"

"I don't know. My mom's on antidepressants. It seems wrong to me."

"Was your mother suffering before?"

"Yes," I said, beginning to weep. Dr. Fangele pulled a tissue out of the air like a magic trick and passed it to me.

"Did you ever think of it as a sign of strength or wisdom that she knew she needed help?"

"No, not really."

"Are you suffering now?"

"Yeah," I whispered.

"Are you able to work and function under your grievous circumstance?"

"I guess not."

"Will you consider taking a sedative for the length of time it takes to write your thesis." This was more of a statement than a question. "You can think about how best to run beyond that first hurdle after you've jumped it. One thing at a time, as they say."

My stomach growled. It was gorging itself on its own walls. "I guess I'll think about it."

"Good, then." She smiled at me and applied some lipstick the color of port without the help of a mirror. "I'll see you tomorrow."

When she left, I turned my head and saw my tattered copy of *The Langston Hughes Reader* next to a bedpan full of my congealing vomit, and in the wallowing hollow depths of myself I pitied me.

"I've known rivers," I said, but I was a phony and I knew it. That night I prayed to Bernie for guidance and when I slept I had a dream. In the dream, I was a guest at Poresh's wedding, in a crowd of apple trees and people waiting for the bride. We all said some words in Latin and she magically appeared on top of a haystack wearing my First Communion dress. She was a little laughing girl. I brought her an apple and laid it at her feet like an offering.

"The body of Christ," she sang, holding out a little white pill. I let her place it on my tongue.

"That's a really pretty dress," I told her.

I decided to read the dream as a sign. When Dr. Fangele returned the following day, I let her write me a prescription.

The Xanax made everything blurry like an ink drawing smudged with rain. I hammered out my thesis in under a week and moved back in with my mother after graduation. The heat was dripping that summer. My brain felt swollen from the humidity. I sat in the shade of the back porch most days, feeling nauseated, drinking lemonade spiked with bourbon, pitying myself and reading endless Russian novels. At night I lay in Bernie's bed, listening to his Coltrane records over and over again. His clothes still hung in the closet but his smell was no longer in them. He'd been dead for over three years. In June, my mother suggested we pack some of his things up for Goodwill, but I threw a temper tantrum and refused. She was unsure of what to say to help me and gave me a lot of space.

One day she came home from her book club with a bag full of artichokes from Deb Levine's garden and a thoughtful look on her face.

"Do you know what she told us today?" she asked. "Adam's leaving her. For one of his graduate students."

"You don't say."

She ran the artichokes under cold water. "Nobody saw it coming. Just like your father."

I noticed there was a ladybug in my mother's hair, but I didn't tell her.

"How's she taking it?"

"She said she's better off. Now she can hunker down and concentrate on finishing her third book."

"That's a healthy attitude."

"You know, I thought so too. I'd really like you to talk to her, Emma. She's an incredible woman. I just know you two would hit it off."

"I don't have anything to say to her."

"Yes, but look"—my mom was peeling the leaves off one of the artichokes, one by one, as if opening a present—"I know I haven't been the best role model for you."

"Don't say that."

"And I thought maybe she could give you some advice."

The only person I trusted for advice was Bernie. I told my mom to forget it. I didn't want to talk to Deb Levine.

I made a wish on the ladybug that something very, very bad would happen to Poresh. It wheeled dizzily from her hair and flew smack dab into the kitchen window screen.

On the last day of July I drank too much bourbon lemonade, fell off the back porch and broke my wrist. My hand was hanging like a sock puppet at a crazy angle. The bone was poking through the skin like a popsicle stick. I didn't feel any pain. It looked like somebody else's accident superimposed on my body.

"Mom," I called. She was pulling dandelion weeds from the grass. "Come see this."

She ran through all the stop signs driving me to the emergency room.

They stitched the skin, set the bone, and swaddled my arm in a sling. The swollen tips of my fingers peeked from the plaster cast. My fingertips reminded me of the litter of newborn mice we had found nestled at the back of a kitchen cabinet one winter, Bernie and I. Little, pink, hairless, blind things. On the drive home I pressed my forehead against the passenger window and began, violently, to cry.

"Does it hurt, honey?" she asked.

"Yes," I wailed in a little girl voice.

❦

During the second week of my recovery, I ran out of painkillers and couldn't find my mother. I went to the liquor cabinet and found it freshly stocked with bottles of tonic water. I slammed the door and phoned my father. My stepmother picked up the phone.

"Mrs. Boudreaux speaking," she said.

"Bullshit," I said and hung up the phone. When my mother finally returned, right before dinnertime, she found me rolling on the living room rug in agony.

"*Where were you?*" I yelled.

"What's wrong, Emma?"

I threw the empty bottle of morphine at her. "Where were you?"

"Oh no! Your prescription, I completely forgot. I'll—"

"Where *the hell* were you all day?"

"Aviation school."

"What?"

"Aviation school."

"You're learning how to fly a plane?"

"Yes, I thought I'd give it a whirl."

"Since when?"

"Since your brother passed away." Flying had been Bernie's dream. She stooped down and picked up the little orange bottle.

For a split second, I forgot about my wrist. "Jesus Christ. Why didn't you tell me?"

"It was a secret." She slipped the bottle in her purse and straightened her shoulders. She tucked her bob behind her ears. "I'll go get your pills."

❧

During the third week of my recovery, the phone rang and my mother answered it. I could hear her from the porch where I sat eating a nectarine, watching the neighbor's cocker spaniel dig a hole underneath our rhododendron bush. I admired the dog's single-mindedness. "Oh my God!" cried my mother. "Oh no . . . Oh Jesus. When?" The dog held something limp between her teeth. I couldn't make out what it was. My mother appeared in the doorway with her hand over her mouth.

"That was Lorna Feferberg," she said. "Deb Levine is dead."

I'm embarrassed to admit my response: I regretted not having met to speak with her, as if by doing so I might somehow have altered the event of her death.

"I just can't believe it," my mother whispered.

I bit into my nectarine. "She's really dead?"

"Lorna found her this morning. They were supposed to go jogging on the towpath."

"How'd she die?"

"Well, apparently . . . she killed herself. She was hanging from the ceiling fan with one of Adam's neckties."

It was so ridiculous I had to stifle a laugh. The irony of it: Deb Levine, bastion of strength, dying of a broken heart.

"How gruesome," I smirked. "I guess that just goes to prove she wasn't so tough after all."

The hand that had been covering my mother's mouth flew out like a startled bird and smacked me so hard I let loose the nectarine I'd been holding in my good hand. It struck the side of the house and left an oily splatter mark.

"You little brat," she spat. "*You selfish little brat.* You think the world revolves around you? Wake up, because it doesn't. Show some sensitivity. Show some goddamned respect. *She was my friend.*" Her face was twisted in pain. It resembled the face Bernie used to wear when he was outraged at our father. She wheeled around and stormed back inside. I heard her yank open the refrigerator door, and then slam it twice in rapid succession.

Over by the rhododendron bush, the neighbors' dog was still furiously digging. I watched the dirt spray out from under her hind legs with my blinking eyes. Upstairs, I knew my mom was crying.

I watched the dog drop the lifeless, inscrutable something from her jaws into the hole. I watched her reverse her stance and scratch at the dirt until the thing was all covered up. She squatted and I watched her urinate on the spot then trot off diagonally through our backyard and bowleg down the neighbors' driveway.

I knew I should go upstairs and say something. I knew that, but instead I stayed there on the porch. I knew that if I didn't apologize I would grow to regret it. I was right about that, but at the time I didn't know what to say. Every word in my vocabulary seemed threadbare, thin enough to fall through. I should have told her she was worth ten Deb Levines, for the simple fact of enduring. I should have asked her how she did it. I should have put my head in her lap and grieved. Instead, I sat motionless watching the earth under the rhododendron bush as if whatever was buried there would resurrect itself. I stayed there, deep in thought, until dusk came and the fireflies and the nauseating smell of someone barbecuing meat a few yards down, and all the while my face burned.

❧

Two days later, Simon Levine said the kaddish at his mother's funeral. I never did see Deb's face. She lay boxed in a pine coffin at the center of the synagogue, surrounded by a hexagon of pews. Dr. Kahn was there, of course, and so was my father, with his new wife. I worried that their presence was disturbing to my mother. I glanced up at her. Her shoulder pads were off-center, but she seemed to be holding up okay. Several people were crying, including Adam Levine who hid his face behind a handkerchief. I was glad he was in pain. The way I saw it, that was the point. He would go home guilt-ridden to a broken house with covered mirrors. I sat wedged between my mother and an elderly woman with a dowager's hump and a turkey neck. There was no air conditioning. The air in the synagogue was hot enough to raise a mound of dough and bake it. Simon walked to the podium beside the casket. His black suit was expertly tailored.

"Is that Simon?" I asked my mother in disbelief. He wasn't the asthmatic boy I had known in high school. He had developed a powerful jaw line. He had either grown a foot or learned to stand ramrod straight. His hair had rusted to the shade of old pennies and his chest was broad as a bear's. The Torah looked like a spindly toy in his large hands.

"Yes, that's him." She sighed. "Poor thing."

"He's changed," I whispered.

"So have you."

I wanted to know how she meant, and I didn't want to know.

"It's the muscles you mean," said the old woman next to me. Her voice was too loud. The skirt of her polyester dress had static-clung to her stockings, which wrinkled around her ankles like an elephant's hide. "You'll excuse me," she said. "I couldn't help overhear. The muscles he got on the crew team at Brown."

"*Shhh!*" hissed a tall man in front of us. She seemed not to hear.

"Handsome, no? Such a *shaina punim*. Like Errol Flynn! But taken." She inspected my face with her watery eyes. "Are you Jewish?" she asked. "A Sabra maybe?"

"No."

"Oh, well. Neither is that one." She sucked her tongue against the roof of her mouth. "That's his fiancée, there, holding Marcos. Also a shiksa." She pointed with her whiskered chin toward a little girl on the other side of the hexagon who couldn't have been six inches taller than four feet. Squirming in the girl's lap was a robust brown toddler, almost half her size.

"But she's just a child!"

"No, no. She's a grown-up, just small. She was the coxswain."

I gathered that Marcos was Deb's last foster child. Under scrutiny he looked how I imagined a baby of Poresh and mine would have looked. Pecan skin. A whorl of thick dark hair.

Simon cleared his throat and began. He snagged on the Hebrew, stopped and started again. I was surprised by the dignity in his voice.

Marcos struggled in the little girl's arms. He seemed healthy to me, kicking out a rhythm to the kaddish with his chunky legs while sucking on his thumb. The little girl tried to wipe some dribble from his chin with a cloth diaper while he squealed and grabbed her braid in his sticky fist. I wondered how long it would be until the virus wasted him.

Simon's voice grew stronger. The acoustics of the synagogue were strange. His words rebounded like the roll of a drum, seeping into my pores, mingling with my sweat. Under the cast my skin was begging to be scratched. I began to cry. The old woman, who had been clawing in her ancient leather purse, pulled out a crumpled wad of Kleenex in one hand and a box of raisins in the other. She offered me both. I separated one of the tissues from the wad and thanked her. It smelled sickly of lavender perfume, but I was grateful for it. I mopped my face.

"You must have cared very much for her that you're crying," the old woman said in a stage whisper. I blew my nose. I was melting.

"Deborah was an angel. For all of us it's hard to let go someone so young and precious. It's dreadful."

"Yes," I cried. I was all snot and hot tears as I listened to Simon's prayer. His voice was the color blue lapping over my limbs. His voice was like liquor. Like Bernie on sax. I didn't understand the Hebrew but under the words was *something* I knew to be true, something heavy, something wet. It threatened to drown me with its brutal weight. It was sucking me into its mouth.

I wondered if my mother could hear what I heard. I looked at her and was awestruck. She had transformed. I cannot describe the sudden beatitude of her face and I won't even try, except to say that it was exposed, the way an icon's face is. It was a lens refracting Simon's song and radiating it. I looked for a trace of my own face in her profile. Slowly, she turned her head to mine and I saw myself for what I truly was, reflected in her eyes—tiny, and insignificant, and loved. Simon's prayer wound down, letting me loose from its undertow, leaving me struggling on the shore of that mercy. I cradled my bad arm in my good one.

"You're all right now, dear?" interrupted the old woman.

"Yes, I think so," I choked.

"So I'm Ida," she told me, presenting me with her hand. It was incredibly soft considering it was just bones and liver spots on tissue-paper-thin skin. It seemed too delicate to shake, so I just held it.

"I'm Adam's aunt. Aunt Ida from Sheepshead Bay."

"Nice to meet you," I sniffled. "I'm Emma."

"How did you know my niece?"

"*Shhh!*" went the tall man in front of us.

"I didn't," I said, returning Aunt Ida's hand as gently as I could. I turned again to face my mother who, in secret, had been learning to fly.

# THE MAN WITH THE
# ONE-STRING GUITAR

Dear Bernie,

How are you finding the afterlife? Balmy, I hope. Down here life is violent and pointless. Maybe you could care less about that, I don't know, maybe you're playing croquet with Coltrane, but if it means anything to you, I'm in New Orleans and you can let Mom know I'm safe if she's still praying to you or if she's hired a detective to find me, which I wouldn't put past her. I would have called her by now but I didn't have enough quarters on account of my laundry and you know how she hates collect calls.

I stole her Toyota and left. I was sick of everybody else leaving—first Dad, then you, then that rat-bastard Poresh (you would have hated him). "Why don't *I* leave?" I said. "Why not? I don't have a job. If Dad can rob the cradle and Bernie can get himself killed and Poresh can pick a bride from a photograph and Mom can fly an airplane, then I can certainly get the hell out of Dodge." So I took Mom's car and look how far it's gotten me down into the deep belly of the country. Of course, someone else stole it from me as soon as

I got here, and I'm forced to ride the streetcar which runs slow as molasses, but that's just desserts.

I was so deluded when I left home, I actually thought I was driving north into Canada because I was looking for snow, but something was pulling me, some equatorial magnet was dragging the Toyota south, and suddenly all I wanted in the whole world was to eat some of those pralines Dad's godmother made us that time we went down to the Gulf of Mexico. Remember that? But I couldn't find her, I guess she's dead, and it's all casinos now, which is tragic, of course, for the landscape I mean, but not entirely tragic, because I won seven hundred bucks at blackjack.

The grand irony of the journey is that I wound up in the very place you always said we'd hitchhike for Mardi Gras and Poresh promised he'd take me on our honeymoon. New Orleans! *Lord,* it's hot down here despite everyday thunderstorms that do nothing to quench the heat. I can tell when the rain's getting ready to come because the dragonflies swarm overhead and the heat gets heavier and thick as soup. When the rain ends, the heat is wet heat. It spills out from the shotgun shacks and the shops selling sequined masks and boils out from the muddy Mississippi. It pours down from the wrought-iron balconies and wilts down from the magnolia trees and seeps out from the crumbling cemeteries. A few days ago I went looking for a place to go swimming, because I remembered how nice it was when you taught me the backstroke at Broadmead Pool, but I stopped when I realized I already felt like I was underwater (I think because you have to move your limbs so slowly or you'll drop from heatstroke).

So I didn't find a swimming pool or pralines or snow, but I did find whiskey and Sweetie Pop, our second cousin twice removed, who is already a divorcée at the age of twenty-three. Would you believe I ran into her on the Riverwalk, watching the barges roll by.

I knew her right away because of the buck teeth. She's an accomplished nurse now—she was in fact the intravenous nurse for the mayor for several months before he gave up the ghost, and despite her teeth and the whitening cream she puts on her face before bed and how she's always boring me with stories about what the mayor said and did, she's really not so bad and I'm staying with her in the heartbeat of the French Quarter in the building where Tennessee Williams used to stay. I don't believe they've renovated since Tennessee's time—there's no hot water and no phone line and the cockroaches are big as my hands but there's a charm about the place.

I've also discovered that although thunderstorms can't quench the heat, bourbon does its best to quench grudges and whiskey washes everything clean and gin makes you forget, and you may as well know, Bernie, that I am piss-drunk as I write this. Yesterday in Pirate's Alley I saw a man with no shirt walking a grinning pot-bellied pig on a leash like it was a dog and I couldn't tell if it was reality or delirium tremens or the heat making me see it.

I got a job waiting tables during the midnight shift at the Café du Monde. It's a tourist trap, but the coffee's good and they were hiring. Most of the other waiters are Vietnamese. They all call me Miss Emma there, except for Luther, the beignet cook with the burned arms, who tries his best to keep the river rats out of the batter with a wooden ladle. He calls me his Octoroon Macaroon and likes to pinch me on the butt. I think I'm getting lung cancer from inhaling powdered sugar all night and the tips are never more than a quarter. They make us wear bow ties and black pants and aprons so we look like domestics from the nineteenth century and these stupid paper hats like at that drive-in Dad took us too in Atlanta after Morehouse gave him that honorary degree—remember when that poor chubby girl on roller skates spilled your milk shake all over the windshield and we couldn't stop laughing? Last night three drunk blind men sat at one of my tables, started arguing over who was first to light his cigar, although none of their cigars were lit, and broke into a sword fight with their white canes.

There is a man who plays a guitar with only one string on the sidewalk outside of the café who says the strangest things. You would love this guy. Aside from Sweetie Pop, he's the only person I really talk to here. Everybody thinks he's crazy, but I think he's a prophet. He told me real manhood is keeping your chin up when the chips are down and never ever shedding a tear. I told him I thought that was the saddest thing I ever heard and burst out crying. I guess that proves I'm a woman. He told me I should sing the blues. (Obviously, he doesn't know I'm tone deaf.) Still, I thought that was sweet and because I was drunk off my ass at the time, I let him tongue-kiss me. When I told him about Poresh, he let me know about a botanica shango where I could get a revenge potion. I'm trying to let go my grudges but it only cost fifteen dollars to make all his hair fall out. This involved the liver of a goat and some foul-smelling liquid. It was way too expensive to make him impotent and impossible to bring you back.

Well, this is the very last piece of Sweetie Pop's rainbow stationery. My lovely roommates, the ten-gallon cockroaches, send their regards and remind me to tell you how much I love you dearly despite your leaving and they dare me not to shed any tears so I can be a real man amidst all this tinsel and sinful sorrow and dripping southern charm.

I hope you are at peace. I don't know why you did what you did. I don't know how you could leave me here like your broken rib. I don't know what to do with myself. I don't know what to be. I don't know how one string can make music, or why I kissed a toothless old bum, or why Sweetie Pop bleaches her skin instead of fixing her teeth, or how a pig can be a pet, or why the rain just makes it hotter, or how I got to the bottom of this bottle before the day is done. I don't expect any answers. I can't send this letter. I don't know your address. I only know that I am

Your Sister,
Emma

P.S. I am thinking of going to New York, where at least there are people who look like me.

P.P.S. Say hello to Jimi Hendrix.

# BEULAH'S QUILT IN
# THE HOUSE OF STICKS

*My disappearance*
*Happened when the sun went down*
*On the house of sticks*

The apartment was trashed. "Is it always this bad?" Fran asked. Fran was a recent lesbian but took it very seriously. Her first girlfriend had dumped her earlier that night in a cruel and messy way and she hadn't predicted things getting uglier when she came over to our apartment to try and have fun.

"No," I said. Then I reconsidered. "Maybe."

Lou was in the other room busting stuff and yelling. Most of the yelling was incoherent, but not all of it. He'd been at it for some time. This was a few hours past his twenty-fifth birthday and the sun was getting ready to come up. I'd thrown a party for him, but Fran was the only one left. It had been a good party while it was contained in our apartment, but when we ran out of liquor around two in the morning everyone but me and Fran went down the street to

The Night Owl at Lou's suggestion, where, as I learned later, things got ugly. Lou's cousins Manny and Hank dragged him home by the armpits and deposited him in the hallway without apology. The wreckage began when Lou kicked in the door.

When I turned twenty-five, a few months before this, I didn't have a party. My mom took me to get my nails done and then to happy hour at this Indian restaurant called The Maharajah. There were some old couples at the other tables, hunched like buzzards, asking the waiter to make theirs without curry because of their digestive conditions. Over dinner, my mom talked about how if I wasn't going to marry Lou, what was the point wasting my best years living with him and didn't I agree I was out of his league. I could have said yes. I could have told her that part of me picked him *because* he was beneath me and that meant he was less likely to leave. I could have talked about how terrified I was of being abandoned again and how belonging to Lou was better than being alone. I could have talked about how he was amazing in bed and made my body alive when normally it was dead, but who talks to their mother about cunnilingus? I talked about Dostoevsky instead. How he specifically chose twenty-five as the cut-off age for his protagonists because he believed that was when human beings lost the ability to change. "That's ridiculous," my mom said, "I've changed." I remember that depressed me (because it wasn't true) and so did my fingernails (painted Midnight Wine), which looked like coagulated blood, and made my hands look like they weren't my hands. My hands looked like vampire hands.

Fran used to think I was a vampire in college. You know the myth about how when a vampire stands in front of a mirror he doesn't have a reflection? It's just dead glass showing the space behind him. Back when we were roommates, Fran used to come and I'd be lying on my bed reading Gabriel Garcia Marquez or Chinua Achebe or

Kafka because I was a comparative literature major, and I'd be turning the pages and a half hour would go by and suddenly she'd scream and say, "My God, Emma, how long have you been here?" as if I'd suddenly materialized out of thin air. This happened all the time, so she came to saying I was a vampire, a demon, or an extraterrestrial being that didn't cast a shadow. Other people have said the same thing more or less, not just Fran. I guess I just don't have a palpable presence or occupy space in the expected way.

It sounded like Lou was ripping the bathroom door off its hinges.

Not again, I thought. He was still yelling—ugly stuff about me mostly, which wasn't anything new. One night when I was locked in the bathroom he called me a stuck-up whiteniggerbitch and a dirty motherfucking whore; then the next morning he fried some eggs and percolated some coffee and when I brought it up he said he didn't remember, which I thought was pretty convenient, and then he left for work. All the ugly things he did and said were just furious scribble scrabble on a chalkboard he could wipe away with a blackout. I could tell Fran was shocked by the stuff coming out of his mouth. I'd been handing her fistfuls of tissues before he came home from The Night Owl but now her eyes were wide and dry.

"How long has *this* been going on?" she asked. We were lying next to each other on the pullout couch in the living room with the blanket up to our chins like two little girls having a sleepover. It sounded like Lou was dragging the kitchen table across the floor.

"Hard to say," I told her. To me it was just a never-ending movie. "Do you think he'll come in here?"

"Probably not," I reassured her. I was thinking about that story—"The Three Little Pigs." *"Little pig, little pig, let me in! Not by the hair of my chinny chin chin! Then I'll huff and I'll puff and I'll blow your house in!"*

254

"Then again, anything can happen," I added.

"Do you think it would make him mad if he came in here and found us in the same bed?"

I knew she was referring to her lesbianism. Ever since she became a lesbian she did that a lot. Lately, she was interested in talking about our identities. About how she'd never been a minority up until now and how strange it was suddenly for everybody to judge her or feel threatened by her when before that hadn't been the case. She thought I would relate to that.

I didn't say anything. It sounded like Lou was overturning my desk. Then it was quiet.

"I think we should go," she said. "Let's go." It was obvious from her voice that she was afraid.

"Okay," I told her, "but I have to get my shoes." My shoes were in the bedroom.

When I got to the bedroom, I saw that Lou had disemboweled it. Nothing was where it was supposed to be; everything was broken. He had indeed overturned my desk and was now underneath it, naked, moaning and pushing against the rug with his heels. I could only see his body from the waist down. He was one of the Shades in Dante's seventh circle of hell, immersed in his own torment. His penis was a snout. My computer was on the floor next to his hairy legs. Its cord, yanked from the plug in the wall, was the long white tail of a rat snaking over the drawerfuls of clothes Lou had dumped from our dresser. The ficus plant was uprooted. The bookshelf was on its side and my dog-eared books were in a great sloppy heap like a Nazi bonfire waiting for the match to come along. My guitar had a bashed in hip and a snapped neck. Here and there, the contents of my jewelry box glittered on top of the jumble. The walls were blank, as they'd been stripped of their pictures. Against the far wall, partially obscuring the door to the kitchen stood the mattress. It was naked and sort of shrugging. Up above, the ceiling fan was dangling perpendicular to the ceiling by its tendons.

Everything was broken. All of it was lifeless. This didn't make me sad really, like you might think, or angry. Actually, it kind of made sense. How can I explain that? For some time I'd been suspecting it was all junk anyway—everything we possessed. Lou had confirmed my suspicion, and he'd done it in a brilliant way. My boyfriend was a very good teacher in that respect.

I stepped over Lou and squeezed past the mattress into the kitchen, which was half-lit by the light from the open refrigerator. The empty fridge was pushed a good four feet away from the wall and rotated forty-five degrees to the side. At its feet lay the kitchen table, on its back, like a turtle someone played a mean joke on. The cupboard doors all stood open and erect like a row of hands frozen in applause. Bravo! The cupboards were bare. Their insides had been flung on the floor along with the refrigerator food, all of it soaking in puddles of spilt beer. As far as I could see, most of the dishes were broken and so was the percolator. I knew that was going to make Lou mad in the morning. It was expensive and he really liked coffee. Then I noticed the bedroom quilt in there too, all soggy and balled up next to the stove.

Lou's grandma Beulah made him that quilt when he was a baby. I met her once before she died, up in Buffalo at the Bennedetti family reunion. She was a tiny woman with enormous glasses thick as hockey pucks. She had a little Styrofoam cup she meant to spit her watermelon seeds into but every one of those seeds ended up in her lap. I've never met anyone named Beulah before or since. It's a strange, beautiful, ugly name, isn't it? I always thought Beulah was a black lady's name, probably because of that Mae West movie where she arches her eyebrow and says to her mammy, *"Beulah, peel me a grape."* I had planned on asking Lou's grandma the story of how she came to get that name but I never got the chance.

This quilt she made was really something magnificent. Every time you looked at it you'd see something you hadn't seen before, even if you slept under it hundreds of nights, like I did. There was the big picture, with angels and sky, sun setting and moon rising at the top and earth and orchards, houses and hills sleeping below. But when you examined one of the angels' wings, say, or one of the roofs on the houses you'd see the pattern on the fabric, that it was slightly different from the other wings and the other roofs. Little details. You might notice that there was a tiny nest on a branch in one of the apple trees, with eggs in it. Or you might be sweating under the quilt with a fever and notice weird things, like how one of the houses was lit up on the inside as if on fire; how on one hill there was this tiny dark patch like a freshly dug grave; or how one of the angels had broken legs.

I'll tell you what made Beulah's craftsmanship truly amazing, though—her houses, trees and angels didn't look flat but three-dimensional. You could easily imagine yourself jumping into that world, swimming in the pond, say, or walking over the hills to see what was on the other side.

Some of that quilt was Beulah's father's parachute silk from World War I and some of it was Beulah's own wedding dress. So, you can see why I didn't like to see it in the condition I found it in the kitchen. It was an inheritance.

I planned to tell Beulah how much I loved her quilt at the reunion barbecue. When Lou introduced us, she looked up at me through those thick glasses. Behind them her eyes swam big as silver dollars, the palest wettest blue. She looked like a little doll in her XXL BENNEDETTI FAMILY REUNION T-shirt. I took her hand and it was as light as a dry husk of corn.

"I'm so glad to meet you," I said.

Her eyes were treading over my face. "What color is she?" she asked. I waited for Lou to answer since the question was put to him. He didn't say anything. I guess he was waiting for me to talk. The three of us were silent for a moment. The moment was a canyon and in it I noticed she had the corded neck of a snapping turtle, the dark teeth of a llama, and yellowing horns for nails. There was roasting meat in the air. Finally, Beulah snatched her hand from mine and spat a watermelon seed into her lap. "Take her away," she snapped. That made Lou so mad he drank enough beer for three men, bent a Wiffle-ball bat in half across a picnic table, and finally had to be restrained by Manny and Hank, who told us we'd better shove off before Gramma Be got upset. The rest of the Bennedettis gaped like carp.

I was hurt but not angry. I told Lou to forgive her. "At least she's honest," I said. "And besides, nobody who made something so beautiful could be all bad." Lou thought I was referring to him, but I meant the quilt.

I reached down to pick it up. It was torn in the front and the batting was spilling out. The tear extended from the heaven to the earth as if an outraged God had destroyed his own creation.

I went to tell Lou good-bye but it looked like he'd blacked out. His legs were bent like a frog's and they weren't moving. I thought briefly about lifting the desk and turning his head to the side so he wouldn't choke on his own vomit. Then I decided against it.

Fran was waiting for me in the hallway, biting her nails.

"Where are your shoes?" she asked.

"I couldn't find them."

"Wear those," she said, pointing to Lou's work boots that were sitting like two cement-splattered ducks on the doormat. Thinking about waterfowl brought that fact about swans to mind—you know, how they mate for life.

"Those are Lou's workboots."

"Put them on. I'm taking you out of here."

I put them on. They were dead weights.

I tramped after her down the stairs. When we got to the next landing our landlord, Hector, opened his door and glared. His boxer shorts were pulled high up over his great round belly, almost to his poker chip nipples.

"I'm taking her out of here," Fran announced.

Hector yelled something in Spanish I couldn't make out because he didn't have his dentures in. I liked Hector. He always called me *Linda* because he couldn't remember my name. He owned the bodega down below and spent most of his time hunched over a card table on the sidewalk out front with three other Dominican guys, playing dominoes and smoking cigars. A few weeks before this, he hung up an American flag the size of a beach blanket in the bodega window over the Goya Sazon, We X-ept Foodstamp, and NY Lotto signs. I could see he wasn't happy about the ruckus.

*"Lo siento,"* I apologized, but it came out in a whisper and I'm sure he didn't hear me.

When Fran and I climbed into her car, the sun was crowning like the blood-soaked head of a newborn infant and the muezzin at the Masjid Al-Farouq on Atlantic Avenue was singing the first call to prayer. His call washed down the street from a loudspeaker and soaked my skin. I can't tell you how much I loved that sound. It was my favorite part of our neighborhood. It was better at calming me than yoga, the smell of baking bread, or a hot bath, even though I didn't understand the words. It was a lullaby. Once I wrote a haiku about it:

*Strange song brings the night*
*Day behind his bleeding throat*
*Blues in Arabic*

The title of that poem is "Muezzin Minus Minaret."

"What a crazy night," Fran said. "Are you okay?"

"Of course," I told her.

"Really?"

"Sure."

"It's just—you're acting like what happened back there was normal. You do know that wasn't normal, right?"

"It's normal for a stick-house. It's to be expected."

Fran was quiet for a minute. She was driving like a sleepwalker, without signaling any turns. "I don't know what you mean."

"If you build your house with sticks, the wolf will blow it down."

Fran thought about that for a little bit. We were making our way out of Brooklyn and heading to her place in Hoboken. The commuter traffic was just beginning. The sunrise was a pink welt.

"Why is he so troubled?" she asked me—but how do you answer that kind of question, really? How do you answer that kind of question for yourself? Language isn't equipped for the range and complexity of human trouble. It doesn't have enough music in it. But since she asked, and I couldn't sing, I had to say something. So I said, "September eleventh." Everyone was saying that at the time. I thought it might mean something to Fran, and as a matter of fact, it did.

"I thought that might be part of it." She nodded. "That's why Yuriko dumped me." Yuriko was one of Fran's architecture professors at grad school. She was an extremely stylish woman with such an exquisite porcelain face you almost forgot she had cerebral palsy, especially when she was sitting down, holding a glass of white wine, with her bad leg tucked under the table.

"She said September eleventh taught her how short life is and gave her clarity of mind about the path she wants to take."

"And you're not on the path?"

"Right. There's no room for me on her path. She's rediscovered the importance of family."

"Because of September eleventh."

"Right. She doesn't want to estrange them anymore. She wants to start a family of her own."

"She's rediscovered the importance of the penis."

"Right." Fran laughed, and I was glad to hear her laughing. Then her voice pitched up like a penny whistle. *But I still love her!*

I didn't know what to say to that, so I didn't say anything. Manhattan rose before us like a face without a nose. Fran started heaving up sobs as big as watermelons. Then I said, "Watch the road, Fran," and buckled my seatbelt because she was driving in two lanes over the Manhattan Bridge.

I didn't know what to say about Yuriko. I didn't know her well but had once spent a cocktail party sitting next to her and found her interesting. She told me that in Japanese, unlike in English, there is a word that acknowledges a baby who doesn't get born, due to miscarriage or abortion. The word is *mizuko*. Loosely translated, it means "water child." Indicating her snifter of brandy, Yuriko explained mizuko to me in terms of a glass only partially filled with liquid—its body is unfulfilled but not without form. Mizukos have presence, and agency. They are capable of haunting; they are capable of being born into another body. At the time, I was tipsy enough to believe Yuriko was telling me about mizuko because she sensed I was unfinished myself, halfway something and halfway something else, without definition.

Later, I decided that wasn't the case at all, that she'd probably lost a baby at some point and just wanted to talk about it. Mizuko is more or less the same thing as a prayer my mom recommended to me in college after my brother died. My mom reads a lot of self-help books. She uses the serenity prayer she learned in Al-Anon as a kind of mantra. You're supposed to say this other prayer she likes before going to sleep at night. It goes like this: *"Lord, teach me a truth this night that I may wake up closer to the knowledge of the person you mean me to become."* Then when you wake up, you write down your dreams in your dream journal and use them as clues to unlock the mystery of your life journey. I told my mom I'd rather use fortune cookies. I kept all my fortunes and taped them one by one to the leaves of the ficus plant in our apartment.

The best fortune I ever got out of a cookie was from a Chinese restaurant in Midtown around the corner from the publishing house I worked at. It said, "You will be loved fiercely for yourself." The day I got that fortune was the same day I met Lou Bennedetti under unusual circumstances. I'd gotten up from my cubicle to photocopy my hands out of boredom when I heard a knocking sound. I turned around to find its source and there he was, in a hard-hat, suspended outside the window of our twenty-second floor office on a plank of scaffolding supported by rappelling ropes. We stayed there on opposite sides of the glass smiling at each other for a miniature eternity. I figured it was a sign. He was hanging from the sky, after all. I went over, exhaled on the glass and wrote my phone number backward in the vapor from my breath.

By the time I figured out linking Lou with the fortune was a mistake, we were already living together. That's not to say he wasn't fierce or loving. The loveliest fierce thing Lou ever did for me was a week after September eleventh when I got assaulted outside the subway by a maniac who mistook me for an Arab, chucked a beer bottle at my head, and told me, in expletive terms, to get out of his country. I remember his eyes, how they were looking through me at something else that wasn't there. This wasn't the first or worst time I was mistaken for an Arab, but after this particular incident, the flag started giving me vertigo. It was everywhere suddenly, broadcast on TV, strung in windows, hung from stoops, worn on T-shirts and hats, decaled on subway cars, painted on truck mudflaps, attached to car antennas to blast in the wind like trumpet flare. It was the newest fad of the millennium. It was a multiplying red, white, and blue vermin. It was farting out of people's mouths behind their doublespeak. I stopped going to work. The bruise above my ear was the size of an infant's foot. In place of pigeons were F-16s. Lou thought I was afraid of being attacked again. He bought me a blue sweatshirt with the flag emblazoned on the front.

"I got it in Chinatown. If you wear this, they won't think you're one of *them*," he explained.

"I can't wear that."

"You could just wear it to and from work."

"I'm not going to work."

"You want to keep living in fear? Is that what you want? 'Cause I'll tell you this much—that's exactly where they want you."

"Who are you talking about? *That's* what I'm afraid of!" I shrieked, pointing at the sweatshirt. "That's what's making me sick and *I can't get away from it*! It's everywhere!"

Lou looked perplexed. "Lemme get this straight. You're talking about the flag?" he asked.

"The flag."

He went out and didn't come home that night. When I woke up the next morning, I found Lou passed out in the rocking chair stinking of whiskey with a load of American flags of every conceivable size spilling off his lap and over the living room floor.

"Lou!" I blurted, "what'd you do?"

Lou came to. "I didn't make it to Manhattan," he slurred. "But I took down just about every one I could find from here to Bed Stuy. You can burn them if you want, baby. I won't tell."

He did that for me.

Fran composed herself somewhere inside the Holland Tunnel but got us lost in Jersey City. We inched along behind a school bus for a while. A little boy at the back of the bus gave us the finger. Fran returned the favor and he mooned us with his little chickpea behind.

"Men," said Fran. She took several wrong turns. "You know what I think?"

"No."

"He feels threatened by your education."

That may have been true, but I enjoyed not having to talk about books or ideas. Lou was unabashedly volatile, but he was also the most virile person I'd ever met. We didn't have to talk at all. There were no pretenses. We could just have hard sex, for hours. I liked the smell of his sweat.

It was about eight when we got to Fran's apartment. Her roommate had one of those untrained yippy dogs that is smaller than a cat and little more than a heartbeat with claws. This dog was an indeterminate breed, but it had a lightning bolt on its forehead for which it was named Flash Gordon. When Fran went to go brush her teeth, it started barking at me in little staccato yelps that stabbed my brain like knitting needles. Then it started baring its tiny teeth and throwing itself at me in weird acrobatic leaps. It was aggravating me so much I kicked it, hard, with the toe of Lou's work boot, like I was punting a football. On impact, the dog squealed, flew through the air, landed ungracefully, and scurried under the couch with its toenails clicking the floor like typewriter keys at 80 WPM.

It wasn't right to kick a thing that was smaller and weaker than you. I got on my hands and knees to look for him under the couch. I thought maybe I'd broken its little pencil ribs.

"What are you doing?" said Fran.

"I'm worried about Flash Gordon. He went under the couch."

"He's fine," she said, going into her room. "Let's just go to bed. I'm exhausted."

I kicked off Lou's work boots and got into bed next to Fran who was asleep as soon as her head hit the pillow, breathing in that kind of asthmatic way people breathe after they've been crying, like there isn't enough air in the whole world to fill them up. I couldn't sleep so I looked out the window. Fran pays exorbitant rent because her room boasts a bay window with a view of the Manhattan skyline. Clouds were gathering out there. The sky was white putty. Manhattan was colorless and flat. Its third dimension had collapsed in on itself. Down at the one end where the towers had been was a smudge—smoke from the fires they couldn't put out.

Fran brought me down to Ground Zero in the third week of September on a special assignment from her design class to experience negative space, which she was supposed to interpret and transform in a drawing. The assignment was ludicrous because that space is the opposite of negative—at least it was then. How can I explain that?

Imagine you are having a normal conversation with someone when, all of a sudden, you blink and this person's body disappears. Now, imagine stepping into the spot where this person had just been. You would feel something, don't you think? You would feel a certain kind of energy, like you were in a magnetic force field. Now multiply that by several thousand.

There was the smell, which carried as far north as Thirty-fourth Street when the wind was strong. Some people said it was the smell of burning flesh and others insisted it was a purely electrical odor. As far as I'm concerned, both interpretations were correct and amounted to the same thing. It was a smell with a charge. There was the dust (the color of coffee with too much cream), which had settled everywhere, so that you could write in it, which people did (God Bless America, Suck My Dick, Shirley Was Here). People wore paper masks to keep it out of their lungs. There was the air. You could touch this air. You could pet it with your hand. There were people watching like me and Fran, and the workers in the rubble, moving in slow motion, coated in the dust. Nobody spoke. The silence was its own language. This was the densest spot I've ever stood in.

Fran agreed Ground Zero was not a negative space. For her assignment she turned in a picture of me called "Vampire in Her Kitchen," which she drew later that afternoon at my apartment before Lou got home from his shift. It is really just a picture of my kitchen. I am not there. Fran's professor gave her a bad grade.

◦╟◦

Outside her window the gathering clouds became one cloud, a newspaper, a dark storm coming. Fran was fast asleep beside me. Her body was a warm loaf of bread. Fran has told me that sleeping with a woman is soft like melting in snow without the cold. That's sort of how it was lying next to her in her bed. Behind the newspaper sky there was roll of thunder. Thunder had new meaning. Soon there was rain and the sound of it brought me to sleep where I had a troubled dream—a dream without sound.

In the dream I am in my bedroom from childhood, in the house I grew up in when my parents were still together. Everything is there—my red and orange rag rug, my unicorn, my dollhouse, my anthouse, my microscope, my colored pencils, my rubber cement, my panda bear. I am sitting at my little writing desk wearing a white nightgown that is also a wedding dress. My brother Bernie is standing behind me, picking the tangles out of my hair with a wide-tooth comb. I am looking past the lemon yellow curtains through the window at our backyard. There is our vegetable patch and there is our garage and the rhododendron bush. Something is coming. Something is descending from the sky. My room grows dark. Suddenly it is nighttime. A great cloud is blowing toward us. It is a black mass with countless little sparks of light. It is the night sky itself with all its stars being exhaled. It is reaching for our house. It is twinkling like an evening gown. Bernie wraps his arms around me but it swallows us. We are torn apart and the walls are stricken down and I am falling through debris. I land in the ruins of our flattened house. I know my brother is dead. I find his hand, severed at the wrist, with its index finger pointing at nothing. As far as I can see, for miles and miles, everything has been destroyed and I am alone in that quiet.

I woke up with my mouth as dry as toast. Fran was still sleeping. Her cheek had a crease on it from the wrinkle on her pillow, but other than that it was in absolute repose. People have said of Fran that she has classic American good looks. Nobody has ever thought to say that of me, even though I wouldn't have resulted anywhere else.

I didn't want to go back to sleep so I thought about my dream for a while. Trying to figure out how the dream was a clue to the person God meant me to become was like the crossword puzzle in the Sunday *Times*. I wondered if Fran was dreaming right then. I watched her face to see if I could tell. If she was dreaming, it couldn't have been about anything bad. Her face was too peaceful, like untroubled water.

The rain had stopped falling and the children were getting out of school. I could hear them laughing down on the street. Fran was knocked out. To look at her sleeping face, you couldn't tell she had a broken heart. "Fran," I said, but she didn't move. "Are you afraid?" Her slumber was a deep spell. Someone would have to come along and kiss her to wake her up. "I have to go now," I told her. I thought about how she used to fetch Yuriko's coat for her and help her into it, like a perfect gentleman.

"Don't worry, Fran," I said, "you will be loved fiercely for yourself."

Flash Gordon bit me on my way out, leaving four little needle marks above my ankle with his incisors. I deserved that, I guess. Some little girls were drawing crooked pastel hopscotch squares on the sidewalk outside Fran's apartment. "Why you wearing man shoes, lady?" asked one of them.

"'Cause it beats bare feet. Where can I get a cab?"

When I got back to the apartment, there were two gifts waiting for me. The first was a bouquet of two dozen irises, purple as cartoon bruises, each with a ripe black eye. The second was an eviction notice. The place was as it was when I'd left it, minus Lou, who'd never missed a day of work in his life. I surveyed the mess for a good while and realized what I had to do. I took off Lou's boots. I took off my clothes. I threw them in the heap with all the other stuff. Then I climbed over it into the kitchen to get Beulah's quilt. Out of all that junk, it was the only thing worth saving, even with the gash down the front. Filthy and wet as it was, I wrapped it around my body like a cape and I went up to the roof.

The last time I was up there was with Hector and Lou. All of Brooklyn was congregated on the rooftops that morning, watching that plume of smoke carry across the perfect blue sky. We rubbed our eyes. The sun shone on us like a benediction. It was picnic weather. It was a glorious day for a family reunion. "Madre de Dios," Hector kept repeating. *Madre de Dios.*

I looked there again, toward Manhattan. This time I was alone among the chimneys. Stretching past the rooftop's lip were the spires and the schoolyards, the brownstone stoops and the bus stops, the empty lots, the hardscrabble gardens, the satellite dishes, the grocery stores and the graffiti, all sewn together with wagging lines of laundry. Beyond that was the dirty river with its Statue of Liberty standing like a little green G.I. Joe, and its bridges stretching like alley cats over to Manhattan. Manhattan was a jaw with jagged teeth. Behind it, the sun was going down and in its wake the sky was a rash. What if I could tear this picture, I thought. What if I could rip it and crawl through? What would be on the other side? Then, when I was thinking that, a piece of paper fluttered from my elbow like a feather coming loose from a bird's wing. I pinned it against the tar with my big toe before it could blow away and bent down to inspect it. Was I dreaming? No. It was a slightly soggy hundred-dollar bill. Stitched in tidy rows inside the quilt, there were ninety-nine more just like it.

Maybe Beulah hid the money fearing another Depression. Maybe she pulled a stocking over her head and robbed it from a bank. Maybe she was saving it to buy the thing she always wanted. Maybe she had forgotten it. I would never know. She would never know that I was her investment.

I stood on the roof, imagining my possibilities. After a time, the muezzin started his fifth and final call to prayer and I turned invisible under Beulah's quilt.

I have been missing ever since.

# THE SCULPTED HEAD

Two letters came. On Wednesday, one from his daughter who had been missing for three months. Her handwriting had changed and the pages were sticky with something he decided was fruit juice. The postmark read, "Bahia."

At the bottom of the eighth page, she explained that Bernie's death had put the wanderlust in her, that her ship had unexpectedly come in and that she'd chosen Brazil because of bossa nova. At the top of page nine, she asked him to please tell her mother she was fine, that she was better than fine because she was learning how to dance, that everybody there looked like some permutation of her, and furthermore that Lynn was wrong about the nature of depression. As far as she could see, it wasn't just anger turned inward, or grief, or something genetic she'd gotten from Bernard's side, or a chemical imbalance in need of correction by a head doctor and pharmaceuticals. Though it might have been all those things, more important, it was a thing you could escape. She was beginning to suspect that there wasn't anything wrong with her head, but rather something wrong with her country.

"It made me invisible. I couldn't feel my body there," Emma wrote on page twelve. "All through the city of Salvador you can buy wax body parts," she continued. "You can purchase a wax hand at the mercado if you're afflicted with arthritis and bring it to Igreja do Bomfim, where the pilgrims go to be cured. You can make an offering and say a prayer for the relief of that suffering. There's a blue hall of miracles there, the color of a robin's egg. Its walls are plastered with passport photos of those who've been healed, and bizarre letters of testimony: a blind child who can see, a woman whose burn blisters have vanished, a teenager who can walk again, his paralysis lifted like a sail. They divide the milagros and hang them in sections up on the ceiling: wax arms, wax feet, wax lungs, wax hearts. I bought a wax head for myself (in case Mom was right) but it cracked into flakes in my canvas bag on the crowded Bomfim bus."

"Is she okay?" Bernard's second wife called from the kitchen. She was only a few years older than his daughter was, and he had a strong suspicion she'd already steamed open the letter with the teakettle and read it for herself. He didn't answer her because he didn't know the answer, even after reading all twenty pages twice.

As a child, Emma had been a habitual runaway. She'd camped underneath the back porch one entire Labor Day weekend, subsisting on uncooked hot dogs and Pepperidge Farm cookies. It had taken a police dog to find her. Another time, they'd had to shut down Quaker Bridge Mall to search for her in every store. Lynn was hysterical, convinced she'd been kidnapped, but after six agonizing hours, Emma had turned up fast asleep inside a circular rack of ladies' dress slacks at Macy's. His relief was so enormous that he'd smacked her. Back then Bernard believed his daughter ran away because she was frightened of him. He experienced her absence like a punishment, as he did his son's death, one that he somehow deserved.

He folded Emma's letter neatly, reinserted it in its tissue-thin airmail envelope, and tucked it in the breast pocket of his tweed jacket, close to his heart.

"Did you hear me before? I asked if she was okay," Barbara repeated. She stood in the doorway, her eyes red and wet with tears.

"Are *you?*" he asked, though he knew she wasn't. By this point it was apparent their marriage had been a colossal mistake. He'd thought Barbara would need him less than Lynn, who hadn't been able to do a crossword puzzle without consulting him, but that wasn't the case. Her body was terrifyingly ripe, her nipples were dark as plums, and she was physically inexhaustible. He found himself missing the dimples of Lynn's thighs, the folds of her stomach, the glove-like softness of her loose upper arms.

"Onions," his second wife explained, exhibiting a knife with her right hand and rubbing her eyes with the left. "I've been chopping onions for the bouillabaisse."

❧

On Friday of that same week, Bernard received the second letter; this one from a Mr. Leonard Zaritzky, Esq., who was writing to inform him that he'd inherited something priceless. "Of infinite value," was how Mr. Zaritzky put it, although he did not state what the item was. The letter was postmarked Mississippi.

"I'll have to go down there for the reading of the will," he told Barbara over dinner. He didn't realize until he said this aloud that he was actually going to do it, that he wanted to.

"Who died?" she asked, though he presumed she'd steamed this one open too and already knew the answer.

"A distant cousin."

"Do you want to tell me his *name?*"

"Roland."

"I'll go with you," she suggested.

"No," he said. "You won't."

Several minutes passed. "I took my basal body temperature this morning," she attempted.

Bernard continued eating in silence.

"Looks like I'm ovulating."

"Don't," he interrupted. "Just don't."

She pushed away her untouched dish of leftover bouillabaisse and retreated upstairs to dissertate in the bathtub. He ate her portion after he'd finished his own. He was full but his stomach felt empty. He was an old man. He was done beginning. Almost twenty years had passed since he'd been home.

❧

He reread both letters on the plane ride south, feeling they were somehow connected, but not knowing exactly how until he sat in a velvet chair in Mr. Zaritzky's air-conditioned office, face to face with his inheritance. He'd been in Hancock County for two days by this point, which was enough time to become acquainted with the staggering developments of that region. He no longer knew anybody. Luscious was unlisted in the phone book and nowhere to be found. A village of identical tract houses, a maze of twirling lawn sprinklers and cul-de-sacs, had been erected in the neighborhood where Nan's pink shack used to stand. The icehouse had been leveled and in its vicinity lay a miniature golf course and water park. The railway had simply disappeared. So had Main Street, or at least Main Street as he'd known it, with the barbershop, the tobacconist, and the five-and-dime. It was now called "Historic Main Street," with a string of new antique shops, a Starbucks, and a Hallmark store. The beach road was flanked with splashy billboards advertising a resort casino. He'd gone there in his rental car, driven by a bottomless sense of his own failure, and lost twelve hundred dollars at blackjack in under twenty minutes.

"As you may know," drawled Mr. Zaritzky, "most of Roland Favre's opus are now traveling the major museum circuit in Europe, but he specified that this particular sculpture be left to you." He patted its scalp, possessively. "It's a real treasure."

Bernard removed his glasses and stared into its eyes. There was a defiance there he recognized as his son's.

"However, as I've been appointed probate counsel, it's my duty to tell you the curators are up in arms. They claim the collection is incomplete without your head, here, and they're wondering if you'd consider selling."

"No."

"Now, wait just a cotton-picking minute, Professor Boudreaux." The lawyer smiled. "They're all willing to pay a pretty penny and I'd be thrilled to serve as acting agent should you choose to auction it off."

"No."

"Before you make your decision, you might like to know what it's been appraised at," the lawyer argued.

Bernard laughed dryly. "I'm not interested."

Zaritzky wasn't willing to give up. "May I suggest—"

"No, you may not. It belongs to me."

"I see." Zaritzky wiped his forehead, unable to conceal his disappointment. "In that case, I'm obligated to ask if you'd consider donating your head to the exhibition on a temporary basis?"

"I don't think so." Bernard stood and lifted his head from the desk. It was the weight of a small child. "I'll just take it with me now," he said.

"You can't just take it with you. You've got to sign this first," the lawyer objected, producing a document.

"Fine."

"And just let me give you my card, in case you reconsider. Hey! Hold on, there. Don't you want a bag or whatnot to tote it in?" he called after Bernard, who was already through the door. "Professor!" he objected. "You forgot your cane!"

❧

Bernard carried it under his arm like a watermelon to the St. Rose de Lima cemetery where he limped through rows of crumbling lime-washed overground graves. Here, at the bottom, you had to put the dead in houses. The land was below the level of the sea and sinking with the country's load. Here, if you buried the dead in the ground, their bones would rise.

He found the grave he was looking for and placed the boy's head at its foot. The salt air had eaten away at the name engraved there. He found a small, sharp stone (a piece of bone?) and dug into the letters, tracing the name until it was legible. It was possible that a burden and a blessing were the same thing.

"Bernie," he said to the boy, "meet your grandfather."

He traced the name until it was legible, all the while thinking about his daughter, who was discovering herself in a new language.

"I love the ocean of Portuguese in my mouth. My favorite word has no English equivalent," Emma had written. "You hear it in all the bittersweet love songs. *Saudade*. A noun with the taste of a rum-soaked lime. Loosely translated, it means 'missing,' or 'longing.' Longing is probably closer in meaning because it's a word touched with loss. You experience saudade for something absent, something gone from you, something stolen or something that left, something close to your heart but far. You feel saudade for the haunting thing that has a hold on you, what blues everything you see. I ran away so you would have the saudade for me. So I could struggle into a name. So I could begin."

Didn't she know? Didn't she know that was his wish? Before he left Mississippi, he boxed the sculpted head in shredded newspaper and brought it to the post office. "This one won't break," he had written her back. "Bring it to that church and say a prayer for us."

"Heavy package," the postmistress observed, and it was true. As she took his head from him, he felt lighter.

# ACKNOWLEDGMENTS

I am indebted to the following for their support during the production of this book: the Virginia Center for the Creative Arts, the Sacatar Foundation, the *New York Times* Foundation, Charles Rowell and the Callaloo Creative Writing Workshop. Thanks also to Melissa Hammerle, director of NYU's Creative Writing Program, my teachers: Katharine Weber, Robert Stone, Paule Marshall, Brian Morton, Thomas Glave, Breyten Breytenbach, Ngugi wa Thiong'o, and Chuck Wachtel. Special thanks to my girlfriends: Nicole, Chastity, and Claire; my brothers: Albert, Charlie, and Martin Raboteau, and my mother (my heart), Katherine Murtaugh. Bottomless thanks to my inimitable agent, Amy Williams, my patient and insightful editor, Jennifer Barth, and finally, my dear mentor, Percival Everett.

# ABOUT THE AUTHOR

EMILY RABOTEAU graduated from Yale University and holds an M.F.A. degree in creative writing from New York University, where she was a *New York Times* Fellow. Her short stories have appeared in *Tin House, Callaloo, The Missouri Review,* and *Best American Short Stories, 2003.* She is the recipient of the *Chicago Tribune*'s Nelson Algren Award for Short Fiction, a Jacob Javits Fellowship, a New York Foundation of the Arts Fellowship, and a Pushcart Prize. She lives in Brooklyn and teaches creative writing in Harlem at the City College of New York.